MARGO HANSEN

GREATLY BELOVED
BOOK 1 - TALL TIMBER TRILOGY

Greatly Beloved
Copyright © 2017 by Margo Hansen. All rights reserved.

No part of this publication may be reproduced, stored in a retrieval system or transmitted in any way by any means, electronic, mechanical, photocopy, recording or otherwise without the prior permission of the author except as provided by USA copyright law.

Scripture quotations are taken from the *Holy Bible, King James Version*.

This novel is a work of fiction. Names, descriptions, entities, and incidents included in the story are products of the author's imagination. Any resemblance to actual persons, events, and entities is entirely coincidental.

Hansen, Margo
    Greatly Beloved / by Margo Hansen.
    (TALL TIMBER TRILOGY: 1/3)
    Originally published: 2015.

Cover Photo by Brooke Streblow

Published in the United States of America

ISBN: 978-1974602780

1. Fiction / Action & Adventure
2. Fiction / Christian / Historical Romance

To Bruce, my ever-loving husband,
and to my family who is the motivation for me to write

ACKNOWLEDGMENTS

THERE ARE MANY great places to visit in Grand Rapids, Minnesota, but three absolutely wonderful sites that should be utilized by every resident and definitely by every visitor to the city are:

The Forest History Center—Minnesota Historical Society
2609 County Road Seventy-Six, Grand Rapids, MN, 55744
Interpretive Center/Museum
Living history tour of 1901 logging camp on the Mississippi River and 1934 Minnesota Forest Service Complex

The Itasca County Historical Society
201 N. Pokegama Avenue, Grand Rapids, MN, 55744

The Gilbert Mansion
719 NW First Avenue, Grand Rapids, MN, 55744
Historic tours of the 1904 home of lumber baron and pioneer resident W. C. Gilbert

These places offer a wealth of information on the beginning of the logging industry in this part of the state as well as relevant history of the town of Grand Rapids and the surrounding areas. My thanks to the actors at the Forest History Center for answering my multitude of questions and to Lilah Crowe, executive director of the Itasca County Historical Society, for pointing me to the proper resources, as well as to Christie Graupmann, current owner of the Gilbert Mansion, who was a wealth of information on the time period.

Also, special thanks to family members, Jon and Betty Stende, who have given me so much encouragement. I just had to use you as characters in this series, and I hope you don't mind that even though you are the inspiration behind my fictional Jon and Betty, their personalities have been tweaked to fit the story.

Although I have made every attempt to be as accurate as possible in my time line of history, I will admit to using my freedom as a fiction writer to "adjust" a few things in the telling of the story, which in itself has been entirely concocted in my imagination. My purpose in writing is not only to entertain, but also to share the love of the Lord Jesus and the precious Gospel of his grace.

The Townsfolk—1888

Daniel Dunn—logger
   Delaney
   Darby
   Daphne
   Didi
   Dylan
Mercy Crane—schoolteacher
Latham and Hedda Bedloe—mercantile
Mr. Hamilton—bank
   Ernestine
Mr. Cranshaw—leather shop
Mr. Hodge—mail-Beckfelt Store
Bernie Clayton—logging camp owner
Murdock—logger
Ralston—logger
Shorty—logger
Jon Talbot—sheriff
Betty—Jon's wife
Jefferson Elwood—deputy
Mr. Olson—lumber mill
Mrs. Ferguson—neighbor
Mrs. Simonson—neighbor
Pratts—neighbors
Ilsa Murdock—neighbor
   Guntar Strahle
Pastor Sampson—preacher
Stanley Crane—farmer (Mercy's papa)

And he said unto me, O Daniel, a man greatly beloved,
understand the words that I speak unto thee…

—Daniel 10:11a

Grand Rapids, MN, 1888

THE CLASSROOM BEGAN filling with her students, and Mercy Crane waited by the door to greet them as they entered and to remind them to stomp off the snow that clung to their boots. The weather was producing plenty of wet snow this winter morning and Mercy was getting weary of trying to sweep the dried puddles off the schoolroom floor. By the time the children were done with their lessons for the day, the dirt had been smeared and ground into the floor and almost always required the mop and bucket to remove it.

Perhaps mopping will be the punishment for misbehavior today.

With an unconscious shake of her head, Mercy quickly dismissed the thought. She didn't want to keep any of the students after school. She knew they all had chores waiting for them and their parents counted on their help. And for most of the children that meant doing the work of their absent fathers who were up north in the logging camps. No, if she had to deal with bad behavior, she would assign the miscreant duties that could be done during the lunch break. Mopping would not be advisable at that time; the floor would only have to be mopped again later.

Mercy sighed. At least this season she had more children in the new two-story building than the first teacher who taught in a one-room log cabin in this northern Minnesota town the previous year. That teacher had only two girls and a few of the Chippewa children. And Mercy counted her blessings on the weather as well. The previous year had produced a devastating blizzard in the west and southern parts of the state and dropped their area into frigid temperatures.

She smiled as one of the older boys stopped by the woodpile and gathered a load to bring into the schoolroom. The school had a chill to it in the early-morning hours, and if the wind became strong during the day, it was downright cold. She already had a fire started, but she appreciated the help in restocking her supply of fuel.

"Thank you, Guntar. That is most thoughtful of you."

The boy nodded and grinned sheepishly. As he passed her, she could see his face redden.

Oh, no! A schoolboy crush.

Mercy's face revealed nothing of her thoughts as she continued to greet the other students. Guntar was a young boy of fifteen, and it was probably only natural that he had become sweet on his teacher, but what he didn't know, Mercy thought as she closed the door, was that a very pretty, very shy fourteen-year-old girl named Leah had eyes only for him.

She walked to the front of the room as the children took their seats. The chattering dwindled to a halt as she turned to address them.

"Good morning, class."

"Good morning, Miss Crane," the students said in unison.

"Time for our Scripture reading."

The day began like all the others: the Scripture reading and a song. She loved every minute of it. Teaching was more than a job to her; in fact, if it wasn't that she needed the income, she'd do it for free, she loved it that much. *God bless Miss Sherman for making me want to study in school,* she thought as she moved to her desk.

She scanned the room as the students went through the morning exercises. The Dunns were not here again. She sighed. She said a quick, silent prayer for the family who had lost their mother so recently. A family of four girls and one infant boy without a mother. So sad.

Mercy loved all her students, but there was a special place in her heart for the Dunn girls. She wasn't sure why exactly. She was an only child herself, so maybe it was that she enjoyed seeing the sisters look out for each other. But, no, there were many other children just like them. More likely it was that the eldest girl reminded Mercy of herself. Delaney was always watching others, wanting to learn, and soaking up knowledge.

"Miss Crane?"

Mercy blinked. She had been daydreaming, and the students were done with their recitation and waiting for instructions. She cleared her throat.

"Time to call roll."

The day moved on at a rapid pace as all the school days seemed to do. There was never enough time to give her pupils all that she so wanted to give. It wasn't an easy task to impart knowledge to the uninterested, but she accepted the challenge to inspire a hunger for it. For those who became excited about learning, she wished for more hours to help them in their quest. All too soon she was at the door waving good-bye, reminding the students of their assigned homework and pointing out belongings that were in danger of being left behind.

She smiled. She was tired, but it had been a good day.

"Uh, Miss Crane?"

She hesitated a moment before turning to face Guntar who was still in the classroom.

"Yes, Guntar?"

"Uh, I could mop for you. I don't mind." His ears were now red as he looked at her, looked away then looked back again.

Mercy glanced out the door. Leah appeared to be walking at a snail's pace as the other children raced off for home ahead of her. *No doubt she's hoping Guntar will catch up to her.* She tightened her lips as she saw Ernestine Hamilton tug at one of Leah's braids as she ran past her.

Mercy smiled at the young man. "I appreciate the offer, Guntar, but I have a meeting with one of the school board members in only a few minutes. You have a good evening and I'll see you tomorrow. Don't forget to study for your geography test."

"Uh, okay. I won't. Uh…which board member, Miss Crane?" The boy's eyebrows drew together.

"I'm meeting Mr. Crenshaw. Do you know him? He has the leather shop in town."

"Yessum, I know him." Guntar's tone changed.

Mercy bit at her lower lip as she guided Guntar to the door. "Thank you, again, for the offer, but you know I don't keep any of my students after school hours. Your mother needs your help at home more than I need it here."

"Yessum," Guntar mumbled. His head was ducked low. "See you tomorrow, Miss Crane."

He nearly collided with the short, stout man coming up the school steps.

"Watch where you're going, young man!"

Guntar only scowled at the man and hurried off. Mercy sighed as she saw him race past Leah without acknowledging her. The young girl stopped and stared after him then she too picked up her pace and headed for home.

"Were you having disciplinary problems with that boy, Miss Crane? Because if you need any assistance, I am only too glad to help in any way that I can."

Mercy glanced at Mr. Crenshaw. She was uncomfortably aware of his interest in her, but something about the businessman didn't sit right with her.

"There is no problem at all." She smiled pleasantly then almost wished she hadn't when she saw his face light up. "What was it that you wished to discuss with me, Mr. Crenshaw? Something about the curriculum, was it?" She cringed as he stroked his waxed mustache. It was then that she noticed his string tie and suit jacket under his heavy outer coat. He appeared to be dressed to go courting.

Oh, no!

Mr. Crenshaw waved her ahead of him to one of the chairs in the back of the room. "If you please."

Mercy sat.

He pulled a chair across the aisle, scraping its legs through the encrusted dirt on the floor, and lowered his portly form onto it so that he could face her. "I have wanted for a long time now to ask you to dine with me, Miss Crane."

She opened her mouth to speak, but he forestalled her.

"Now, I know you haven't had much time to think about it, but I have taken the liberty of reserving a table for us at the hotel. I think it's high time we get better acquainted." He pulled at the curl on his handlebar mustache again as he watched for her reaction.

Mercy did not consider herself to be an attractive woman. She was fairly plain and she readily admitted it. Her father never agreed with her in her estimation of her appearance, but he knew he had to instill in her a confidence in herself that beauty never could have given her. It was with that learned confidence that she was able to reply to Mr. Crenshaw.

"Uh…"

Actually her father was never able to build any self-confidence in his stubborn daughter's head. In front of a classroom she shined. When faced with a dinner invitation from a man, even a man she knew she would never be interested in, she faltered. The thought of having any man want to court her unnerved her, especially as she had vowed to herself never to allow anyone to court her again.

Just imagine him as one of the students. She stood to her feet and Mr. Crenshaw rose also. *If only he didn't have that ridiculous mustache.* Mercy tried to dispel the image of one of her students with a mustache from her mind, but she felt a bubble of laughter building inside her.

"I'm afraid my schedule is far too busy to…uh…to…be dining." *Argh! That came out wrong!* "I mean, thank you for the offer, Mr. Crenshaw, but as you know, the teacher's code of conduct forbids…uh…forbids…me dining with a man, so I must decline." *There, I said it.*

Mr. Crenshaw tilted his chin up as he eyed her. "I see." He fingered his mustache again. "I will respect your schedule and will ask you again when the school term is over. As far as the code goes, since I am on the school board I am sure we can work something out. Good day, Miss Crane."

Mercy fought to stifle a laugh as the paunchy man made a slight bow and turned to leave. The urge to laugh was more a release of tension than ridicule, but it would be hard to explain either way, so she kept her control until he had exited the schoolroom then she collapsed back on the chair and released her breath and the inevitable *snort* erupted. She clasped her hand over her mouth and nose and turned quickly to the window to be sure he hadn't heard.

That stupid snort! It was Mercy's misfortune to have a snort added to any laugh she tried to hold in or that came out unexpectedly. She shook her head. It had caused her more trouble than she cared to think about.

She tackled the rest of her work with a vengeance. It felt good to push the mop back and forth over the wood floor as she replayed the uncomfortable scene with Mr. Crenshaw again in her mind, and that in turn caused her to recall the last painful scene she had with Jefferson Elwood.

No! I will not think of him. It's over!

She gathered her schoolbooks and bundled up in her warm outerwear to begin the long walk back to the Pratts' house where she boarded. There had been a time when she thought maybe someday she would be able to consider a suitor if she felt the right person came along, but no more. Those dreams had been shattered. She was content in her position as a schoolteacher, even though many considered her an old maid at twenty-two.

Grand Rapids was devoid of men most of the winter months due to logging, although with seventeen logging camps within a few miles of Pokegama Falls, there was a constant flow of wagons carrying supplies and provisions about the town. Then in the spring when the water started flowing in the rivers, the men were all out guiding the logs downstream to the various mills along the way. But when they finally were paid and freed to go home, the town was suddenly filled with loggers hungry for drink and a good time. It was then that Mercy closed the school and hurried back to her father's farm, which was a couple hours walk from town, on the Mississippi River. Boarding in town during the school term was the only way she could be available to teach.

Thundering Rapids or Long Rapids, the area had once been called, and Mercy thought of that as she walked as swiftly as possible through the snowy streets. Right now, the Mississippi and Prairie rivers were frozen and all boat travel halted, but goods still managed to get through as men hauled them by dog sled, wagon, or sleigh over the frozen areas. In fact travel was almost easier when the ground was frozen; most other times the residents had to deal with muddy conditions or stumps, rocks, and roots on the tote roads. Her mind had wandered as she walked, and she nearly bumped into a man coming around the corner.

"Oh, excuse me, please," she said as she backed away.

The man kept his head down as he mumbled something and moved past her.

Mercy watched him go. The slumped shoulders and trudging footsteps revealed his weariness, but something else caught her attention—despair.

Mr. Dunn.

Mercy felt tears prickle behind her eyelids as she moved on again and her thoughts returned to the Dunn family and their recent loss. She sighed as her thoughts turned to prayer for the man who now bore the burden of caring for his children on his own.

Dunn Home

DELANEY WAS AWARE of the baby crying, but it was her father's command that had her on her feet and leaning over the small wooden cradle in the dark hour of the night.

"Delaney! I need my sleep. See to him!"

"Yes, Pa. Sorry 'bout that."

She picked up the infant and put him to her shoulder while she patted his back. *He's hungry again.* Making her way to the woodstove in the kitchen, she tested the temperature of the water she had left in a pot there before going to bed. It wasn't long before she had the goat's milk warmed and ready to feed to her little brother.

Her little, motherless brother.

At only eleven years old, Delaney was now mother to her four siblings.

She sighed as she lifted Dylan to her shoulder to burp him. She missed her mother so much, but there never seemed to be time to think about her except for these moments in the middle of the night when she was up with Dylan. Then the tears would fall.

And she was so tired.

Pa had found a wet nurse to come in and feed the infant during the day, but the nights were up to Delaney. And with the responsibilities of the household mainly on her young shoulders, she never seemed to have time to mourn.

Delaney's eyes drooped as she rocked with her brother, but she forced herself to rise and gently place Dylan back down in his cradle. Night after night of experience had taught her that if Dylan woke again, he'd be up for the rest of the night. A fussier baby she had never seen, and that included all three of her sisters, at least as far as she could remember. Of course, Ma had always been there to see to the babies in the middle of the night before, but Delaney was sure she would have remembered all this crying if it had occurred.

Delaney was asleep as soon as she rolled over onto the little makeshift mattress beside the cradle in the small room next to her parents' room. Pa needed his sleep to go work with the ice cutters every day so it only seemed right for Delaney to leave her sisters in the cold upstairs bedroom and stay close by Dylan downstairs near the stove where the baby could be warm. Pa now slept alone in the room he and Ma had shared until she died just weeks ago.

The doctor said it was Dylan's birth that weakened the already thin and sickly woman. Ma never recovered from the birth and never left her bed again until she was carried out by Pa and the undertaker. And Pa wouldn't have been there at all for Ma's last days, except he and another man pulled an injured logger out of the woods on a sled just a few weeks ago. Delaney figured that Pa volunteered to leave the logging camp to do the job because he knew the baby was about due and he hoped to make it home in time to be with Ma. Instead, he got there in time to watch her die.

Delaney struggled to open her eyes when she heard the front door open and close. Instead of heading back to the logging camp, Pa had decided to work with the men who cut ice for storage for the summer so he could be here with the children and still earn some money. The trouble was that the work was only temporary. Delaney didn't know what he would do when they had the icehouse full and the work was done for the season. *At least this winter is cold enough so they can cut ice.* Delaney recalled one winter when temperatures were so warm that the ice was too thin to fill the icehouses completely.

Pa was up and would be back from the well soon. She checked Dylan before she slipped from her bed and began pulling on her coat over her nightdress. She was just getting into her boots when Pa opened the door and carried in two buckets of water. He only nodded at her as she passed by him to make a journey to the little building behind their house. Soon she was back, washing up in the icy water on the front step before hurrying back into the warm house to begin breakfast preparations.

It was still dark. Pa had the lantern lit and the cook stove heating. Delaney glanced again at Dylan and was relieved that she could get to her work unencumbered. Many a time she had tried to hold the baby and cook at the same time, but his cries at being made to wait for his own meal usually had the whole house in an uproar and it was too much for Delaney. Pa helped more now. Those first few days when everything was in turmoil, Pa would sit and stare into space. Delaney couldn't understand why he didn't at least hold Dylan and feed him while she got the girls settled back into bed and worked on his breakfast. But Pa didn't seem to want to hold the baby and Delaney ended up working one-handed and scolding the little girls for causing more trouble with their whining. It was more than the eleven-year-old could handle.

But Pa came around. Young as Delaney was she could understand in her own way the effort it took for him to go on. She understood because that was what she had to do. It was what they all were going to have to do from now on.

Delaney stirred the mush before moving to the counter to slice bread and warm it in the oven. Pa liked to break the toasted bread into his mush to eat it. While she worked on preparing the lunch he would take to work, she started warming the goat's milk for Dylan. He would be waking again soon.

Pa was just finishing his breakfast and as he pushed the bowl away from him, he spoke, "Delaney, come sit down."

Delaney was surprised. Pa hadn't said much to her lately and he rarely talked in the early morning hours before leaving for the day. She slid onto the bench across from him and watched his face expectantly.

"The ice cutting job is over," Pa started without preamble. He rubbed his knuckles against the bristle on his chin, but he avoided looking at his eldest daughter.

Delaney's heart sank as she waited for his next words. Would they have to move? They hadn't been in town long. Pa worked with some of the other logging camps farther south before moving to Grand Rapids, and they had moved several times as he worked with different groups, but how could they manage now with a newborn to be fed? It was too much! She was tired; she couldn't do this, not again, not without Ma.

"I'm going back to the camp and leave you and the others here. You're settled in here and the baby is going to need that wet nurse for a time." He paused and glanced at her for her reaction.

Delaney knew what he was thinking. The family had always hated the constant moving about. The girls could never make friends and rarely kept up in the schools, so Ma had schooled them on at home as best she could. Here they were attending school regularly until Ma died. It would be good to stay in one place longer, but what was really on Delaney's mind was how they could possibly do so without their father. Surely he wouldn't leave them alone, not with their mother gone also.

"Mrs. Ferguson will live in with you while I'm gone. I should be back after the log drive and we'll figure out what to do then."

He's already planned this out.

Pa rose from the table. "And instead of Mrs. Simonson coming here to feed the baby, you can drop him off at her house while you're in school. You'll pay her at the end of each week. That way Mrs. Ferguson can go home during the day and take care of her own house."

Dylan started to whimper and they both turned at the sound.

"We'll talk more tonight," he said as he started for the door.

Delaney stood slowly. "But…when, Pa? When do you leave?"

Her father faced the door, his hand on the knob. Without turning, he said, "Tomorrow." Then he opened the door and left.

Delaney stared at the closed door. Her whole being was numb. She didn't even realize she was gripping the edge of the table until she started to move toward the now crying baby and had to consciously release her hold.

He's going to leave us. We'll be alone.

Mrs. Ferguson was an older woman and even though her presence would give the children some reassurance, especially during the nights, Delaney didn't expect much more of her than that. The woman mostly sat in her rocker now.

Dylan was soaked, so Delaney automatically changed him and wrapped a clean blanket around him. She jostled him while she prepared his bottle and sat with him in the rocker. The lantern and the fire were the only lights in the dark room, and the creak of the rocker and Dylan's attack on the bottle were the only sounds.

Delaney's thoughts whirled through her head.

Alone. It couldn't be true. She was dreaming, that was it. Pa wouldn't abandon them, not now with Ma gone, with spring just around the corner, with four children left to her care, plus all the cooking and cleaning and managing of a house. They had hoped to start a garden, but she couldn't do that alone. What would they live on? Pa always put his earnings in the tin by the dishes and Ma carefully planned out her shopping to make each penny last until the next pay day. She had even made it a part of Delaney's school assignment to help her with the figures. But now, how would the money even get to the tin with Pa gone? Delaney had no idea.

She shivered as she pulled the baby up to her shoulder to burp him. Even though he had just been fed and should be sated, he started in with his whimpering.

Maybe the goat's milk isn't agreeing with him.

Delaney stood and tried bouncing Dylan to quiet him, but it was no use. She sighed as she heard the others moving about upstairs. The girls would be crabby and Delaney was in no mood for their arguing today. As she heard them tromp down the steep staircase, she made up her mind that she wouldn't say anything about their father's decision. Maybe Pa would still change his mind.

Darby was first to appear. At nine years old, she was the beauty of the four girls. Her natural curly hair was in contrast to Delaney's straight locks, and whereas Delaney had blonde hair, Darby sported the golden brown hair just like their mother's. Delaney often wondered at Ma and Pa's choices of names for their five children, but remembering her mother's imaginative stories and fanciful tales seemed to explain it. Ma's name before she married Pa was Dee Doherty and with Pa's name being Daniel Dunn it must have seemed natural for them to decide to christen each of their offspring with a name beginning with a "D" to carry on the tradition.

Delaney liked her name and its connection to the Irish heritage of her father, but there were times when her family shortened the name to Laney, and she liked that as well. Darby was rather a masculine name for the pretty girl who bore it, but the nine-year-old's femininity was so evident that she could never be mistaken for a tomboy. Daphne was the six-year-old member of the family. She was blonde like Delaney and their father, and Didi, who was three, had their mother's brown hair much like Darby's. Dylan, the newborn and only boy in the family, sported a head of black fuzz, like many newborns. Delaney recalled Ma saying that a baby's hair color often changed, so no doubt Dylan's would too.

Delaney nodded over Dylan's head to Darby as the girl left the house to use the privy. She turned as her next sister appeared.

Didi stumbled into the room still not fully awake and Delaney's heart wrenched when the child cried out, "I*th* Ma up, Laney?"

With Dylan crying on her shoulder, Delaney held out an arm to her little sister. "No, Didi. Remember? Ma's in heaven now. It's just us."

The young girl wrapped her arms around her sister's leg and held on tightly. "*Th*ee ain't nevah comin' back?"

Delaney choked back the tears that threatened. They went through this every morning and she didn't think she could do it again. Not today. Not with Pa's declaration going through her head over and over. She squeezed Didi's shoulder.

"Preacher says we'll see Ma again someday. Right now we just have to get along without her." She looked up as her other sister slid down the last few steps. "Get Didi's coat on her and take her out back," she directed Daphne. "I've got to get you some breakfast." She turned as the door opened and Darby returned. Gratefully Delaney handed the unhappy infant to her sister and moved quickly to prepare mush for their first meal of the day.

"We going to school today, Laney? We've missed a lot."

Delaney turned from the stove, considering Darby's question. "Are you ready to go back?"

Darby shrugged as she bounced the wailing baby up and down. "It would be better than sitting here without Ma," she reasoned.

But Delaney was still considering her father's announcement. Her voice shook a little as she answered. "Let's wait one more day. We'll have to make arrangements for Dylan to go to Mrs. Simonson, and I suppose Didi will have to come to school with us."

"I never thought about Didi. Will Miss Crane let her come?" It was hard for Darby to talk over Dylan's increasing volume. "What's the matter with him anyway?" she shouted as she paced the floor.

"Be careful," Delaney warned. "Remember when you almost dropped Didi and Ma scolded you but good?"

At Darby's sudden intake of air, Delaney turned and then hurried to her side. "I'm sorry." She patted Darby's shoulder as tears flowed down her sister's cheeks. "I miss her too."

"Why'd she have to die? We need a Ma. We need *her*!"

Delaney couldn't answer. She just nodded and wiped at her own eyes with her sleeve. "Quiet now. The girls are coming in." She cleared her throat. "Are you girls washed? Good. Breakfast is ready. Let's eat and then get dressed before we clean up."

"Ma always makes us dress first."

"Just today we'll do it different, okay?"

"Can I *th*ee Dylan?" Didi pulled on Darby's arm. "Why i*th* he cryin' *th*o much? He *th*ure i*th* loud."

The day moved forward in slow motion for Delaney. Tasks seemed to take longer than usual, and the girls helped with what they could and moped and argued with each other when they didn't have tasks to do. Dylan was silent only when he was sleeping, which wasn't for very long. It was a welcome relief when the woman they found to nurse Dylan finally arrived.

Mrs. Simonson was a large woman, a mother of six. She lumbered into the house carrying her newest in one arm and a basket of bread in the other. A child a little younger than Didi hung on to the woman's skirts as she dropped into the rocker and wiped at her forehead.

"I brung Ervin along to play with Didi today," she announced. "Get me a glass of water, will ya, Delaney? Here ya go, luv," she said to Darby as she handed over the baby bundle to her. "Stick Myrna in the cradle while I take care of this hungry mite." She reached for Dylan and soon had him suckling.

"I could hear him caterwaulin' clear down the road, I could. Are ya feedin' him thet goat's milk often enough? He sure appears hungry."

"Yes, Mrs. Simonson." Delaney stepped forward. "I check the temperature when I heat it to be sure it's just right and he seems to drink it fine, but he just cries all the time when he's not eating or sleeping. I don't know what's wrong with him."

"And yer 'bout ready to drop to sleep yerself, ain't ya? I can see the shadows under your eyes. Poor little ones. Well, it will help some to drop him by when ya go to school agin. Ya might as well leave Didi with me too. She and Ervin get along well enough. I already mentioned it to yer Pa when he stopped by, and he said to let ya decide for yerself."

Pa's already spoken to her! Delaney felt a chill down her spine. It really was happening. And Pa was leaving decisions—important decisions—up to her. She would have to get used to it.

"Maybe that would be best for now, if you don't mind."

The woman nodded and then rested her head on the rocker and closed her eyes. Delaney realized that it was an effort for her to come twice a day to take care of Dylan's feedings. Having the baby in her own home would certainly make things easier for her, and even more, it would help Delaney. The responsibility of taking care of a newborn plus her other tasks was wearing on her, and Dylan's constant crying was making her want to scream. But she couldn't help wondering what kind of care Dylan would receive at the hands of Mrs. Simonson. She was a nice enough woman, but not once had she really looked at the baby. She'd never changed him or even burped him. As soon as she was done with the feeding, she'd hand him over to Delaney or Darby and pick up her own baby and leave. There was none of the cuddling or cooing that most of the neighbor women did when they held Dylan.

Supper was quiet except for Daphne and Didi jabbering about playing with Ervin twice that day. Pa nodded a few times when the girls told him about their playtime, but even though he seemed distant, Delaney caught him staring at each one of them as if he were memorizing their faces. He turned to look at her and she quickly looked away. Then suddenly she realized something. *He never looked at Dylan.* Delaney made up her mind. If Pa was leaving, he needed to see his son before he left. He needed to really see him. She rose from the table and went to pick up the sleeping infant. Almost instantly he began crying, but she jostled him and returned to the table.

"Here, Pa. He wants you."

She watched as Pa's shoulders stiffened and he placed an elbow on the table as if to block her from handing the baby to him.

It's Dylan! This is why he wants to leave. He blames Dylan for Ma dying! Wisdom beyond her years made Delaney act.

"He's asking for you, Pa," she said over the baby's cries.

"Delaney!" Pa's tone was a warning. The other girls at the table stopped eating to see what was wrong.

"Just hold him. Please."

Pa's eyes never left Delaney's face as she held the boy out to her father, but just when she thought he was going to take him, Pa stood and mumbled, "I've got things to see to." And he left the house.

Pa didn't come back to the house until they were all in bed, and when Delaney woke the next morning, he had already gone.

Dunn Home

IT WAS ONLY a few days after Pa left and Delaney was still trying to answer her sisters' questions, but she was finding the answers hard to come by. She didn't know where the logging camp was or when Pa was returning. All she knew was what he had written in a note he put on the table for her to find the next morning. But unfortunately that didn't tell her much. She was at least gratified to know that the mercantile owners would handle their rent and give them credit at the store until Pa returned at the end of the log drive with his pay. Mrs. Ferguson was now staying with them and would be watching out for the children's well-being. But Delaney didn't understand how the elderly woman could possibly be of much help.

That first day was the hardest. With Dylan's constant crying and the girls' panicked faces as she explained their situation, Delaney could hardly keep from crying herself. She was frightened. They had never been alone without one of their parents to care for them. Now they were. And if the pattern of their days was to be set by the first one, then Mrs. Ferguson was going to be more of a burden to them than a help. She moved in and immediately took over the rocker and sat and knitted and slept through most of the day, expecting the girls to do the work including the cooking for her. Their grief over losing their mother was still ever present and now they felt tossed aside and left to their own devices by their father. Delaney knew that she had to be strong for the others, but what she didn't tell them, what she kept completely to herself, was the nagging fear that someone was going to put them all in an orphanage if Pa stayed away too long and they couldn't get by on their own. If they could just stay unnoticed by the rest of the town, maybe they would be okay. At least Mrs. Ferguson's presence could alleviate some of those fears.

So with that thought in mind, she laid out her plan to her family.

"We'll go back to school today after we drop off Dylan and Didi at Mrs. Simonson's. You are not to tell the others that Pa is gone. If they ask about him, just say he'll be back soon. If they get nosey, you send them to me. Do you understand?"

Daphne chewed at her fingernail. "But he will be back soon, right, Delaney? He won't stay away too long."

"Of course he will be back soon. We just don't want people talking about us, that's all. And I don't want any trouble at school either. We don't need Miss Crane poking her nose into our family's business, so you girls behave yourselves, you hear me?"

"You're not the boss of us, Delaney." Darby challenged her.

"For now I am." Delaney's voice was firm. She shook her head at Darby when the younger girl would have said more. "Let's get our coats on. I'll get Dylan and we'll go." She motioned for Darby to follow her to the other side of the room while the younger girls did her bidding.

"Darby! Please, let's not argue! I need your help now. If you don't listen to me, the others won't either, and right now we only have each other," Delaney pleaded.

Darby's pretty face held her stubborn look until she realized that her sister was shaking. "You're scared. Isn't Pa coming back, Delaney?" Fear was now in her voice.

Delaney willed herself to calm down. "He's coming back. We just have to stick together now and not argue anymore, okay? I can't do all this by myself." She picked up Dylan and patted him to keep the crying from getting louder. "I don't know what to do with Dylan either. I can't get him to quit this crying."

Darby seemed to see how tired her sister was for the first time. She nodded as if deciding to work with her rather than oppose her further. Turning to her sisters, she said, "Okay, let's go. Take my hand, Didi. We don't need you slipping on the ice."

Delaney breathed a sigh of relief. In the past, she and Darby often got into squabbles over any little thing and their mother would have to intervene. How foolish and how long ago it all seemed! Now Delaney knew there was no time for such things.

"We'll be home right after school, Mrs. Ferguson." Delaney stopped in front of the rocker and the old woman opened her eyes and stared at her.

"School?" She looked around at the children with their coats on. She pushed herself up from the chair slowly. "Then I will go back home for the day. No sense sitting around here."

Delaney nodded.

There were no questions at school. No one yet seemed to realize that their father was gone, and the Dunn children didn't volunteer the information, but Delaney had underestimated the gossip of a small town. It was only a few days before Miss Crane took her aside and asked the dreaded question.

"Delaney, is your father at home with you?"

Delaney kept her eyes on her teacher's face. "He works at a logging camp."

"So he's not home every night?"

Delaney swallowed. "He's gone for a while, but he'll be back soon." She watched as the teacher thought about her reply.

"How long have you children been alone?"

"We're not alone," Delaney quickly formed her answer. "Mrs. Ferguson is looking after us."

"I see."

Delaney clasped her hands behind her back so the teacher couldn't see them shaking. Out of the corner of her eye, she saw Darby stop playing a game with the other children to watch them.

"Does she care for the baby and your other sister? What is her name again?"

"Di…Di…Didi" Delaney stammered. "She and Dylan are at Mrs. Simonson's while we're here."

Miss Crane looked at her intently. "I see," she repeated. She seemed to be making up her mind about something. "Run along, Delaney. Class will begin shortly."

Delaney moved away quickly but she avoided going directly to Darby, who she could see was bursting with curiosity. The teacher was indeed getting too nosey. What if she learned that Dylan cried all the time? What if she found out that the girls didn't always get the beds made and the floors swept? What if the teacher discovered that she only knew how to cook a few things and that the pantry was starting to get bare? What if she found out that Mrs. Ferguson sometimes didn't come back to the house at night, as had happened once or twice now? What if she decided that Delaney couldn't take care of the other children and she put them all in an orphanage?

Delaney's heart was thumping as she ran all the possible scenes through her mind. She had to do a better job. She had to protect her family.

The remainder of the day passed slowly. It was Friday and Delaney breathed a sigh of relief as she left the building and headed for the Simonsons with her sisters. She wouldn't have to face the teacher for two days. And a good thing too.

When the small family entered their house that afternoon they found a letter on the table from the absent Mrs. Ferguson. Delaney carefully read the contents and folded the letter before turning to her sisters.

"She says her sister is ill and that she has to go to her. She's not coming back."

"Well, she didn't do anything anyway," was Daphne's quick comment. She moved to open the pantry doors. "What's for supper, Delaney?"

Darby shared a look with Delaney, but Delaney shook her head. It would be better to discuss things later when the younger girls couldn't hear, but for now Delaney's worries increased. *How could she just leave us like this? What if the people in town find out?*

Delaney watched the sun rise the following morning. She had been up most of the night trying to calm her brother into sleeping, but to no avail. Her eyes were dry and scratchy from lack of sleep and she groaned as she got up from the rocker and made another attempt at laying Dylan in his cradle. This time he seemed to finally give in and he settled down to sleep. Not so for Delaney.

She had to do something. She couldn't go on like this— not getting any sleep, trying to keep up with the household chores, and worrying about their future. Later in the day, she yelled at Daphne for dawdling when she was supposed to be helping Darby carry in firewood. She even slapped Didi's hand when she reached for a second helping of stew without asking. Didi bawled like she had been given a whipping instead of a hand slap, and Darby glared at her older sister but said nothing as she calmed the distraught girl.

Delaney felt horrible. She was so overwhelmed with it all, and she couldn't seem to stop herself from being angry at all of them. Her head hurt. She was so tired.

Finally she had enough.

"I'm going for supplies." She grabbed the list she had made earlier off the shelf. "Darby, you clean up here and get more wood in the house, we're running low." Her voice brooked no argument, and she watched Darby tighten her lips at the commands, but she ignored her as she prepared to leave.

"Then you have to take Dylan and Didi." Darby walked over to wrap the crying baby into a blanket.

"How am I supposed to watch Didi and carry the supplies and Dylan at the same time?" Delaney demanded.

"I don't know! But you can't leave them here if you want me to get the wood in. All Dylan does is cry, cry, cry! Maybe taking him for a walk outside will make him stop." Darby thrust the baby at her sister, daring her to refuse to take him.

Delaney pulled Dylan into her arms and started patting him. She glared at her sister then grabbed Didi's hand and without another word she turned and walked out of the small house.

Their rental house was on the outskirts of the rugged town. She walked fast through the packed down snow trail made by other pedestrians until the extra weight of the baby and the fact that her whole body seemed to ache made her slow her steps. She was already sorry for treating her sisters the way she had and she almost turned to go back and tell them so, but she had cooled down somewhat and knew that they really did need supplies and she was almost to the mercantile by now. She would hurry with the shopping and fix something extra special for their supper to make it up to them. And the walk had settled Dylan down as Darby suggested.

"You awright, Laney?" Didi's trembling voice told Delaney that she was still upset over the scolding earlier that day. She patted her little sister's shoulder.

"I'm fine, Didi. I'm just really tired. Dylan's crying keeps me up most of the night and I'm not getting enough sleep. I'm sorry I yelled at you today."

"Okay." Didi wiped at her eye and leaned her head against Delaney's side.

"Hi there, Delaney," Mrs. Bedloe greeted her as she entered the store. "Have you got Dylan there with you, dear? Oh, is he sleeping? Why don't you lay him down back here where it's warm while you do your shopping? Don't worry, you'll be able to keep an eye on him."

Delaney walked over to where the storekeeper indicated. A blanket was folded and placed behind the counter and another baby was sleeping on it.

"Who's that?" Delaney whispered.

Mrs. Bedloe smiled. Sharing newsy tidbits was her specialty. "He belongs to some folks passing through here." She lowered her voice and bent forward to Delaney's ear. "I think they're rather rich. That's the nanny for the baby over there. The missus is next door at the dressmakers and the milliners looking at hats." She seemed excited to tell someone and since Delaney was the only one around at the moment, she apparently would have to do.

"See that sleigh over at the hotel? Have you ever seen anything so fancy in all your born days?"

Delaney glanced out the window at the fancy vehicle and the beautiful horses.

"Are they staying at the hotel?" she whispered again. She swallowed and winced when she felt pain in her throat.

"They did. I heard the lady tell the nanny to stock up on supplies as they would be leaving soon. Their name is Blackmore and Mr. Blackmore is involved with the railroad and plans to see to it that the rails get all the way to Nealsville. Oh, I keep forgetting, they call it LaPrairie now, don't they? I only hope they bring it on to Grand Rapids. Anyway, this is their third child. Imagine, hiring a nanny to care for your children! Mrs. Blanchard—she's the nanny— confided in me that the baby is a perfect angel, but not having any children of my own, I wouldn't know much about that. Mr. Bedloe and I—well, never mind, child." Mrs. Bedloe's expression soured before she returned to her subject. "They have to be rich to hire a nanny for a child like that. Maybe the two older boys are the reason."

Delaney bent down to place Dylan next to the other infant.

"Why, don't they look sweet!" Mrs. Bedloe commented with a smile. "Do you have a list, Delaney? Would you like some help?"

"Yes…please." Delaney pulled the list from her pocket and let the storekeeper move away to gather the items for her. She felt dazed and just wanted to close her eyes to rest them.

"I'll watch Dylan, Laney." Didi pulled on Delaney's arm.

Delaney swallowed again and put a hand to her sore throat. *I can't get sick now!* "Sure, Didi. That would be nice. Thank you."

The bell over the door jingled, announcing another customer. Delaney turned to see who it was and found a young boy about her age craning his neck to look for someone. He caught her looking at him and stared back at her until Delaney felt her face grow hot. She was suddenly aware of her plain dress and the heavy woolen stockings that were starting to droop.

He strode over to her and looked past to the babies on the blanket. "Well, Shawn is here anyway. That must mean that Mrs. Blanchard is around here somewhere." He cocked his head at Delaney. "You're kind of cute. If we was stayin' in this backwoods town, I'd be your feller, but we're moving to the big city in Minneapolis, so I'll have to find someone else. Have you seen Mrs. Blanchard?"

Delaney only gaped at him in astonishment.

"There she is." He pointed to the woman with Mrs. Bedloe. "Say, what's your name? I'm Ben Blackmore."

Delaney lowered the shawl she still had covering her head. She tried not to wince as she swallowed and felt the pain in her throat. "I'm…Delaney Dunn," she managed to stammer.

"Oh, Delaney! Delaney, what does this say, dear? I'm afraid I can't read your writing."

Delaney turned toward the storekeeper. Her head was throbbing. Mrs. Bedloe was looking down at the list in her hand.

"Excuse me, please. Mrs. Bedloe needs me." She made to move past the boy but he stepped forward and blocked her path.

"I hope to see you again someday, *Delaney*." He grinned as he emphasized her name before moving to speak to the woman he had pointed out. Then he made his way to the door but before he exited, he looked Delaney's way again and winked.

What a cheeky boy!

Delaney swayed a bit as she stood and took one last look at Dylan and Didi before she walked over to Mrs. Bedloe.

"Um…that's molasses," she murmured. Her throat was tight and suddenly she felt sick. "Excuse me, ma'am. I need to go out back." She turned and raced for the door.

Delaney was sick. She expelled her breakfast in the outhouse and tried to calm herself as she broke out into a cold sweat. She had to go back and get the children and get home as soon as possible. She didn't dare let the storekeeper know how sick she was or worse, have her find out that Mrs. Ferguson was gone. She pressed her hand to her aching head. If only she wasn't so tired she could think clearly.

A knock on the privy door startled her.

"Delaney! Are you all right, dear?"

Delaney pushed open the door and collapsed in Mrs. Bedloe's arms.

4

Dunn Home

No one could have been more surprised than Delaney when she opened her eyes and saw Miss Crane's concerned face looking into hers. She stared at the teacher as she tried to figure out what happened and where she was.

"Well, hello there, Laney. Welcome back."

Laney? She called me Laney?

The teacher's voice was soft and soothing, and Delaney became aware that the woman was dabbing at her forehead with a cool cloth. She looked past the teacher and saw Darby approaching with a glass of water in her hands.

I'm in Ma and Pa's bed!

Delaney attempted to sit up, but Miss Crane gently pushed her back. It didn't take much effort because Delaney felt extremely weak. She smiled faintly at Darby as her sister brought the water to her lips. Darby's look of relief told Delaney that her sister had been worried about her. Miss Crane raised Delaney's head and she swallowed the cool liquid gratefully.

"My throat hurts." Her voice came out as a raspy whisper.

"I'm sure it does." Miss Crane stroked back Delaney's hair. "You've been sick for several days."

"Days?" Delaney closed her eyes. The water made her throat feel better and the bed felt so good and sleep was welcome after so many sleepless nights getting up with Dylan.

Dylan!

Delaney groaned and rose up on one elbow.

"Where's Dylan?" She choked out the words. She tried to throw off the blankets and get up, but the teacher kept her restrained.

"I have to get Dylan! I left him…and…Didi in the mercantile!"

"Shhh, Delaney. Dylan is at Mrs. Simonson's along with Daphne and Didi. We didn't want them to get sick too." Miss Crane made the explanation as she tucked Delaney back into the bed.

Delaney burst into tears and sobbed until sleep overtook her once again.

It was the next morning that Delaney woke to hear a woodpecker tapping on a tree outdoors. She felt so much better as she stretched her arms above her head, but there was still the nagging feeling that something was very wrong.

Delaney swallowed and her throat felt fine. She flipped the blankets back and stood to her feet. She waited until she felt that she could step forward; then she padded quietly out the bedroom into the living area of the small house. She stopped in her tracks at the sight of her teacher sleeping in the rocking chair.

What is she doing here? Where is everyone?

She looked around the room but no one else was in sight. It was early, too early for the others to be up, so she moved silently to the staircase and began the climb, taking each step slowly and carefully, avoiding the spots that creaked, until she reached her sisters' bedroom. Darby was the only one there, huddled under the covers with only her head peeking out at the top. Delaney sat on the edge of the bed and tapped her sister on the arm. Darby's eyes flew open at once.

Delaney put her finger to her lips to silence her, but Darby pulled herself up to sit upright in the bed and opened the blankets to allow Delaney to climb in to get warm. The sisters looked at each other. Finally Delaney spoke, her voice only a whisper.

"What's Miss Crane doing here? How long have I been ill?"

Darby kept her voice down too. "She was in town when you got sick and she heard Mrs. Bedloe yelling for help. All I know after that is that she got Mr. Bedloe to bring you home in his sleigh and she took Dylan, Daphne, and Didi to the Simonsons. She wanted me to go too, but I wouldn't leave you. I think she decided she had to stay with us until you got better, especially after she found out that Mrs. Ferguson was gone."

Delaney studied Darby's face. She knew that the impact of having the teacher know about their situation hadn't hit her sister yet, but she was well aware of the predicament they were in now that Miss Crane knew they were on their own.

"You okay, Delaney? You look like you're going to be sick again."

Delaney took a deep breath. "I'm fine." She looked around the room at the other bed. Empty. "We need to get everyone back here. I don't want Miss Crane to have to stay any longer." She slid out of the bed and took Darby's arm as they began the descent to the lower level of the house. "You say she's been here for days? What about school?"

"Miss Crane told the board to keep everyone home so that no one else would get sick. I heard that the doc has been called to several homes."

"She's been here the whole time then?"

"Yep."

Delaney peeked around the corner to see the teacher was still asleep. It was odd to look at Miss Crane in this setting. Her light brown hair was loose around her shoulders and it softened her features. She was almost pretty.

"She called me Laney," she whispered to her sister.

"I know." Darby made a face and Delaney couldn't help it. She giggled.

Miss Crane's eyes flew open. Delaney watched as she twisted her neck from side to side as if to get the kinks out of it before turning to greet the girls.

"Good morning, Delaney. You must be feeling better today. Good morning, Darby." Miss Crane rose to her feet and pulled her shawl closer to her. She reached for Delaney's forehead and felt it. She smiled. "Much better. Thank the Lord for that."

Delaney wasn't sure what to say or do. This was her schoolteacher. To see her standing in their house with her hair mussed up and knowing that she had been tending to her while she was sick was a bit unnerving. But apparently Miss Crane wasn't uncomfortable with the situation.

"I'll expect you to take it easy for the next couple of days. Darby and I will prepare breakfast and then we'll go for the other children. I'm sure you'd like to see everyone. But before that we'll heat water so you can bathe. You'll feel a hundred percent better after that."

Before Delaney knew what was happening, the teacher had her back in bed. The girls looked questioningly at each other. Darby shrugged and started after the teacher out the door while Delaney stared up at the ceiling wondering what to do. She needed to get back control of her family and that meant getting rid of Miss Crane. She appreciated what the teacher did in helping out while the family needed her, but now that Delaney was better the presence of the teacher was no longer wanted.

Getting cleaned up lifted Delaney's spirits and refreshed her. She wanted to go with Darby to get the other children, but Miss Crane insisted that she remain at the house and wait for them to return. But she couldn't sit still. She had an overwhelming desire to make sure her brother and sisters were all right. Even though taking on their responsibility was a huge task, she loved them all dearly, and she knew she would do anything to keep them all together.

She got up and began pacing the small room. She couldn't help but worry about what was going to happen to them. *If only Pa would come home!*

She stopped suddenly when she recalled that boy in the mercantile. What was his name? *Ben Blackmore.* She wondered if he had witnessed her dash to the outhouse to be sick, but, no, he left before that happened. She felt herself blush again as she remembered him saying that he would be her feller. She shook her head. She'd never had a boy talk to her like that. He must be the reason that family needed a nanny. It seemed he was a troublemaker. Still, it gave her a funny feeling inside to wonder if he really did think she was pretty.

Finally she heard the voices of her siblings as they walked toward the house. She ran to the door and was nearly knocked over as Didi flung her arms around her.

"Laney! We thought you wuh gonna die like Ma!"

"Hush, Didi! We told you she was all right." Darby's scold was gentle.

Delaney hugged her little sister. "I'm okay now, Didi. I missed you."

Daphne hugged Delaney next. "I'm glad you're better. I don't like staying at the Simonson's. They make us do their chores for them and Mrs. Simonson can't cook as good as you." Daphne set down the belongings she was carrying and went to the pantry to look for something to eat.

Delaney's eyes were on the bundle in Darby's arms. She reached eagerly for the baby, hardly hearing Darby's next words.

"Miss Crane said she'd be by later after she did some errands in town. Oh, and Mrs. Simonson said to tell you that Dylan is finally getting his days and nights straight. He's slept through the night three times now. I guess it was the goat's milk that didn't set well with him at first."

Delaney pulled the blanket away from the baby's face and stared at him. He looked so peaceful, sleeping with a small smile on his face.

"He looks different."

"What do you mean?" Darby stood on tiptoe to see the baby's face.

"Older. He looks older." Delaney smiled at her sister. "I mean it's only been a few days, but already he's changed. Remember how Didi changed so quickly, especially when she started to crawl?"

Darby nodded. "Yeah, and when she got her first tooth too."

The sisters shared a special look. Having the responsibility of raising their brother and younger sisters might seem overwhelming, but as children themselves they could appreciate the rewards in their tasks as well.

Delaney looked down at the baby in her arms. She stroked his cheek and his lips curled into a smile as he opened his eyes and studied her. She smiled back.

Darby left her to settle a dispute between the younger girls, and Delaney leaned down to whisper to the baby.

"I'm going to take good care of you, Dylan Dunn, because you're my brother."

She was awarded with another smile.

5

Logging Camp
Several Weeks Earlier

DANIEL DUNN TRUDGED down the path back to the camp. He pulled a sled of supplies behind him as he had promised to do when he and Ralston brought Shorty in to town to see the doctor. It took two of them to pull the injured man. Having the name Shorty was a misnomer as the man was over six feet and built like a block house. But such was the way of the men in the woods. The grumpiest was called Smiley and the thinnest was Moose. Daniel was weeks later than expected, but Ralston had returned right away with the first load of supplies, and Daniel knew that he had passed on the information that Daniel's wife died.

The trail wasn't easy to navigate with the heavy sled and having to pull it by himself. Daniel strained to pull it up hills and fought to keep it from getting away from him on the downward sides. The physical exertion was just what he needed, but being alone with his thoughts was not. He grieved over losing his beloved Dee.

His thoughts went to his children. Leaving them on their own was probably considered a terrible thing to do but no one could understand his torment. Daniel couldn't walk into that house night after night and sleep in that bed alone. And the baby—he had wanted a son, and Dee was so hoping that this baby was the boy he was waiting for, but she died giving him his son, and for that very reason he couldn't even bear to look at the baby. It was his fault that Dee was gone.

He knew it was wrong to leave Delaney with all the responsibility of caring for the newborn, but he just couldn't bring himself to even hold him. He stayed with the ice cutting work only long enough to find someone to stay with the children and then he had to leave even though they really had more work for him contrary to what he had told Delaney. He had to get away, and at the first opportunity he did.

But his demons followed him.

Daniel knew he should talk to God. The only thought that was keeping him sane was knowing that Dee was in heaven. They didn't talk about their faith much, but before they married, Dee had questioned Daniel about his beliefs. She told him she couldn't marry someone who didn't believe in God and who hadn't trusted Jesus Christ as his Savior. Daniel had grown up going to church and knew enough to convince her that he believed, but after they were married he was too busy working and providing for the family to go to church with her and the children. Dee kept going when she could and she read Scripture to the children.

Daniel heaved the sled up the last of an incline and leaned back against a tree, panting for air. He used his coat sleeve to wipe away the sweat on his forehead as he looked at the scene before him. The camp was quiet except for the smoke coming from the cookhouse. The jacks were out piling more logs on the landings and would be in just before nightfall for the meal the cook was busy preparing. He squinted.

Looks like they put the wanigan together already.

Over by the riverbank was a crude structure on a raft that the cook would use when the men began the log drive down the river. On the drive the previous year, the wanigan had gotten crushed and broken into bits when it got caught in a log jam. This new one would be pushed into the river as soon as the ice disappeared.

It was time to go and get immersed in the backbreaking work that he needed to restore his soul, but before he started the sled down the last slope, he had to have his say with God.

Daniel pulled his wool hat off his head. He didn't bother closing his eyes or dropping to his knees. He looked to the treetops and spoke his thoughts out loud.

"I don't know why you had to take her." He didn't raise his voice, but each word pierced the silence around him. "I have never been more angry in my life, but because she loved you and believed in you, I know she's there with you." No tears fell but his jaw tightened as he continued, "But I loved *her*. I don't know if I can ever forgive you for taking her from me."

He waited as if expecting a bolt of lightning to strike him dead and he almost wished one would, but having said his piece, he tugged his hat back on and pulled the sled forward.

The men who worked in the logging camps were a rough lot. Some were there of their own free will because they needed the job, but many had been tricked into the work. Some of these unsuspecting men were given free drinks in one of the many saloons and taverns in the small towns in the area. The drinks would be laced with knockout drops and when the men woke with their heads hammering in pain, they would find themselves dumped in a snow bank in the woods, their money gone, and nothing but the clothes on their backs. They could either freeze to death in the snow or follow the trail to the camp and be put to work.

The wages were not good, but for those who completed the drive to the mills and received their pay, it was a living, *if* they could keep the pay in their possession long enough to get it to their families. Too often the rowdy men hit the taverns again and the unscrupulous bartenders made sure the money was spent on liquor, gambling, and women in their establishments. Again, many were drugged and their money stolen so that they had no other recourse but go back to the woods again.

Daniel learned his lesson early. The first pay he received, he gladly joined the others at the saloons, but he was quick to see what was happening and got out of that environment before he became one of the victims. Dee was waiting and they needed the money. Once, walking the roads to home he was set upon by thieves who were waiting for one of the jacks to stroll by. They had clubs and came at him with the intent to maim or kill to get his roll of bills, but Daniel was fit and agile from his winter in the woods and was able to dodge their blows and strike soundly with his own. He had sweat and toiled for every last penny in his pocket and he was not about to lose it to some thugs.

The men welcomed Daniel back to camp in their own ways. A nod of the head was the usual gesture of sympathy, occasionally a pat on the shoulder as one walked by him. No one mentioned his loss and he was grateful for that. The work was what Daniel wanted and there was plenty of it. And Daniel went after it with reckless vengeance, so much so that some of the men were uneasy working near him, fearing his wild look and careless regard for safety. And to make matters worse, Daniel's once easygoing manner was now replaced with a simmering anger that exploded to the surface at any provocation. Fistfights were not uncommon in the camp, but Daniel was now the catalyst to most of them.

There were no sounds but the scraping of forks on tins as the men ate their evening meal. Talking was not allowed in the cookshack and the time to eat was limited, so the men shoveled in the food as fast as they could and often filled their pockets with whatever food they wanted to take to eat later. The food was abundant, for the men needed the fuel to do their work, and the cook was generous with the pies, cakes, and cookies and the blackest of coffee to wash them down. It was the coffee that started the latest fight.

Daniel was sitting between a huge jack named Murdock and Ralston, the man who helped him bring the wounded man named Shorty to town. Eating was serious business and the men devoured their meals with gusto. Daniel ate without tasting the food. He only ate to keep up his strength so he could push his body to work all the harder.

Ralston reached past Daniel to grab the freshly baked rolls at the same time as the beefy arm of Murdock reached for them. Daniel's scalding coffee sprayed him as his tin cup was knocked on its side.

"Murdock!" Daniel was on his feet and lunged at the man. He missed the surprised expression on the giant's face and the smirk on Ralston's, but he didn't miss the blow when Murdock backhanded him alongside his head.

Fists pounded bodies as the two men wrestled between the tables, but the cook wasn't about to allow his domain to become a battleground for the pugilists. He grabbed Daniel by the collar and used the force of shoving him into Murdock to send them both toward the door.

"Get out! You wanna fight, you do it out there!" He was surprisingly strong for a man who worked in a kitchen all day, but then hefting sides of pork and fifty-pound bags of potatoes and meal made as much muscle on the cook as on the men who swung axes or pulled on saws all day. "You fight in my mess and you don't get fed. Ever!" He slammed the door behind them.

Daniel hardly noticed where he was. He just kept swinging at Murdock and landing blows and receiving them. Some of the men who were done with their meal came out to watch and place bets on the winner, but the fight was finally broken up when four men came into the camp and one of them called for the foreman.

Daniel's face and fists were bleeding from cuts. His beard and hair were as wild as his eyes when he looked up into the faces of the four men. He recognized the tall form of Shorty, the injured man he and Ralston brought to town months ago, and he saw that one of the men was wearing the badge of a deputy. He had no idea who the other two were; all he knew was that he was angry that they were the reason the fight was over. He glared his hatred at them.

"Looks like you've come just in time, Preacher," the older man commented to one of the others.

"And there's no time like the present," agreed the man. He looked up as more men filed out the cookhouse. "Men! As soon as you can get gathered in the bunkhouse. I'm going to preach your first sermon." He looked down at Daniel and Murdock. "I believe you two will have a front row seat."

"Who are you to tell me what to do?" demanded Daniel.

The older man stepped forward. "This is Pastor Sampson, and you show him some respect, mister."

Daniel eyed the preacher with suspicion before turning back to the older man. "And who are you?" Daniel spat blood into the mud.

"I'm Bernie Clayton, the owner of this camp and your boss, and you'll do as I say or you're out on your backside!"

Daniel struggled to his feet and without realizing it, he held out a hand and helped Murdock up as well. He missed the look that passed between the preacher and the camp boss at his action.

"Mr. Clayton, sir?"

The camp boss looked at the lawman as if just remembering his presence. "Oh, that's right." He stopped the men who were headed to the bunkhouse. "Men, Officer Elwood would like a word with you too, so I expect everyone to be present. No excuses!"

A few splashes of water in the trough outside the bunkhouse helped clear his head, and Daniel entered the long narrow building and flung himself down on his bed. By now, he was used to the bedbugs and fleas that lived within, but he didn't think he would ever get used to the odors of sweat and the smell of drying woolens that the men threw over the ends of their bunks. Even now as they worked in the warmer weather, the woodstove was kept hot to help dry out the men's clothing. The room was stifling as the preacher took a bench and placed it by the door.

But before the preacher spoke, Deputy Elwood gained the men's attention with some astonishing news. He stood tall with his feet slightly apart. The gun on his belt appeared to be new, shiny with scrollwork, definitely not issued by the county, which made Daniel wonder if the man was a greenhorn. He didn't recall seeing him before.

"We've had some robberies in town lately and I'm here to question you men. I expect you to give me your time and attention. I'm planning to stay in camp until I've heard from every one of you. Now I'll let the preacher have his say."

The far end of the room was almost completely in the dark, but a sliver of the night sky appeared when the end door was opened slightly and quickly closed. They all knew there were men among them who were fleeing the law and working in the logging camps to keep out of sight. Daniel didn't know who slipped out the door and he didn't care.

Elwood moved aside and motioned for the preacher to take over, and the pastor stepped up on the bench and began to preach.

Daniel was in no mood for a sermon, but he was curious about this Pastor Sam, as the men called him. He had heard of him. Usually if a preacher showed up at the camp, the men did their best to run him out, not sparing his tender ears with their foul language and behavior. But Clayton was here. The boys weren't likely to put their jobs in jeopardy with the boss watching. Daniel put an arm over his eyes. If he didn't like what he heard, he'd just go to sleep.

But sleep wasn't possible with the booming voice of the preacher expounding on God's Word to the men. Daniel found himself listening despite his intention not to. Pastor Sam told them things that Daniel only vaguely remembered from his childhood. Things he heard Dee saying to the children. And when Pastor Sam got to the end of his sermon, he challenged the men to believe the Gospel message for themselves.

"Jesus didn't have to take the whippings and beatings that he did," the preacher proclaimed. "He could have stopped that awful crucifixion, and with a word he could have destroyed mankind completely. But he didn't. He didn't because of the great love he has for every human being including wretches like you and me. He didn't because he wants each one of you to accept his sacrifice for your sins by faith. He took your place, men! He died for you! He wants you in heaven with him. Won't you today place your faith in him? Won't you give your life to him and let him walk beside you?"

Daniel kept his arm over his face as he thought about the man's words. Dee talked like that. She knew God in a personal way that Daniel never had. He knew *about* God, but he didn't know God.

Soon the bunkhouse was dark and quiet except for the snoring and deep breathing of the sleeping men. Daniel rose from his bunk and stepped outside for a breath of fresh air. He needed to think. He rubbed a hand over his face and winced at the swollen cuts and bruises. This fighting wasn't right. It wasn't what Dee would have wanted him to do. He needed to get control of himself. He had to think of his family.

His family. Daniel walked down the dark trail a ways while he finally let his thoughts return to his children. He knew they needed him.

When the drive is done this year, I need to go home and get a job in town.

There had to be something he could do to earn enough money to stay with his family. Maybe the lumber mill would hire him.

These new thoughts settled him down. He didn't know if it was the preacher's words that had an effect on him or if Murdock's punches finally knocked some sense into his head, but he made up his mind that he was going to change.

The cook had smoke pouring from the chimney of the cookhouse the next morning by the time the jacks began rolling out of their bunks when a sudden shout caught their attention. The men hurried to the door in their long underwear to see what the commotion was about.

"He's dead! Murdock's dead!"

Daniel pushed his way through the throng to find Murdock's body leaning against the side of the bunkhouse. Daniel's heart started thumping wildly when he saw the knife in the man's chest—not any knife—*his* knife.

6

Grand Rapids

MERCY CRANE MOVED through the town, trying to avoid the icy patches on the road. She didn't want to leave the Dunn children alone for too long, especially now with what she had just learned.

Being the town's schoolteacher, she heard a lot of the town gossip. Most of what she heard she dismissed. She preferred to approach her students without the prejudice of rumors about them, but the Dunn girls were different. Not that she had favorites, but there was a connection between her and the three girls under her tutelage of which they knew nothing. She too lost her mother at a young age. Her father raised her just as Mr. Dunn now would have to raise his children—alone.

Mercy fingered the message in her pocket and her brow puckered in concern. With Delaney as sick as she had been, Mercy had taken it upon herself to send word out to the logging camp with one of the suppliers to inform Mr. Dunn of his daughter's condition. The reply she received back worried her more than she was going to let on to the school board members who were about to meet with her at her request.

She entered the empty schoolhouse and began arranging chairs for the men. She was nervous about her request, but it made sense and it would help those children. She needn't reveal to anyone what the message contained. It would only make the situation worse.

She heard footsteps outside the door and hurried to greet her guests.

"Afternoon, Miss Crane." Mr. Bedloe, the owner of the mercantile, slid his hat off his bald head.

"Hello, Mr. Bedloe. Won't you take a seat, please?" She motioned to the chairs set in a half circle near her desk.

"Fine thing you've done taking care of that Dunn girl when she was ailing," he commented. "My wife was pretty near frantic to know what to do until you happened by and took charge."

"You were a big help too by offering the use of your sleigh to get her and the baby home, sir." Mercy returned the compliment.

The other men were coming and Mercy stood uneasily watching the door for Mr. Crenshaw to arrive. She hadn't expected to face him so soon after rejecting his dinner invitation and she was nervous about his reaction to her. But she relaxed when he entered and merely nodded his head in her direction.

She was about to begin when she overheard the conversation going on among the men.

"You heard about the robbery at the lumber mill last month, didn't you?"

"The lumber mill too? Someone got away with money from my store, I know."

"It's those criminals who work in the camps, that's who's done it!" declared Mr. Crenshaw as he joined in the conversation. "Someone broke into my shop and I know it was one of those men. They steal from the towns and then they hide out in the woods where the law can't find them. We need to—"

"Gentlemen," Mercy attempted to gain their attention. The men turned to her. "If you'll allow me to interrupt, I don't want to keep you too long. As you know I've been staying with the Dunn children during this time of illness, and I think you'll all agree that closing the school until this contagious disease passed was a good idea."

The men nodded.

"Wise decision. Wise. I commend you for making such a wise decision."

Mercy's face reddened at Mr. Crenshaw's praise, but she cleared her throat and continued. "My reason for calling you here today is to discuss a couple of matters, if I may. First, I believe it is safe to open the doors to the children once again and allow them back to school. We only have about a month left before their break, and we still have a lot of material to cover in that short time."

"I agree," Mr. Hamilton from the bank spoke up. "And if I may say, you have been doing a fine job with the children, Miss Crane. My Ernestine is a testimony to that."

Mercy hesitated a moment. Ernestine Hamilton was a difficult student. Her family's social position in the small town caused her to put on airs with the other children, but Mercy kept her in line. Interesting that her father thought she was doing so well. Ernestine was dumb as a post in most subjects.

"Thank you, sir. Next, I would like to speak to you in regard to my living arrangements."

"Are you not happy at the Pratts?" questioned Mr. Olson, owner of a lumber mill.

"The accommodation at the Pratts has been satisfactory." Mercy didn't expound to the men that she shared a bed with the Pratts' two-year-old twin girls and that she rarely got a good night's sleep. No, they didn't need to hear about that. "My suggestion is that, in light of the Dunns' recent loss of their mother and the fact that their father is away for a time, perhaps the board would consider allowing me to room with the Dunns and be an adult presence for the children."

She watched the men look at each other as if seeking out the others' thoughts.

"Having been there these past few days, I feel that I can speak informatively on their conditions. The oldest girl, Delaney, has been doing quite well for her age, but as we've recently seen, illness can interrupt daily routines, and in the case of the Dunns, it left them vulnerable to needing outside help. I feel that having an adult with them would ease their burdens somewhat, and I believe they could use the money you provide for my room and board to help with their expenses."

"I didn't realize the father left them." Mr. Hamilton frowned.

"Didn't you hear? He's back at the camp and left the children to their own devices," Mr. Olson was quick to inform him. He turned back to Mercy. "Wasn't Mrs. Ferguson staying with the children?"

Before Mercy could answer, Mr. Bedloe spoke up. "She left about a week ago to help an ill relative, I believe."

"Well, if he has abandoned his family, then the children should be sent to Owatonna to the orphanage. Surely this shouldn't become Miss Crane's responsibility." Mr. Crenshaw insisted.

It was what Mercy feared. She knew it wouldn't be long before the town stepped in and did their civic duty by the family. The message in her pocket would certainly seal the fate of the children if the contents were known to the others. She couldn't let that happen.

"Excuse me, please, gentlemen, if I may." She waited for their attention again. "I have it on good authority that Mr. Dunn's absence is a temporary one, so I don't believe there is any reason to discuss orphanages. And if I should be permitted to board with the family, I believe there will be no cause for concern about their welfare."

She waited.

"What happens when their father returns? You can't stay there with a widower," Mr. Crenshaw voiced his disapproval as he furiously twisted his handlebar mustache.

"When Mr. Dunn returns, I shall move back to the Pratts or return to my father's farm."

"They have an infant, don't they? What do you propose to do about that? You can't have an infant in the school and be productive in your teaching duties."

"Arrangements have already been made for Mrs. Simonson to tend to Dylan and the youngest of the sisters while the older three attend school. And as we've already said, gentlemen, there are only a few weeks remaining in this term."

The banker stood and fingered his lapels as he walked to the front of the room and stood beside the teacher. "Have you forgotten, Miss Crane, that you do not receive compensation during the summer months? Will you be more of a burden than a help to the family by staying with them and not paying them?"

"I believe we can manage, sir. I do expect their father to be back by then."

"Then I vote yes." He turned to the others and one by one they nodded in agreement. Mr. Crenshaw was the last to acquiesce, and Mercy wondered if his reluctance was because he knew it would make her even more unavailable for courting. She breathed a sigh of relief as she closed the door behind the last man. She did a quick survey of the schoolbooks on her desk, gathered what she needed, and hurried to the Pratts to collect the rest of her belongings. If Mr. Pratt would lend her his horse and sleigh, she could get everything to the Dunns in one trip and be finished before nightfall.

As her long strides quickly took her on the way to the Pratts' home, her thoughts returned to the message she carried in her pocket and that in turn led her to prayer.

Dear Father, please, please don't let it be true that Mr. Dunn is being accused of these thefts.

7

Dunn Home

DELANEY WASN'T SURE what to think of the new living arrangements. One day she and her sisters and brother were on their own, and the next they had Miss Crane as a permanent fixture in their little house. It was unnerving to have the schoolteacher at their table for every meal, sometimes correcting grammar, sometimes settling squabbles, always reminding them of their manners.

The meals were better though, Delaney had to admit, and giving over that responsibility didn't really bother her. Miss Crane could cook. Menus were simple and meals after school were prepared and eaten quickly so the girls could attend to their homework, which always got done now, even before chores.

But life wasn't the same. Part of Delaney wanted to rebel at having her position as head of the house usurped by the teacher, but part of her was relieved not to bear all the burdens any longer on her own. Miss Crane didn't actually take over, she just made everything so much easier for the eleven-year-old.

It was Delaney, who after accepting that Miss Crane was truly moving in with them, insisted that the teacher use her parents' bedroom for her own. It was an uncomfortable moment. Somehow Miss Crane seemed to read Delaney's thoughts. Delaney didn't want her upstairs. She wanted her sisters to have their own space without the teacher's constant presence, and understanding that, Miss Crane graciously accepted the room to herself. Delaney continued to stay close by Dylan's cradle in the small room next to her parents' even though the baby now slept peacefully through the night. She found it difficult to allow anyone else to care for him but her, and leaving him every day at the Simonsons was actually painful for her.

School was no different than before. Miss Crane treated them the same as she did the other students, but Delaney could see that having the teacher live with them would improve their skills in all their subjects. Having their homework assignments done and having Miss Crane as a ready resource for their questions at night made their learning more enjoyable. She could see a new confidence in her sisters and in herself.

The other students accepted the change without comment. Teachers always boarded with one family or another, so it was nothing new to them to see their teacher come and go with one of their own, this time the

Dunn girls. Only Ernestine Hamilton heckled the girls behind the teacher's back, calling them teacher's pets. But Delaney knew Ernestine's ways, having been tormented by her before.

The biggest immediate change was that the teacher was able to bring laughter back into their home, and when she surprised them one night with a peppermint candy each after supper, Delaney thought it was one of the best days they'd had since their troubles began. Didi expressed her appreciation by climbing onto the teacher's lap and hugging her.

"I love you, Mi*th* Cwane."

Delaney inhaled sharply and met Miss Crane's eyes with her own. She hadn't counted on the teacher stealing the affections of her family. But before she could decide how she felt about it, Miss Crane spoke.

"I love you too, Didi." She looked around the table. "I love all of you." Her gaze rested on Delaney.

Delaney felt a warm glow fill her. It felt so good to feel loved, to feel safe, and to feel happy again. *Except for…*

Miss Crane studied her a moment before speaking again. Then as if making up her mind, she leaned forward. "Can I tell you a secret?"

The girls nodded eagerly.

Miss Crane smiled. "I think it would be all right if you stopped calling me Miss Crane when we're alone and instead call me by my given name."

Delaney opened her eyes wide. "Really?"

"Really. Are you ready? My name is Mercy."

Delaney closed her mouth and out the corner of her eye she saw Darby put her hand over hers. She could see that Miss Crane waited for their reaction and that she too had a grin on her face.

"Don't you like my name?"

Delaney heard the teasing in her voice and was about to answer when Didi spoke up.

"I like Mer*thy*."

They all burst out laughing when suddenly a *snort* caused every head to turn in Miss Crane's direction.

Mercy clapped her hand over her mouth, but her eyes danced with merriment at the looks on the children's faces. Then a muffled *snort* escaped past her hand.

The girls' expressions revealed their delight in finding this oddity about their teacher.

Mercy hugged Didi tighter.

"Mercy?" Delaney smiled. "I don't know if we can call you that, Miss Crane. It would feel funny."

"We will all get used to it soon. Now, how about we get this cleaned up and get ready for our story time."

Later, Mercy pulled Delaney aside. "Is everything okay with you, Delaney? Are you worried about something?"

Delaney didn't meet her teacher's eyes as she pondered what to say. She was holding Dylan and feeding him his bottle of goat's milk before putting him to bed, and as if to protect him, she held him even closer to her.

"I worry about Pa," she finally spoke. She glanced at the girls who were busy at the table before looking at Mercy. "The money tin is almost empty. I'm glad I don't have to pay Mrs. Simonson anymore. Dylan seems content with the goat's milk now."

Mercy nodded as she watched Delaney. "That's a lot to think about, but worrying about it won't help. The school board will pay for my room and board here. And we can plant a garden in the spring and have fresh vegetables this fall. Meanwhile I have some money put away to help us get through until we hear from your father."

"No, Miss Crane—I mean, Mercy. We can't take your money. Ma never wanted people to give us charity."

"Not charity, Delaney. I'm paying for my room here. Now, don't you worry. We're going to be fine and we're going to trust the Lord to take care of us."

Delaney glanced again at the woman beside her. Her confidence was reassuring. "I'm glad you're here."

"I'm glad too."

8

Dunn Home

"We need some supplies," Mercy announced as she wiped her hands on a towel, having just helped Daphne with the morning dishes. "How about if we all walk into town together after our Bible story?"

"Yeah! I want to go!"

"Didi, don't holler so," Delaney scolded.

"I like your *th*torie*th* about Je*thuth*," Didi lisped.

Mercy put her teeth together and hissed an "s" sound to Didi. "Remember, Didi, say it like this." She demonstrated.

"*Ththth*," Didi attempted.

"No, keep your tongue behind your teeth, sweetheart, not between them." She smiled as Didi tried again. "Yes, that's better! Keep trying."

Delaney smiled with the others. "Daphne used to lisp too," she explained. "Ma did the same thing with her that you're doing with Didi."

All eyes turned to her and there was a pause as the girls remembered their mother. It wasn't as painful as it was at first to talk about her. Mercy sat down and pulled Didi onto her lap.

"I'm so glad you girls are old enough to remember things about your mother. I don't remember mine, but I asked my father so many questions that I feel that I knew her." She looked at the baby on the floor. "You'll have to do the same for Dylan now. In fact, it might be a good idea for you to write down some of your favorite memories to keep for him."

They all looked at the little boy as he tried to roll over.

Mercy took her Bible and read to them, much as their mama had done, but Mercy had a way of making the stories come alive and she had answers to their many questions. Delaney was always quiet during these times, especially when Mercy encouraged the girls to place their faith in Jesus. The others wanted to know more, but Delaney could only think that God took their mama away from them. She had no need for him.

"Well, shall we get going?" Mercy was on her feet. "You girls get ready while I finish cleaning things up here."

Delaney reached for Dylan and checked his diaper. She rarely allowed anyone else to care for him and they all seemed fine with that. Even though the others held him from time to time, it was Delaney who Dylan wanted when he was upset or tired. And Delaney was willing to take the responsibility for him. She would be his mother.

The walk to the store was fun. The girls spotted an unusual bird in the frosty treetops, and Mercy said they would have to see if they could find out its name. They learned so much from Mercy, and her love of nature rubbed off onto them. Having a schoolteacher around was helping them grow in a lot of ways.

The mercantile was quiet when they entered. Mrs. Bedloe was stocking some shelves and turned to greet them.

"Why, if it isn't the Dunns and Miss Crane! Good day to you all."

"Good day, Mrs. Bedloe." Mercy and the storekeeper visited a bit while the girls walked around the store. Delaney stopped by the spot where Dylan rested that day she got sick. Her thoughts went immediately to the boy who winked at her and she wondered where he was now. She smiled to herself. It was fun to have that little exchange between them in her memory, something no one else knew about. Out of the corner of her eye, Delaney saw Didi reach toward a decorative kerosene lantern.

"Didi, don't touch that!" Delaney scolded her sister. Holding Dylan made it difficult for her to look through the store.

"Delaney, can we have peppermints today?" Daphne asked.

Delaney shook her head and whispered. "No, and don't fuss. We don't have enough money."

Daphne scowled. "I wasn't going to fuss. I'm not a baby, you know. Maybe Mercy will buy us some."

"Don't you ask her to, Daphne! We can't have her spending extra money on us." She saw her sister's face darken. "And don't look at me like that!" Trying to think of some way to diffuse Daphne's potential outburst, she said, "Remember that story Mercy told us about the ten lepers that Jesus healed and only one of them came back and thanked him?"

Daphne's anger turned to puzzlement. "Yes?"

"You should be thankful for what we have now and not expect more."

"But I told Mercy thank you."

"I know, but…but you always want more, and we just can't have more." Delaney sighed as she shifted Dylan in her arms. "I wish we could, but…I'm sorry."

Daphne studied her as if trying to make up her mind. Finally she smiled at Delaney. "It's okay."

Relieved, Delaney smiled back. She looked over at Mercy who was reading her list to the storekeeper. The items were stacking up on the counter, and Delaney wondered how they were going to pay for them. The tin was empty and had been for some time. The credit the store allowed them was used up. Mercy had been paying now, but Delaney didn't know how much money Mercy had or how long it would last them. She couldn't allow her to spend more than they absolutely needed, even though the thought of peppermints was enticing to her as well.

And it was her birthday tomorrow.

Delaney thought about that. Ma had always managed to make a cake for each one of them on their special days, even when their larder was low on supplies. Birthdays were celebrated with good wishes and a special treat to eat, but not with presents. There was never enough money for those, but the girls didn't mind. Being made to feel important on that special day was enough.

But now, unless one of her younger sisters remembered, Delaney fully expected the day to go by without notice. It would be just another one of the many changes she had to get used to.

The bell on the door jangled and they all turned to see who entered.

"Miss Crane, thought that was you," Mr. Hodge panted as he took out his handkerchief and wiped his brow. He pulled two envelopes from his inside vest pocket and checked them carefully before he handed one of them to her. The girls gathered around, curious to see what their friend had received. "This one came in to Beckfelt's Store today in the weekly mail delivery." He pointed to the second envelope and then turned to look for Delaney. "And this one here is for you, Delaney. This was brought in from one of the suppliers to the camp where your pa is. Is it from him?"

Delaney held the wrinkled envelope in one hand as she balanced Dylan in the other. Her heart pounded as she stared at it. The writing didn't look familiar. "I don't know." She turned when Mercy spoke.

"We'll read it at home. Thank you, Mr. Hodge." Mercy efficiently paid Mrs. Bedloe for the supplies and handed parcels to each of the girls except Delaney, who carried Dylan. Taking a load herself, she thanked the storekeeper and herded the girls out of the building.

"But who's it from?" Mr. Hodge called after them.

Delaney clutched the envelope and Dylan tightly as Mercy led them toward their house. They didn't speak until they reached the door and then Mercy said, "We'll just set the supplies on the table. Delaney, do you want some privacy to read your letter?"

Delaney looked at the teacher with wide eyes. "I don't know." She looked at her sisters' expectant faces. "Maybe."

"Go on into the other room and read it. If you feel like sharing it with us, you may. That will be up to you. Darby, will you take Dylan, please? And, Daphne and Didi, will you help me put things away?" She nodded to Delaney over their heads as if to reassure her, but the only thing that registered in Delaney's mind was that Mercy was behaving like a teacher again. That must mean that she was worried too.

Delaney stepped into the other room and sat on the edge of her parents' bed and looked at the envelope. Taking a deep breath, she carefully opened it and pulled out the paper inside.

Regarding Daniel Dunn:

Daniel Dunn is in custody on the suspicion of a crime. He will be transported to the Grand Rapids jailhouse on Thursday next to await a hearing date.

Jefferson Elwood
Deputy

"No! No! No!" Tears began rolling down Delaney's cheeks, and she wasn't even aware that she had spoken out loud until Mercy ran in the room and reached for her. Delaney flung herself into her arms and sobbed. Her sisters hovered near with fear in their eyes as they waited to hear what bad news the letter had brought them.

"What did it say, Laney?" Daphne said through tears. "What's happened to Pa? Is he dead too?"

Delaney inhaled sharply and pulled away from the teacher. She opened her arms to Daphne who ran to her. She gathered the others close as well and finally was able to speak.

"No, he's not dead. Don't even think that!" Her voice shook. Her tear-filled eyes looked up at Mercy as she handed the letter over to her. "What does this mean, Miss Crane?" She didn't even notice that she used the teacher's formal name.

Mercy picked up the paper and read it carefully. Her brows knit together at the news and she seemed to stare at it a long time. She then folded the letter carefully as she looked at the children.

"Your pa is alive." She paused, and Delaney could see she was trying to find a gentle way to explain. "There is a…situation…and it appears that your pa will be in jail for a while."

The girls gasped and Didi began crying in earnest.

"I want Pa! I want Pa to come home!"

Mercy stroked her brown hair. "We'll pray, darling, that God will show him a way to get here. We'll all pray, and we'll start right now."

9

Dunn Home

Mercy didn't sleep well. How could a man with the responsibility of a family get involved in a crime? What was the man thinking? Was he really the town thief? The girls were distraught with the news about their father, but Mercy knew they didn't fully understand the implications of that letter. Depending on what crime Daniel Dunn was accused of, he may never be able to return.

As she dressed and prepared for the day, her mind was on the name at the bottom of the letter—Jefferson Elwood. How long has it been since she thought of him? If she were perfectly honest with herself, she would have to admit that he was often in the back of her mind though she wished she could eliminate any memory of him. She sighed in resignation. It looked like she would have to deal with him once again.

Next, her thoughts turned to the children. She had come to love them and she saw a bleak future for the five Dunns unless someone stepped in to help them. And she believed that responsibility was falling on her shoulders. She closed her eyes in thought as she coiled her brown hair and began automatically pinning it up. A noise in the next room got her attention. Delaney was up with Dylan.

She frowned. Delaney had an obsessive desire to be Dylan's sole caregiver. It was sweet that she loved her little brother so much, but it almost seemed that she was trying to compensate for the baby losing his mother. Delaney shouldn't need to bear that responsibility at her young age. She should be enjoying her youth. The stresses of being an adult would be hers before long.

Mercy had breakfast almost prepared by the time the girls came downstairs. They were a somber group, their eyes swollen from the tears of the night, and their feet dragging from weariness. Delaney and Dylan joined them.

"Good morning, everyone." Mercy was careful not to sound overly cheerful, yet she wanted to get the children back to some normalcy. "Let's have breakfast and then we'll talk about what we're going to do next."

"I*th*n't Pa comin' home?" Didi put her elbows on the table and leaned her chin on her hands. Her lower lip trembled as she looked up at Mercy.

Mercy wanted to prevent them from all breaking into tears again, so she responded positively. "We'll pray that he will be able to come home." She looked down at their pensive faces. "I think that's what he would want you to do."

Darby wiped at her eyes. "Who was your letter from, Mercy?"

Mercy blinked. "Oh. I forgot about my letter." She looked around the room searching for it. "Where did I put it?" With the upsetting news from Delaney's letter and an evening of comforting the distressed girls, Mercy had neglected to read her own mail. "I'm sure it's from my father." She looked through some items on the shelf where they put away their supplies the day before.

"Here it is." She glanced at the writing. "Yes, it's from my father. I'll read it after breakfast. Let's sit down and pray now, shall we?"

It wasn't until after the dishes had been cleaned up and the morning chores underway that Mercy took time to look at her letter. The girls were doing better with duties to occupy their minds and Mercy was relieved, although she knew they had a long way to go to recover from this latest blow. She sat down in the rocker and leaned back, ready to enjoy the news from her father. Suddenly she sat up straight and grasped the letter with both hands. She quickly swept over the second page and then stared into space as she thought. The girls stopped what they were doing to watch her.

"What's wrong, Mercy?" Delaney asked.

The nervousness in the girl's tone caught Mercy's attention and she turned to her and the others. She folded the letter and put it back in the envelope while she thought.

"Girls, I need to go to town briefly. Will you finish your chores and get the bread started, please? I promise I won't be long."

"Something's wrong, isn't it?" Darby dared ask.

Mercy stood and smiled at her. She put out her arms to Daphne and Didi, who ran to her and clung to her side. "It's nothing to worry about." She looked over their heads to Darby and Delaney. "Let me take care of a couple of things in town and we'll talk when I get back, okay?"

The older girls nodded, but Mercy could see the uneasiness in their expressions. She couldn't leave them with so much worry on their minds.

"I think I'll have some good news for all of us," she ventured to say. She saw the girls visibly relax and she continued with a smile on her face. "Let's have a special supper tonight. How about I get a chicken from the mercantile and we fry it up?"

"Yeah!" Daphne squealed. "Can we have a cake too? It's Delaney's birthday today and Ma always made us cake for our birthdays."

"Well, I didn't know that. Yes, we'll have to have a cake for Delaney." Mercy reached for Delaney and gave her a hug. "You are growing up so fast, honey." She then went to the other room and was gone a short while before coming back with her handbag. "I'll try not to be too long." She saw the anxious looks return to their faces, but she smiled confidently at them and let herself out of the small house.

Mercy prayed during her walk to the store. She didn't want to share her father's news with the children until she had more answers herself. She needed a little more information first. For instance, if Mr. Dunn was going to jail, what would happen to the money he had coming to him for his work at the logging camp? The children needed that money. She headed to Beckfelt's Store first to talk to Mr. Hodge about sending a message to her father. Often some of the Chippewa, even the women, were willing to run errands for a fee. Since it was early enough in the day, she may be able to receive a reply by evening.

Next, she needed to talk with the mercantile owners. Mr. and Mrs. Bedloe owned the house that the Dunns rented and Mercy had been concerned for some time about their situation.

Her greatest fear was that as soon as it became known that Mr. Dunn was in jail, the courts would send the children to an orphanage or to homes where they would be split up, and who knew what would happen to them. And should the townspeople find out, especially the gossipy ones, they most certainly would bring their opinions about the children's care to the judge's ear.

Now this latest news from her father gave her an idea on how to get the children away from Grand Rapids and the prying of well-meaning people.

The bell announced her entry into the store and Mrs. Bedloe greeted her with surprise. "Why, Miss Crane, I didn't expect to see you back so soon!" She came around the counter, placed her hands on her generous hips and questioned, "Did the Dunn children receive bad news then?" Curiosity rather than concern filled her voice.

Mercy was well aware of the flow of gossip in the small town and was sure that most of the rumors came from the woman she faced.

"The children did receive some news, and they've sent me to see what is owed on their rent and their bill."

Mrs. Bedloe raised her eyebrows. "Really? Well, that's a relief. I don't mind telling you, Miss Crane, that there has been speculation for some time in this town about those poor children being without mother or father. I know it is a Christian thing you are doing by taking on their care, but it really shouldn't be your responsibility and as far as I'm concerned, I think you are an angel. Yes, an angel of *mercy* I tell everyone for being so selfless and…"

Mercy barely listened to the woman rattle on as she continued to think through the plans she needed to make. It only required an answer from her father and she could set things into motion. She waited impatiently for Mrs. Bedloe to finish her harangue.

"…and as I told Mr. Bedloe just the other day, I told him that if those children didn't hear from their father soon, someone was going to need to take action and do something about it and—"

"The rent?" Mercy finally interrupted the long-winded lady.

"What? Oh yes, the rent. Well, let's take a look here. I know for a fact that it's behind three months, but I want to show you so that you can see it for yourself. I usually don't worry since I know that the men get paid after the drive in the spring, but under the circumstances with Mr. Dunn taking off the way he did…" Her voice trailed off as she opened the ledger and pointed at the figures for Mercy to verify her words.

Three months! That will lighten my purse by quite a bit. Mercy didn't let her thoughts show as she calmly paid the storekeeper for the rent and for the amount due on credit at the store.

"There you are, Mrs. Bedloe. Thank you for your patience. Excuse me, please. I have some more errands to tend to."

"Of course, Miss Crane." Mrs. Bedloe waved her customer off without looking up as she carefully counted the money that had been handed to her.

Mercy exited the store, nearly bumping into a woman in a shawl on her way out.

"Pardon me! Oh, hello." She stepped back to get a better look. "You're Guntar's mother, aren't you?"

The woman mumbled something back and would have kept on, but Mercy continued, "I want to tell you how much help Guntar has been at the school and how well he has been doing with his studies. You must be very proud of him."

The woman simply nodded and again moved on. Mercy watched her, puzzled at her lack of cordiality, but shrugged. She had other things to think about.

For the next few moments, Mercy walked slowly through the snow-packed street. She was formulating a plan in her mind and interlacing each thought with prayer. She paused and took a moment to sit on one of the many benches in front of the stores, needing the support as the immensity of what she was attempting to do threaten to overtake her. It was a good idea, but it depended solely on Mr. Dunn and his situation. She would go to the jail now, a building she never had a cause to enter before this, and talk to the sheriff to see what he knew.

Her biggest fear was that she might see Jefferson Elwood. She hadn't heard anything about him becoming a deputy, and she sincerely hoped that he wasn't working in this town.

Grand Rapids was a town in its infant stages. Some of the buildings sported new logs in their construction, but others were roughly put together with the chinking falling away, leaving huge holes in the sides. In contrast, brick and stone had been used along with sawed and planed lumber in the grander buildings like the mercantile and the hotel and also the jail.

Mercy shuddered as she saw the iron bars in the small window of the jailhouse. She didn't know Daniel Dunn, but she didn't wish for anyone to be imprisoned in such a place. She entered the small office to find no one there. She hesitated a few moments then walked to the doorway at the back of the room that led to the cells. She peeked around the corner.

"Looking for someone, miss?"

Mercy jumped and spun around. Her hand flew to cover her mouth and the shriek she couldn't contain.

"You're the teacher." The man with a sheriff's badge stated as he entered the jail and crossed to his desk. "Is there something I can help you with, miss? I'm Jon Talbot." He remained standing while he motioned her to a chair.

"Thank you." Mercy sat and the sheriff settled into his chair. "I was…I was wondering what you might know about…about Daniel Dunn."

The sheriff was a big man and when he leaned back in his chair, it squeaked so loudly Mercy was concerned that it would snap in two. His graying hair was cut close to his head and there was already stubble on his chin though Mercy surmised he had shaved that morning. "What do you know about Dunn?"

"I take care of the Dunn children and they received a note that said their father was guilty of a crime and would be brought here. I need to know what has happened."

Mercy jumped again when the sheriff sat forward suddenly and his chair banged onto the floor. "That Elwood!" He shook his head. "I've got me a new deputy and I'm afraid he's trying to impress me." He rummaged in a drawer and pulled out a piece of paper. "Was this what the note said?"

Mercy took the note he handed her across the desk. Her heart was thumping at hearing Jefferson Elwood's name again and she was dismayed to know that he had returned to the area.

Is she *with him?*

She tucked a loose hair in place as she opened the note and read the exact same message that Delaney had received. She nodded to the sheriff.

"Yes. This is what the children received. What is this all about, Sheriff Talbot?"

"I wish I knew. We've had some robberies in town—"

Mercy nodded. She had heard.

"—and I sent Deputy Elwood to the logging camps to sniff around and see if he could learn anything. I guess he thinks this Dunn fellow is the offender." He took the note she handed back to him. "I apologize for worrying the children, miss. Elwood is a greenhorn and acted without my knowledge on that."

"It has frightened the children," Mercy admitted.

"Until Elwood brings Dunn in, I have nothing to tell you. You know as much as I do at this point. Is there anything else, miss?"

Mercy twisted her hands in her lap. "I…uh…" She cleared her throat. "I just learned that my father has a broken leg and needs me to come home. I'm taking the

Dunn children with me." She watched for the sheriff's reaction. "You see, they need my care, and I planned to leave word with people in town to tell Mr. Dunn where the children will be, but now—" She looked down as she formulated her thoughts. "Now I'm not sure what to do. What happens to children when their only parent is in jail, if that is what is happening?"

The sheriff's look was intense, but for the good of the children she kept eye contact with him and ignored her own nervous reaction to his stare.

"We don't know what is involved here." The sheriff appeared to hedge his reply. "I suggest we wait until we learn more."

"I can't wait. My father needs me and these children need me." She rose and the sheriff stood with her. "Could I send a message to the logging camp so that Mr. Dunn knows where I've taken his children?"

"Now hold on. You can wait until Thursday when Deputy Elwood brings him in. Then you should be able to talk with the man himself and sort these things out. I don't suggest that you take the children without his permission or you could be accused of kidnapping."

Mercy inhaled sharply as she stared wide-eyed at the man.

"That's right, miss. You can't just walk off with someone else's children. And if Dunn is guilty of something and has to go to jail for a time, the children will go to an orphanage or to families the judge selects as the best place for them. I'm sorry, but they wouldn't be given into the care of a single woman such as yourself."

There was real fear in Mercy's eyes at this statement, but she recovered and turned to the door. "Then I will see you again on Thursday, Sheriff. It seems imperative that I speak with Mr. Dunn."

10

Logging Camp

My knife?

How can this be?

Daniel became aware of the murmuring around him. The men knew his knife. It had a distinct handle, different from the ones most of the jacks carried. Daniel had even let some of the men take a closer look when they became curious about the design engraved on it. A gift from his father, it bore an emblem much like a family crest on its side.

The muttering was getting louder and Daniel could hear his name being mentioned. His heart felt like it was pounding in his ears as he realized they thought him guilty. The fight the night before didn't help matters. He turned as the men moved aside to allow Mr. Clayton and the preacher in for a look. Daniel watched as the boss studied the body of Murdock, but it was the preacher who caught his attention. Pastor Sam was looking from one man to another until his scrutiny rested on Daniel. There it stayed and Daniel felt as if the man were looking into his very soul.

"Whose knife is this?" demanded Clayton.

There was dead silence. Daniel knew every man there who could see the knife knew it was his, yet none said a word. It was not their way to inform on each other.

"It's mine."

Clayton stood to his feet and looked down at Daniel where he knelt beside Murdock. "So you admit to killing this man?"

"No, sir!" Daniel stood so swiftly the older man took a step backward.

"You just said it's your knife." He took a closer look at the cuts on Daniel's face. "And weren't you the one fighting with him last night?"

Daniel's eyes bore into those of the camp boss. "I am, and it is my knife, but I didn't kill him."

Clayton matched Daniel with his own penetrating stare. "We'll see about that." He looked over the rest of the group still standing in the chill of the early-morning air, some just in their long johns.

"This man smells of bad booze, and liquor is prohibited in camp. I want answers. Where did he get it? Who else has been drinking? Did anyone see or hear anything suspicious last night?"

Again, silence.

Daniel could see the camp boss was infuriated with the lack of response.

"If I have to sit down with each and every one of you to get to the bottom of this, I will. Do you hear me?"

Not a word.

"And if I have to withhold your pay until I get answers, I will. Do you hear that?" he shouted.

Pastor Sam put a hand on Clayton's arm, and Clayton swung around in anger, thinking one of the men was trying to stop him, but the preacher just calmly motioned with his head. Deputy Elwood was rushing over.

"What happened here? Whose knife? Who did this?" He reached for the gun on his hip.

"Hold on, Deputy," Clayton stopped his hand. "Looks like you'll have more questions to ask." He rubbed at the whiskers that had sprouted on his chin overnight as he looked over the group. "But I need these men out there working too." He pointed at Daniel. "I suggest you start with this one, and you—" He pointed at the man beside Daniel. "And you, and you, and you. The rest of you men get to your work."

"Sir, if you let these men go now, the guilty man will take off into the woods and we'll never see him again," protested the lawman as he looked over the men. "He may have taken off already."

"I can't afford to lose a day of work while you question men."

"You have to let me do my job, Mr. Clayton. A man has been murdered."

"He's right," agreed Pastor Sam. "I'll be glad to help in any way I can," he offered.

Elwood nodded. "Appreciate it." He raised his voice. "Men, get dressed and get to the cookshack for your breakfast. I will start questioning you there."

Daniel hoped the trembling he was feeling wasn't showing. As he turned to go back to the bunkhouse with the other men, he saw the camp boss point him out to the deputy. His instinct was to disappear into the woods along with the men who already had taken off when the lawman appeared in camp, but he was innocent and it went against his grain to run.

Why is it when I decide to change my ways I find myself in a mess of trouble?

Daniel wasn't too surprised to find that he would be the first man questioned. More men had disappeared into the woods and the tables in the cookshack sported several empty spaces on the benches.

Shouldn't the deputy be going after them instead of looking at me?

Daniel kept his expression free of his thoughts as the deputy sat down across from him. He continued eating his breakfast of potatoes, ham, beans, prunes, and pancakes, all the while aware that the men were watching them with interest without appearing to be listening. Daniel's thoughts were divided. He poured blackstrap molasses over the cakes while he was trying to assess the man who stared at him across the table, but at the same time his thoughts were racing, trying to figure out what had happened. Murdock was a good worker, a bull of a man as Daniel knew from fighting with him, but not a friendly man. Given his size, he wasn't afraid of any conflict and never backed down from a fight, but Daniel didn't know of anyone in the camp who would want to kill the man.

"What were you and Murdock fighting about last night?" the deputy finally spoke.

Every head turned at the sound of his voice, speaking out loud being a prohibited activity in the cookshack.

Daniel spoke around the food in his mouth. "He spilled blackjack on me."

The lawman raised an eyebrow. "Blackjack?"

Daniel held up his tin cup of coffee.

"You got into a fistfight over spilled coffee?"

No comment.

"Where did you go last night when you left the bunkhouse?"

At Daniel's questioning look, the deputy continued. "You were seen leaving."

Daniel wondered who had reported that fact to the deputy. "I took a walk to clear my head."

"Was Murdock out there with you?"

"I never saw him."

"Did you see anyone else?"

"No."

Daniel was aware that the normal noise of the forks and knives on the tin plates was silent as the men in the room listened to their exchange.

"I have no choice but to detain you as my prime suspect." Deputy Elwood looked around for the camp boss. "Mr. Clayton, is there a place I can jail this man while I question the others?"

Daniel said nothing as he watched the boss, but his mind was working. *Jail? Since when is a man guilty without proof? What will happen to my children? God, is this your punishment for what I said to you?*

"Deputy, if I may." Pastor Sam forestalled Mr. Clayton's reply. "I understand that evidence seems to point to Mr. Dunn as the guilty party, but I don't believe you should lock the man up while you continue questioning the others, which may take several days yet."

"I can't allow him to run free. He'll disappear into the woods!"

The pastor leaned forward. "Deputy, you are aware that several men have already done so. Wouldn't that indicate guilt?"

The lawman didn't reply.

"And Mr. Dunn is still here. Doesn't that tell you something about his innocence?"

"He's got a point there, Elwood," Mr. Clayton agreed then his face darkened. "But I want this mess dealt with immediately and someone has to be held accountable." He pointed at Daniel. "It was your knife and you had a fight with the man. As far as I'm concerned, that's enough to bring you before a judge."

Daniel saw the preacher shake his head.

The boss continued, "And I don't want this one running off into the woods like those other criminals, so I guess we'll have to lock him up somewhere. How about the root house?"

"Now, Bernie, think about this. You can't lock a man in a cold, windowless place like that. He's not an animal, and I'm going out on a limb here and say that I don't even think he's guilty of this crime."

Bernie Clayton stared at the preacher. "Why not?"

"Think about it. Wouldn't it be stupid to use such a distinctive knife, one that everyone knows, for all to see? It seems apparent that the killer is trying to set this man up."

The men around the table were silent as they thought about the preacher's words. Daniel's face remained impassive as he continued to eat his meal, but his heart was racing and his stomach was rebelling at the food. He glanced at the preacher. He didn't know why the man was helping him, but he was grateful for any help he could get, even from a preacher. And if what the man said was true, then someone was trying to make him look guilty. But who? And why?

"I still need to hold him for trial, and it's going to take some time to talk to the other men. What do you suggest?" Deputy Elwood turned back to Pastor Sam.

The pastor looked around the room. "How about if I take responsibility for him?"

Clayton made a noise that sounded like a grunt mixed with a laugh. "I can't let him back into the woods, Sam."

"Then how about here at the camp? Isn't there enough work here to keep a man busy?"

Clayton shrugged.

The preacher faced Daniel. "Mr. Dunn, will you give me your word that you will remain in camp with me until the deputy finishes his questioning, and that if he decides to take you back to town that you will go willingly to stand trial?"

Daniel's fork stopped midway to his mouth. He carefully set it down then lifted his eyes to the pastor. "I didn't do it."

"That remains to be seen," interjected the deputy.

"Will you promise me, Mr. Dunn?" Pastor Sam questioned again. His intent eye contact with Daniel unnerved him and finally made him give in.

"I promise."

The preacher turned to the camp boss and the deputy. "That's good enough for me, gentlemen. I will stay here until Deputy Elwood has finished his questioning and Mr. Dunn will be my charge until then." He waited for the others to agree.

The deputy stepped over the bench as he stood up. "Just keep an eye on him, that's all I can say."

Men started filing out of the cookhouse, but Daniel remained in his seat and waited. When he and the preacher were the only two left besides the cook, he repeated his statement.

"I didn't do it."

Pastor Sam sighed as he stared at his charge. "Unfortunately, I'm not the one you have to convince." He started to rise. "Well, Mr. Dunn—"

"Name's Daniel."

The preacher nodded. "Daniel, what do we do now?"

"We?"

"As long as I'm responsible for you, I might as well work with you."

Daniel hid his surprise. He was grateful to the man for keeping him out of the root house, and he appreciated that his innocence was accepted even if only by him, but he hadn't expected the preacher to offer to work alongside him. He stood.

"Work at the camp usually means working with the blacksmith or the dentist, helping the teamsters with the horses, cutting firewood, or—"

"You're helping the cook!" Clayton stepped around Daniel. He pointed a finger at Daniel's chest. "You do whatever he wants, you hear? I want you where more than one pair of eyes can watch you, so don't even think of disappearing."

"A cookee?"

Clayton nodded at the burly cook then directed his next comment at the pastor. "I don't like this, but as long as you've agreed to keep an eye on him, I'll do as you've asked. But if he runs…" He left his threat dangling.

"I have confidence in Daniel's word."

Daniel remained silent. He felt trapped. He needed to get out and see what clues he could pick up regarding Murdock's murder that could exonerate himself, but how could he do that penned up in the kitchen? He wondered what would happen to his pay as a result of this latest development. His family needed that money.

"There's a pile of dishes waiting to be washed." Grunted the cook. "Since yer my helper now, ya might as well get water heated and get busy. I'll have the cookee bring the dishes to ya."

A young man in a grayed linen apron was hurrying back and forth between the tables gathering the tin plates and cups from breakfast. Daniel gave the cook a quick nod and walked over to get the water buckets. He nearly tripped over the preacher as he turned to go out the door.

"I'll get these," Pastor Sam said as he reached for another two buckets.

Guess he means what he says. Daniel shrugged and headed outside.

11

Dunn Home

THE EVENING MEAL could not be called festive. Mercy tried to make the atmosphere as pleasant as possible in light of the children's recent shocking news about their father and their nervous anticipation about the contents of her letter. The fried chicken was delicious, and the cake for Delaney's birthday was a treat that should have brought more enjoyment than it did, but Mercy could see that the children were too uneasy to find pleasure in it. It was time to share her news with them.

Mercy pulled the letter out of her skirt pocket and opened it while the children watched her expectantly. She smiled to reassure them.

"My father has a small farm several hour's walk from town. He has a few fields that he is clearing to begin planting hay because he plans to have dairy and beef cattle soon, plus he grows some other crops to sell. He always has a hired hand come in the spring for planting and the fall for harvesting, but the rest of the farm work he manages on his own now that I'm not there. We raise pigs and chickens. We have goats for milk for the local store and we supply some of the logging camps."

She paused as she glanced at the letter again.

"My father somehow got tangled up with one of the sows, and it managed to crush him against the fence and break his leg."

The girls gasped.

Mercy quickly continued, "He says in his letter that he is doing fine. The doctor told him that his leg is healing well, but he needs to have his hired hand there all the time now to do the chores for him, and, well, my father is wondering if I would come home and help him. You see, I usually go home for the summer after school is out, but I wrote him earlier to tell him that I would be staying with all of you when school ended."

Before Mercy could go on, Daphne exclaimed, "You're not going to leave us too, are you?"

Mercy pulled the young girl to her side. "Absolutely not! I'm going to ask a big favor of all of you." She looked around at the faces intent on hers. "What would you think if we closed school early and went to live at my house and help out my father?"

"But…" Delaney began. She searched her sisters' faces. "But what if Pa comes back and we're not here?"

Mercy nodded in understanding. "We still don't know what is happening with your pa, but I plan to either talk with him or get word to him so he knows where you are. I know you want him home with you as soon as he can be."

A knock on the door startled them and Mercy went to see who it was. A Chippewa woman handed her an envelope and waited until Mercy went for the coins needed to pay her. Quickly Mercy scanned the note and looked up with a smile.

"He is eager to have you all at the farm. Oh, I know you will love my father!"

Delaney picked up Dylan off the floor and began rocking him in her arms. Mercy watched the emotions cross her face and tried to imagine what she was thinking. The only link she had left to her mother and father was this house, and the family didn't even own it. It was a lot to ask of the children. Mercy had little choice left to her now that her father needed her help, but she wouldn't leave the children, and she needed them to be willing to come with her.

"I paid the rest of the rent that was owed to the Bedloes," Mercy spoke mainly to Delaney. She watched the young girl glance at the empty tin and then back to her. They both knew the money was gone and that they couldn't depend on more coming from their father. It left the girl with no other options but to agree. Delaney snuggled her head close to Dylan's before looking at Mercy and giving her a slight nod.

Mercy released the breath she was holding. "Okay, girls, we're going to have a lot to do to get ready. If things go as planned I would like to leave on Saturday."

"That's only five days from now!" Darby exclaimed.

"I know." Mercy pulled out another paper she had in her pocket. "I've made a list of the things we need to get done in a very short time. The reason we have to make the move now is that we're almost into a new month, and I know we don't want to pay any more rent here than we have to. Also, my father needs us as soon as we can get there." Mercy paused. "There are chores to do and a house to care for."

"And we'll help too," Daphne volunteered.

Mercy smiled. "You are going to love the farm," she told the girls, and the love for her home warmed her voice. "Besides the other animals, we have the sweetest collie named Sugar."

"A dog? You have a dog?" Didi jumped up on the bench and clapped her hands.

"Didi!" Delaney scolded her sister.

Mercy grabbed the little girl's hand so that she wouldn't fall. She was glad to see some excitement in their faces. It would make the changes of the next few days more bearable for all of them.

Mercy was busy answering questions until the girls were tucked into their beds upstairs. As she descended the narrow staircase, she remembered again that it was Delaney's birthday, the first without her mother. How could she make the young girl feel special with all the changes and upheaval in her life? So far all she'd been able to do is make a cake that none of them could really enjoy as they had so much on their minds.

Delaney was settling Dylan down for the night, so Mercy went quietly to her room. She knew what she wanted to do. Searching through a small case she kept beside the bed, she found the item she wanted. Taking a plain piece of paper and a bit of hair ribbon, she made an attractive package. She stepped to the door of the small room next to hers.

"Delaney," she whispered.

Delaney turned and followed Mercy. She was in her nightgown and had already braided her long blonde hair for the night. But before Mercy had a chance to speak, Delaney surprised her with her words.

"We'll work hard for you, and we'll pay you back for everything you've spent on us."

Mercy was astonished. She took Delaney by the hand and led her to the table where they both sat down. She didn't release the girl's hand as she looked into her fearful eyes and smiled.

"There is nothing to pay back, Delaney. My father and I want all of you to come and live with us, and even though we will all have to help out, you are not to think that I am asking you to work to pay me back. We're just going to think of each other as family for now. Do you think that would be okay with you?"

Delaney exhaled as if she had been holding her breath. "I don't know what we would do if it weren't for you."

Mercy smiled and patted Delaney's hand. "And I don't know what I would do without all of you either." She brought the small package up to the table and set it in front of Delaney. "I should have given you this in front of all the children, but I didn't want to let you go to bed thinking that you wouldn't get a present for your birthday. Happy Birthday, Delaney."

"A present? For me?"

Delaney carefully untied the gift and gasped when she pulled out the small locket within. She fingered it gently as she stared at it. "I've never gotten a birthday present before."

Mercy blinked.

"Then it's time you did. You're growing up into a lovely young lady."

Mercy was even more surprised when Delaney threw her arms around her. Usually the oldest Dunn girl was not demonstrative with her affections, and it touched Mercy's heart to know that she had brought her some pleasure amidst all her troubles.

"Thank you so much."

"You're welcome. Now, we both better get some sleep; we have a lot to do tomorrow. And, Delaney."

Delaney looked into Mercy's eyes.

"I don't want you to worry about your father. We have to believe that he is innocent of whatever he is being accused of, and he wouldn't want you and the other children spending your days in worry. I'm counting on you to be an example to the others."

Delaney nodded. "I'm scared for him," she admitted.

"I know, sweetheart. We will keep praying that the Lord helps him through this mess."

Delaney's expression was doubtful, but she gave Mercy a quick nod. "Good night and thank you again for this. It's lovely and I'll take really good care of it."

"I know you will. Good night."

Mercy didn't expect much difficulty getting packed, but she was nervous about how she was going to get permission from Mr. Dunn to take the children. She would have to wait until Thursday and see if he was in the Grand Rapids' jail to talk to him. Meanwhile, she arranged to meet with the school board the next day and after explaining to them about her father's injury and why she had to close the school early, the men seemed satisfied, all except for Mr. Crenshaw who scowled at her during her explanation. However, when she mentioned that the Dunn children would be leaving the town with her, the men's attitude turned in a different direction. Mercy was unprepared for their reaction.

It was Mr. Hamilton, who first voiced his concern. "Miss Crane, you have done a fine job caring for the Dunn children during this time, but you can't simply walk off with them as if they were stray cats that you've taken in. There are laws that must be obeyed. If these children are without parents then it is our duty as citizens to place them in a home for orphans to be legally adopted."

"Well, I don't know as we need to send them off to that orphanage in Owatonna. I hear tell that the Ellis's are looking for a girl. Maybe that youngest one could go there if we got legal papers and all from the county judge. He's due here next week," Mr. Bedloe spoke to the others. "And I hear that the Pratts are having an awful time with those twin girls. Maybe they'd take in the oldest girl. She's used to caring for small children."

"My wife and I could use a girl to help out around the house too," Mr. Olson stated. "But I don't know about that infant. Anyone know who'd take him? I hear he cries all the time."

Mercy was horrified. She had to do something and quickly. She struggled to keep her body from shaking with rage as she tried to think. She couldn't just claim to have legal guardianship of the children; she was unwed and, according to the sheriff, the court would never allow her to have them. As far as she knew, the men were unaware of the accusations against Mr. Dunn so that might buy her some time. The men were rising to leave and she knew she had to stop them from doing more damage to those children. It was now or never.

"Gentlemen, you haven't given me a chance to explain."

They turned back to her but didn't return to their seats. She knew she had to convince them now before they left the schoolroom and started spreading the news that the children were up for grabs. She took a deep breath.

"I will see to it that I have Mr. Dunn's permission before I leave, so, you see, there is no need to talk about splitting the children up. I will be able to take them all." Two bright red spots appeared on her cheeks, but with the children's welfare at stake, she held her ground as the men gaped at her.

Suspicion was in Mr. Crenshaw's eyes as he studied her.

"That's what Hodge said," commented Mr. Bedloe.

Mercy suppressed her irritation at hearing about the gossipy store clerk. "I've had contact with Mr. Dunn." She knew that Mr. Hodge must have talked about the message she sent to the camp regarding Delaney's illness and more recently about the one Delaney received.

"I still don't think that it's right for a single woman to take the children," Mr. Hamilton said. "But I think it would solve a lot of issues involving the courts and getting them new homes."

"So you see, gentlemen, it will all be taken care of, and if you will excuse me now, I have much to do before we leave. Remember, my father is awaiting our arrival." She motioned to the door.

The men seemed uncertain by this turn of events, but finally Mr. Hamilton tipped his hat at Mercy as he started out the door. "Best wishes to you, Miss Crane."

"This is most unusual." Mr. Bedloe shook his head at her as he started for the door. "Wait until the missus hears about this. Guess we need to find a new renter for the house."

Mr. Crenshaw walked out without a word or a backward glance. It was Mr. Olson who lingered a moment and quirked an eyebrow at the schoolteacher. "You're a brave woman." He studied her a moment then said quietly, "God be with you," before he too left the building.

Mercy collapsed onto the nearest chair. What had she done? Then she jumped up and gathered her things and hurried to the Dunn home. She had to explain the situation to the children before anyone from town spoke to them.

"So it's okay for us to go with you?" questioned Darby.

"I will talk to your father on Thursday and hopefully find that he is not going to be jailed after all. But whether he is or not, I will get written permission from him to take you with me. Don't worry. I am not leaving you. I'm going to do everything I can to keep us all together. Do you understand?"

Four pairs of eyes continued to stare at her as they had since she swept into the house and gathered them all at the table to tell them what happened.

"I don't want to frighten you, but I have to have your father's permission, especially if he is jailed or the townspeople will feel that they must place you in an orphanage and then you could very well be separated." She hated scaring them, and seeing the reaction her words produced, she knew she had. "Please try to understand, girls, I'm only trying to protect you so that you'll all be together when your father comes for you."

"You'll do that for us?" Delaney concentrated on Mercy's face. "You'll take care of all of us?"

"I already have."

Mercy watched as the girls thought about her announcement. She didn't dare tell them more about the risks she was taking. She didn't know what she would do if Mr. Dunn refused to let her take the children. If she tried to take them without getting permission, she could be found out and actually be put in jail for kidnapping and the children could still end up in an orphanage and their family split apart. She never thought she could get in trouble for helping out the Dunn children, but apparently the people in town did. And the people in LaPrairie might feel the same way. She must do this right. She breathed a sigh of relief when she saw the trust the children had in her until she caught sight of Darby's face. Uncertainty marred her pretty features.

"Darby?"

The young girl glanced at the faces around her before turning to Mercy. "What will Pa say when he gets here? I mean, we won't have a house or anything."

"There's no need to worry about that, dear. When he gets back to you again, he'll find you a new home and you'll all be together again."

Darby faced Mercy, her expression serious. "And you'll come with us, right?"

Mercy caught her breath as she knelt before the girl. "I will be with you as long as you need me." She waited until Darby nodded then she stood. "Okay, we have more to pack in the morning. I've arranged with Mr. Bedloe to rent his wagon on Saturday to help us transport everything to the farm. I'll have Jemison, our hired man, return the wagon later. Fortunately, the frost hasn't come out of the ground yet or it would be too muddy for the wagon."

It was Delaney who asked the question she had been expecting.

"Can we go with you to see Pa?"

Mercy smiled gently. "I know how much you all want to see your pa, but I think it would be best if I go alone and find out what is happening. The jailhouse is no place for you children, and I dare to guess that your father would not want you to see him there."

"What did Pa do?" Daphne asked.

Mercy pulled Daphne to her. "We don't know that he's done anything, sweetheart. This may all just be a big misunderstanding. Remember, the note said that there was a *suspicion* of a crime not that one has been committed. There could be several men that are being brought in for questioning, so let's not worry."

"Je*th*u*th* wa*th* cwu*th*ified, but he didn't do anything wong eithuh!" Didi exclaimed. Her lower lip trembled as she grabbed Mercy's leg for comfort.

Mercy patted the little girl's head. "Yes, you're right, Didi, but do you remember that I told you that Jesus came to earth just for that purpose? He knew he was going to be crucified, but he was willing to do it for us, to pay for our sins." She knelt to look in Didi's eyes. "Do you believe that he did that for you, honey?"

The little girl hung her head. "*Th*umtime*th* I do bad thing*th*."

"We all do. That is why Jesus was willing to pay for our sins, because we couldn't do it for ourselves. But he didn't stay dead! He arose because he's God. And we can go to heaven to live with him if we just believe that he did that for us."

Didi looked up at Mercy. "I wanna be in heaven with Ma and Je*th*u*th*. I'm glad he paid for my *th*in*th*."

Mercy hugged her. "I'm glad too. You are pretty young to understand about salvation, but I can see that you know Jesus is the way to heaven." She turned to the other girls. "How about you girls? Have you accepted Jesus as your savior?"

Darby looked at Daphne and Delaney before answering Mercy. "Ma talked to us about it, but I guess I didn't really understand what that meant. Do you do something?"

"It's all about placing your faith in what he has done. It's like this, you trust me to take care of you, right?"

The girls nodded.

"And I will. But I am only human and can't promise you everything. God is capable of doing what he says he will do, so when you trust him, you can be sure that you belong to him for eternity." She took Darby's hand. "It's not something you do, Darby, it's what you believe. You are the only one who can make a decision to believe that Jesus took care of your sins and rose from the dead for you. When you accept that, you become a child of God and you can know you'll be in heaven with him."

Darby nodded but remained silent.

Mercy waited a moment more. She knew she could press the girls to make a decision right then, but she wanted them to understand, and she knew it sometimes took a while to sink in. She smiled at them.

"Whenever you want to talk about this again, I will be glad to talk with you. For now, let's get our supper and do some more packing, okay? Tomorrow I'll see what we can find out about your pa."

12

Logging Camp

It was only two days later, but Daniel felt as if weeks had gone by with the preacher at his elbow at every turn. It was true that the man proved to be helpful and pulled his weight and then some, but it was also true that he never stopped talking, and Daniel was feeling himself weakening. The preacher got up on his stool every evening and preached a fire-and-brimstone sermon to the loggers, but Daniel had the full impact of constant sermonizing throughout every hour of the day. He was thankful that the cook's rule of silence during meals gave him a much-needed break.

But the man's words were having an effect on him. He chewed on his thoughts while he chewed on the sow bellies served for supper. Pastor Sam kept stressing to him that heaven was a gift not a reward that he could obtain by doing good things. Daniel tried to recall what Dee believed. She used words like *trust* and *faith*, much like the preacher used. Pastor Sam said that he needed to make a decision about trusting Jesus—that he needed to accept salvation for himself.

But concentrating on that thought was difficult with the nagging fear in his gut about being brought to jail for something he didn't do. Deputy Elwood was questioning the others, but no one else had been confined to the camp like he was, and he wondered if that meant he was going to be the only suspect. How could he expect to get a fair trial if the lawman believed him to be guilty?

Men started filing out the door so Daniel rose and grabbed the buckets to get water. He stepped aside quickly to avoid tripping on Pastor Sam as he hastened to join him. Daniel wondered if the preacher actually wanted to be helpful or if he was taking his job of keeping an eye on him that seriously.

Does he really think I'm going to run?

"Daniel, I heard one of the men mention wanting *swamp water*. What's that?"

The preacher had been peppering him with all kinds of logging questions, the first was when he expressed surprise that there was a dentist in camp. Daniel explained that the term "dentist" went to the filer who kept the teeth on the saw blades in good shape.

"It's tea."

"Tea. I see. I must say you have interesting names for things."

"Hold on, Dunn."

They both turned at the command, and Daniel watched the deputy make his way through the men to him. He had a determined look on his face, a warning to Daniel of the news he was about to hear.

"I'm taking you into town with me tomorrow to await a hearing."

"The drive starts soon. I'm going with it."

Elwood actually smiled. "I'm the law. You'll do as I say."

Daniel stared stone-faced at the lawman. He could hear triumph in the man's voice, and he caught a glimpse of a sneer in his expression.

Pastor Sam bumped Daniel's arm as he swung around to face Elwood. "What happened to your investigation, deputy? You haven't spoken to all the men, have you?"

Elwood maintained eye contact with Daniel as he answered the preacher. "I've talked to enough. No one saw anything or heard anything, so that leaves me to go on the evidence I have, and that leads to you." He pointed at Daniel.

"But even you can see that Daniel hasn't tried to escape. Surely a guilty man wouldn't stay here to be brought to jail."

The lawman's head remained still, but he pierced the preacher with a sideways look. "What do you mean *even you?*"

Pastor Sam ignored the question. "I think you're making a grave mistake if you think Daniel is a murderer."

"Oh, I'm bringing him in for the murder all right, but I'm also charging him with the town thefts."

"What? What proof do you have?"

Jefferson Elwood crossed his arms over his chest. "I found a gold watch in his belongings, and it's just like the gold watch missing from the mercantile."

"Oh, now that's ridiculous! Even—you must see that someone is trying to frame Daniel. Why on earth would he leave a stolen article where you could find it?"

"It's my experience that criminals aren't too bright. Dunn, I'm locking you in the root house until we leave in the morning."

Daniel hadn't spoken throughout the exchange, but the lawman's words had started a rage burning in him. His features were hard as he spoke.

"No."

Deputy Elwood uncrossed his arms.

"What did you say?"

"You heard me."

Pastor Sam laid a hand on Daniel's arm, but one look from Daniel made him drop it.

"If I say you're going, you're going!" The lawman took a step forward.

"You think you can put me in there?"

Something about Daniel's tone must have gotten through to Elwood because he hesitated. Daniel watched for the move he knew the man had no choice but to make, and when the lawman reached for his gun, Daniel grabbed his arm.

"Take the pistol, preacher," he commanded.

"Now, Daniel. Think about this," Pastor Sam admonished.

Daniel grinned, but there was no humor in it. "If the man wants to put me in the root house, he's going to have to do it under his own power. Just get the gun out of his reach so it's a fair fight."

The preacher slid the gun out of its holster while the deputy tried to yank free of Daniel's grip.

"I'm not fighting you! Preacher, you're in a heap of trouble for helping a criminal!" He struggled against Daniel's hold.

When the gun was out of reach, Daniel released the deputy. "Now, what was that you said about the root house?"

Elwood rubbed at his arm while he glared at Daniel. "You are under arrest! I'm going to see to it that they put you away for the rest of your life!"

Daniel now crossed his arms over his chest as he studied the lawman. He was aware of the jacks gathered around to see what would happen. It was time he had his say.

"I've stayed in camp these past days, and I've done all the work I was asked to do and then some. I've even put up with listening to all-day sermons. I could have run, but I didn't, because I am not guilty," he said the words slowly and loudly. "I don't know who killed Murdock, I don't know where he got his booze, and I don't know who's been robbing the stores in Grand Rapids, but I do know that it's not me. So if you want me to go to town tomorrow to clear this thing up, I will, and then I'm coming back here for the log drive. All you had to do was ask. But I will not be holed up in a root house like a criminal. Unless you have something else to say, I've got work to do."

Daniel stared down the deputy until Elwood looked away. Then he picked up the water buckets and headed for the door, the jacks clearing a path for him.

"You don't really think he's the one, do you?" asked Pastor Sam as he handed Elwood's pistol to him.

The deputy grabbed the gun and holstered it. He put his hands on his hips as he faced the preacher. "You're coming with me tomorrow too. I believe you have some explaining to do to the sheriff." Then he turned on his heel and left the cookshack by the backdoor. They didn't see him the rest of the night.

Daniel only half listened as Pastor Sam preached a final sermon to the jacks that night. He would go with the hotheaded deputy to see the sheriff, he'd stop by and see how his kids were doing, and then he'd get back for the log drive down the river. He wouldn't even contemplate there being any other outcome to the situation. The sheriff was a reasonable man, as far as he knew. Surely he would be able to size up the facts and see that Daniel was innocent. And the preacher would vouch for him. He told him so. He turned his head as Pastor Sam's words caught his attention.

"…Jesus Christ was unjustly convicted of crimes he did not do. He was cruelly punished and put to death when all along he was innocent…"

Daniel sat up on one elbow.

"And he could have stopped it all with one word. He could have destroyed the entire world, but instead he gave his life for it. He paid the death penalty that we deserved, he took our place, and he died for our sins. Men, accept what he's done as a gift to you. Believe that he rose again and made the way to heaven open to all who will believe. It's so simple, a child could do it. And once you trust him, you have a friend who walks beside you through any trial or tribulation you might face."

Daniel lay back down again. If only he could have the confidence the preacher talked about. He was tired. He was weary. He was facing his own trials and tribulations without the friend he had always relied on—his wife. He was alone, but he didn't need to be. He closed his eyes and let the preacher's words of the past days run through his mind. One verse that penetrated was "Believe on the Lord Jesus Christ and thou shalt be saved." He needing saving, not only from the trials he was facing, but also from the emptiness of his soul. He needed a savior, but even though part of his heart wanted to accept what the preacher was saying, the other part fought against the very idea. He had experienced nothing but hard work and misery the last few months since losing his wife. And now he was facing criminal charges for things he had no part in. What kind of a God did that to a person? Why should he give his life over to him? God hadn't been of any help to him so far.

The next morning Daniel was up early. He didn't know what the day would bring, but he wanted to be ready for it. He stepped outside in the cold morning air and took a deep breath.

He was tired. He had wrestled with his thoughts most of the night and woke feeling worn out from the struggle. But his decision was made. He would fight his own battles.

He turned to the wash basins on the bench outside the bunkhouse and began washing up, more by feel than by sight as the morning was still shrouded in darkness. He wanted to shave. He didn't want to return to town and have his children see him in his present condition. His hair and beard were not out of place in the logging camp, but he looked a little too wild even for his own liking.

"Turn around, Dunn!"

Daniel swung around at the deputy's voice.

"I've got my gun on you."

Daniel could make out the man's form now.

The lawman kept his distance as he motioned for Daniel to move ahead of him.

"I was about to shave." Daniel was almost amused by the man's determination, but he wisely kept his features controlled.

"No time for that, we're leaving now."

Daniel raised his eyebrows. "No breakfast?"

"Get moving!"

"Now, hold your horses, deputy. I said I'd go with you and I will, but first I'm going to get my jacket and my things. Do you have a problem with that?"

Pastor Sam stuck his head out the backdoor of the cookshack where he had bunked. "What's going on?"

"You stay out of this, preacher! I'm taking Dunn in and I don't want you getting in the way again."

Pastor Sam tugged his arm into his coat as he walked over and sized up the situation. He looked at Daniel and then did a double take when he saw his haggard features.

"You ready to go, Daniel?"

Daniel nodded. "As long as the deputy lets me get my things, I guess we can go. I'd kind of like a shave though." He rubbed a hand over his bearded face.

"No shave!" Elwood nodded his head to Pastor Sam. "You go with him and make sure he doesn't go out the back way. We're leaving now!"

The bull cook was lighting the lanterns and waking the men when Daniel and Pastor Sam entered the bunkhouse. Daniel sensed that some of them had overheard the conversation outdoors. He moved to his bunk and gathered his belongings while the preacher waited by the door.

"What's going on?" Ralston pulled on his pants over his long johns as he watched Daniel reach for his coat.

"Leaving. I'll be back though. You can count on it."

"Good luck then."

Daniel just grunted.

The trip back to town took longer than Daniel anticipated. He hadn't counted on pulling the sled with Murdock's body through the woods over some snowy and some muddy tote roads. The preacher spelled him so that he could catch his breath, but the deputy kept behind them and kept a guard on his prisoner the entire way. It was obvious that he was out for revenge against Daniel for relieving him of his gun the day before. Each step made Daniel feel angrier at the injustice of what was happening to him. He could easily slip away from the lawman and disappear, but it wasn't his way to run from a fight and he needed to clear his name if for no other reason than for the sake of his children.

It was nearing nightfall when they stumbled wearily into town. After dragging the body to the undertaker, the deputy directed them to the jail. Warning bells went off in Daniel's head when the deputy pulled out his pistol and shoved him through the door. The man seemed determined to give the impression to the sheriff sitting at his desk that Daniel was a guilty man.

"What's going on here, Elwood?" The sheriff was a big man and when he rose to his feet, Daniel had to look up at him. He caught himself before he tripped and landed at the sheriff's feet. Out of the corner of his eye, he saw someone jump out of the way and back against the wall.

A woman.

She looked familiar but he didn't know who she was and though he should feel embarrassed at his unkempt appearance and unwashed state, he was only irritated that he had an audience, a woman at that.

"Well, Miss Crane, he's finally here," the sheriff stated unnecessarily.

The deputy and the preacher entered and they both began talking at once. The sheriff held up his hand to silence them when Deputy Elwood noticed the young woman in the corner.

"Mercy?"

The woman seemed shaken by the presence of the deputy.

"Hello, Jefferson."

13

Grand Rapids

Mercy held her hand over her mouth to keep from screaming when the door flew open and the man fell into the room. She had been waiting at the jail for hours to talk with Daniel and she was concerned about the children being alone for so long. They were in good hands with Delaney, but she knew that they were worried about their father and what she would discover after visiting with him. The sheriff was growing impatient with her presence, but she refused to leave until she knew what was happening. Too much was at stake for her to give up now.

Her worse fear was that she would have to face Jefferson Elwood again, which was likely, but she put aside her personal distress to help the Dunn children.

And now, here he was.

And with every eye in the room on her, she choked out his name.

"Jefferson."

There was a long pause as the others looked between the two then finally the sheriff spoke. "Elwood, what's your report? I got your note last week that you were bringing in Mr. Dunn on suspicion of a crime. Have you got proof that he's the thief?"

The deputy kept staring at Mercy.

"Elwood!"

The deputy jumped and stepped up to the desk. He grabbed Daniel by the arm. "Not only is this the thief, he's also a murderer."

"No!"

They all turned as one to Mercy who again clapped her hand over her mouth.

The sheriff scowled. "What's this all about?"

Mercy listened in horror as Jefferson began telling about the murder at the camp and finding the watch in Daniel's belongings. The other man kept shaking his head as if he disagreed with everything, but Daniel stood by silently. He cast looks her way occasionally as if puzzled by her presence there.

Oh, dear God, he can't be a murderer! What will happen to the children if it's true?

The voices of the men were getting louder and for the first time Daniel spoke.

"A month? I can't stay in jail a month. I have to get back to the log drive. I have children to provide for." He leaned forward on the sheriff's desk. "This idiot deputy you sent has made up his mind that I'm guilty, but I had nothing to do with any of these crimes and I'm not about to be put in jail for them."

Mercy tried to squelch her own thoughts and follow what the men were saying.

"The judge can't hear your case until then and I can't, in good conscience, let you loose. If what my deputy says is true, we have enough to hold you. The only other thing I can do is transport you to Stillwater and maybe your case will get heard sooner, but there's no guarantee."

"But, Sheriff, if you would only listen to me," the man with Daniel said. "I don't see that there is any evidence at all and that what the deputy thinks is evidence has been planted there to convince others that Daniel is guilty. I think—"

"It don't matter what you think, even if you are a preacher. It only matters what the judge thinks." Sheriff Talbot turned to Elwood. "I want you to get over to the undertaker and tell him that I want to see Murdock's body before he does anything to it."

The deputy glanced at Mercy again. "I'll talk to you later."

"Get going!" The sheriff barked.

Mercy watched as Jefferson scowled and slammed the door behind him.

Oh no, he thinks I'm here to see him!

She met the sheriff's eyes briefly before he turned back to the other two men. "Dunn, come with me."

"Where?"

The sheriff glared at Daniel. "You don't want to give me trouble, mister. I'm tired and I've missed my supper. Now I'm going to lock you up until we get to the bottom of this and that's that."

Mercy watched nervously as Daniel sized up the sheriff as if debating how to tackle him. The man referred to as a preacher put a hand on Daniel's arm to stop him.

"We've come this far. Fighting now will only make it worse for you."

But it was obvious Daniel wasn't going to go willingly, and the sheriff sensed it too. Faster than Mercy believed possible for such a large man, the sheriff pulled out his pistol and aimed it at Daniel's chest.

"I can save the judge the trouble if you want to end this here and now."

Daniel appeared stunned by the turn of events and the man with him again tried to persuade the sheriff to listen, but the sheriff waved Daniel ahead of him and led him to the back room where Mercy heard a cell door open and shut. She waited with the preacher for the sheriff to return.

She was shaking. Daniel had a wild look about him with his beard and his unkempt hair and clothes, yet he seemed genuinely concerned about his children. Maybe it wouldn't be too difficult to convince him to give her guardianship of the children until he was released.

But murder?

The sheriff walked back into the room and faced her and the preacher. "It's getting late, miss. I suggest you come back tomorrow to talk to the prisoner."

"No, sir." Mercy stepped forward. "I need to talk to him now and get the matter settled."

The sheriff sighed and rubbed the back of his neck. "I know you've been waiting a long time, but I don't think he's in the right frame of mind to discuss anything tonight. He needs to cool down."

"Excuse me. Miss?"

Mercy waited for the preacher to continue.

"I'm Pastor Sampson—Pastor Sam is what most people call me. Uh…may I ask what you need to speak with Daniel about?"

Briefly Mercy told the man about the situation with her father and with the children needing someone to look out for them.

"The sheriff tells me that with their father in jail, the children could be sent to an orphanage or split up and given to different people. I can't let that happen to them. I've been praying and praying for a solution."

The preacher nodded in understanding. "And the way the law is written, you can't legally take them because you are unmarried, is that correct?"

"Yes."

He appeared to think about it. "What about your parents? Could they—?"

"My mother is deceased."

"I see." He studied her a bit longer. "Let me go talk to Daniel about this for you, if you don't mind. Sheriff, would that be all right?"

"How long is this going to take? Like I said, I haven't had my supper."

Just then, Jefferson Elwood swung open the door. He seemed pleased to see that Mercy was still there, but his pleasure was interrupted as the sheriff gave him another order.

"Elwood, go to the hotel and get me some supper and bring a plate for the prisoner too."

"But I—"

"Get!"

Elwood glanced at Mercy again and stomped out the door.

The sheriff waved a hand at Pastor Sam. "Okay, go talk to him and while you're at it, try to knock some sense into his head. That hotheaded attitude will only make more trouble for him."

The preacher nodded and hurried to the back room of the jail.

Mercy was puzzled. She sat down again while she and the sheriff waited, one for answers and one for sustenance. Her stomach growled. She had missed supper too.

Father, please help us work out a solution to caring for the children. It would devastate them to be split up or to go to an orphanage. I know you care about them even more than I do, but I need help knowing what to do for them. Please, let it not be true that Mr. Dunn is a criminal—

Her thoughts were cut short when they heard raised voices coming from the cell.

"Are you crazy? I just lost my wife or did you forget that?"

Mercy and the sheriff looked at each other.

Daniel's angry voice continued, "Did you get a good look at her? She's nothing but a skinny scarecrow with big eyes! Why would *anyone* marry her?"

The preacher answered in an urgent tone, but his words were muffled. Mercy felt her face blaze with heat, and the sheriff shuffled some papers on the desk in front of him as if he didn't want to look her in the eye.

Mercy rose to her feet.

"Perhaps I *will* wait until tomorrow—"

She was cut off by the preacher hurrying back into the room.

"Miss Crane, please don't leave." He held a hand out to stop her as he turned to the sheriff. "Is it true that with their father in prison, the children become a ward of the state since there are no other relatives to care for them?"

The sheriff nodded. "Yes, 'fraid so."

Pastor Sam changed his focus to Mercy. "Miss Crane, I know this is a lot to ask, but would you consider marrying Daniel for the sake of the children? I know, I know," he continued as she gasped. "Daniel is reluctant too, but once I got through to him that it was for the good of his family, he finally agreed. I assure you, Miss Crane, I can help you get it annulled when Daniel is released from jail. And he will be released. I have every confidence that he is an innocent man."

Mercy stood very still. She didn't wring her hands or twist at her handbag or give any indication of her thoughts to the two men watching her, but inside…inside she was quaking at the thought of marrying a man who had nothing but disdain for her. Hadn't she already been cast aside once? Was she going to allow herself to be put in a position to have it happen again?

Skinny scarecrow!

She couldn't help it. She tried to squelch it, but it came out anyway.

Snort.

The men's eyes opened wide.

She covered her mouth with her hand, but her eyes gave her away and the preacher smiled at her. Then it could no longer be contained. She laughed and she laughed hard enough that she had to gasp for air, and she snorted again.

This time both men grinned and even chuckled along with her, although the sheriff cast a wary glance at her that only made her laugh harder.

She sank back into the chair. "I take it Mr. Dunn isn't too pleased with his choices," she finally managed to say.

Pastor Sam pulled another chair over and sat down beside her. He leaned forward as he spoke. "He's mad as a caged wildcat and he's saying all sorts of things without thinking, miss, but believe me when I tell you that Daniel is a good man, a hard worker, and a father who truly cares about his children."

"Are you trying to sell me on him, Pastor?"

The preacher grinned again. "I'm glad you're not offended, Miss Crane."

Mercy snorted, but this time in derision not in mirth. "You must think I'm addled, laughing like that, but it did strike me funny." She straightened in the chair. "But there's nothing funny about the situation. The children need protection and I need to leave in two days. If there is no other solution and if you are sure the marriage can be annulled…" She waited for the preacher's nod. "Then let's get it done. I must get home to the children." She stood.

The men stood with her, but as they started for the door, Mercy turned back.

"May I speak to him alone first?" she asked.

The sheriff gave a quick nod. He stepped into the opening leading to the cells and called out to Daniel. "Dunn, this here is Miss Crane and she needs to speak to you." He turned to Mercy. "I'll be right outside the doorway, miss."

Mercy saw that Daniel sat with his head in his hands, but he rose to his feet when she approached. He squinted his eyes as he studied her.

"Do I know you?"

Mercy's mouth was suddenly dry, but her sense of humor remained despite the awkwardness of their situation. She wondered if he knew that she had overheard his comments. "I'm Miss Crane, your children's schoolteacher."

She saw recognition dawn as he nodded his head. "Is everything all right with the girls? School isn't over, is it?"

"Yes. Mr. Dunn, I—"

"You sent the note about Delaney."

"Yes, I—"

"You said she was doing better. Is she worse?"

"Mr. Dunn! Please, let me talk." Mercy felt her face heat to a deep red as the man across from her stared at her. "Delaney recovered very well and the other children are well. I have been taking care of them for a couple of weeks—"

"*You* have? What happened to Mrs. Ferguson?"

"She left to take care of an ill relative, and then I moved in with the children. But now—"

"She *left*? Were the children alone?"

Mercy took a deep breath. She understood that Daniel was distraught and behind bars for murder, but if he didn't give her a chance to finish saying what she came to say, she was going to scream.

"Who's with my children now?"

Mercy couldn't help it. She stamped her foot. "If you will give me a chance to tell you, I will!"

They stared at each other.

"I'm waiting."

Mercy released her breath in a whoosh. "Okay. Your children are fine. Delaney is watching the others while I'm here. The reason I've come is to tell you that my father has broken his leg and I need to go to him. Our farm is almost a half-day's walk from town. I came here because I wanted to get your permission to take the children with me, but as you now know, the only way I will be allowed to take the children is if you and I…if we…." She couldn't say the words.

Mercy let the silence lengthen while the man in the cell stared at her. She noticed the bruising on his face and the cuts.

"I don't want them leaving town."

Mercy stepped closer to the bars and lowered her voice. "Mr. Dunn, you should know that the money you left for the children is gone. I paid off the last three month's rent on the house and the bill at the mercantile out of my own money."

"Gone? There should have been enough to last them until the end of the log drive! What happened to it?"

His suspicion was evident and Mercy bristled.

"I assure you that when I arrived to care for the children, the money was already very low. Delaney did her best, but with paying Mrs. Simonson for caring for the younger two children during school and buying supplies—"

"Still there should have been enough." He interrupted her again. "I wouldn't have left them without enough money." He seemed truly puzzled.

Mercy was relieved to hear that. She had begun to wonder about the man and his seeming irresponsibility. She didn't know what he was thinking, but it had been in the back of her mind for some time that the money had mysteriously disappeared about the same time Mrs. Ferguson did.

Daniel rubbed at his whiskered face. "I don't understand." Then as if remembering why she was there, he continued, "I can promise you that I will pay you when the drive is over." He looked at his surroundings. "At least I hope I can." He paced the small cell. "So what do we do now?"

Mercy grabbed the bars in front of her, causing Daniel to stop and turn to her. "I want an honest answer, Mr. Dunn. Did you murder that man?"

Anger flashed across Daniel's face then he stepped up to her and looked down into her eyes. She could have stepped away, but she stared steadily back at him.

"No."

"And the thefts?"

He grabbed the bars above her hands and shook them. "No!"

She stared almost nose to nose with him until finally she nodded. "Thank you. I'll marry you now, and I promise to look after your children as if they were my own."

Daniel bristled. "Just remember that they are not."

The comment should have angered Mercy, but she told herself that the man was in no mood to be polite. The only sign of her annoyance was the tightening of her lips. "You're welcome," she said as sweetly as she could.

He cocked his head at her.

They both turned as the sheriff and the preacher joined them, obviously having eavesdropped on their exchange. Pastor Sam looked from one to the other. "Are you ready to begin?"

Mercy turned to the preacher. "It can be annulled?"

He nodded.

She turned back to Daniel. "Then for the sake of the children, yes."

Pastor Sam smiled. "If you two will join hands."

Mercy's heart started pounding but she reached through the bars and let Daniel take her hand. His grip was firm and she could feel calluses and see cuts on his knuckles. He didn't look at her. His eyes were on the pastor, but somehow his touch calmed her. The pastor spoke some words that Mercy didn't hear. Her thoughts were racing with the unexpected turn of events.

I wonder what the children will think of this. I wonder what my father will think!

"Do you—I'm sorry, Miss Crane, what is your given name?"

Mercy cleared her throat. "Mercy."

The preacher nodded. "Do you, Mercy Crane, take Daniel Dunn to be your lawfully wedded husband?"

Mercy hesitated and Daniel squeezed her hand painfully as if to hurry her answer and get rid of her. She looked him in the eye for the first time since the preacher started speaking. She was unprepared for the anguish she saw there.

He's thinking of his wife.

"I do."

"And do you…"

The preacher continued, but Mercy barely heard Daniel's response. She was suddenly praying for the man holding her hand. It no longer mattered what he thought of her; it no longer mattered that she had vowed never to marry; what mattered was that the children would have a home as long as they needed it. She shook her head to clear it when she realized that the men were patting their pockets as if searching for something.

"What?"

"We should have a ring for you."

"Oh." Mercy looked down at her right hand. "I have the ring my father gave my mother."

"Excellent." Pastor Sam waited until she tugged it off her finger. He handed it to Daniel. "Now place this on her finger, please."

Mercy held out her left hand.

"I now pronounce you husband and wife. What God hath joined together, let no man put asunder." The preacher grinned. "Or at least until the annulment. I won't ask you to kiss the bride, but maybe you could shake hands. Now, if you don't mind, I would like to pray."

Mercy felt Daniel squeeze her hand again but gently this time. Then unexpectedly, he kept hold of it while the pastor prayed for them. When he was through Daniel released her and she felt self-conscious as the men looked at her.

"That should take care of it then." The sheriff nodded to them and headed back to his desk.

"I'll prepare a marriage certificate for you in case you should need any proof," the preacher said as he backed down the hallway. "God bless you both for what you are doing."

Mercy fingered the ring on her left hand. It felt odd to have it there. She kept her head down, embarrassed and shy now that the ceremony was over. Daniel shuffled his feet.

"Thank you for doing this for the children. I realize that it is a lot to ask of you, taking my family on the way you have, but I want you to know how much I appreciate it. I shouldn't have left like I did. I know that now.

"When I get out of here, I'll come and get them. I'll try to get a job in town so that I can be home with them from now on. Just thought you should know that, miss." He again rubbed at his bearded face. "You best not bring the children here. As much as I want to see them, maybe it would be better they not see me like this. I think it would upset the little ones."

"I agree. I'll tell them that you are well and we'll be praying for you to be released quickly."

It was awkward talking to the man who was now her husband, but Mercy told him a little more about the children and about the farm and her father.

"I guess I should go now."

"Thank you, Miss Crane. You've saved my children."

Mercy felt tears glisten her eyes as she turned away from the man. She took one last look as she rounded the corner and saw him slumped again on the bunk with his head in his hands.

14

Crane Farm

Delaney held Dylan tightly as the wagon bounced over the ruts in the road, some still frozen and others soft enough to cause the wheels to sink. The jarring and swaying was making her feel slightly ill, but the baby seemed contented by the motion and had slept most of the way. She looked at her sisters. Didi cuddled in Mercy's lap, and Darby and Daphne walked on either side of the ox, directing it to follow the trail. They looked back from time to time as if for reassurance of Mercy's presence. Delaney felt squished next to all the belongings they had packed on the wagon, but she didn't complain. She didn't want to do anything to make things more difficult for Mercy. If it weren't for her, she didn't know what would have happened to them.

Mercy's head bobbed forward and Delaney could tell she was dozing. No wonder. Mercy had been up most of the night before, finishing their preparations. Delaney tried to help, but Dylan was teething and his fussiness required her attention so that she couldn't do much else but try to comfort him. But Mercy managed to get everything done and ready for them to leave.

It hurt a little to walk away from the house where her Ma and Pa had lived with them. It was Delaney's last connection to her Ma and her memories of her. They had lived in many rented houses in Delaney's lifetime, but they had stayed the longest in this one. She tried not to shed a tear when they left the house. Like Mercy said, she had to be an example to the others.

Mercy's hat was crooked from being jostled by not only the wagon ride, but also by Didi clinging to her neck. Delaney studied her for a moment. She could easily accept Mercy as a stepmother. Already she had come to depend on her and she felt close to her during all the troublesome times they had gone through.

She's not as pretty as Ma.

Delaney's forehead crinkled as she tried to remember her mother's features. Already they were beginning to fade and that worried her. If she couldn't remember, how could she help her siblings remember? She fingered the locket around her neck. Maybe she could put a picture of Ma in there.

Delaney felt someone touch her knee and she looked up to see Mercy watching her. She gave her a wobbly smile and Mercy smiled back, but there was concern in her gaze. Delaney suspected Mercy thought she was worried about the move, and that was fine with her.

"Mercy? I mean, *Mama* Mercy." They all smiled. It had been agreed that calling her Mama would help convince others that the marriage was official. It was coming easier, but still awkward to address her as such. "I've been meaning to ask you, what did Guntar want?"

Delaney watched as Mercy hesitated before answering. The night before they left, Guntar had appeared at the Dunns' door and Mercy had stepped outside to talk with him.

"He was disappointed to hear that I wouldn't be teaching school there this fall."

"Oh." Delaney thought there might have been more to it than that, but she let it go. Darby asked the next question as she dropped back to walk beside the wagon.

"Why didn't you stay in LaPrairie to teach school? Why did you come to Grand Rapids? Isn't LaPrairie closer to you?"

Mercy smiled. "There isn't a school in LaPrairie and I wanted to get a job, so I took the position in Grand Rapids. It was hard to leave Papa alone at the time, but I'm so glad now that I did." She smiled at them. "I wouldn't have known you otherwise."

Daphne smiled at Mercy. "I'm glad you were there."

Mercy then told them all about the people in the town and the neighbors closer to the farm and kept them entertained with stories.

Delaney relaxed. Their worries weren't over, but Mercy had certainly made them easier to bear.

They took turns riding in the wagon and walking alongside until Mercy directed the ox toward a tall white house nestled in a grove of trees. Surrounding the grove were open areas that Delaney thought must be the fields. A golden brown dog began barking and ran toward them. Mercy jumped down and let the excited dog greet her with leaps and wagging tail. She rubbed the dog's neck. "Down now, Sugar. Meet your new family." Then she stood and pointed.

"There he is! There's my father!" She shielded her eyes. "Oh, look! He has crutches."

Delaney heard the concern in Mercy's voice. She looked at the man and was pleasantly surprised. He had a big smile on his face as he watched the wagon approach. Delaney wondered what Mercy had told her father about them coming. Somehow with all they had to do to get here, the subject hadn't come up.

"Mercy! Where's my little girl? Mercy!"

The girls started giggling as Mr. Crane started calling for his daughter in a loud, comical way.

"Oh! I forgot how embarrassing that man can be!" Mercy sounded mortified, but Delaney could see delight in her eyes. Mercy held out her arms to Didi and helped her down to the ground. Taking her hand they ran together toward the house, leaving the others to follow at the slower pace of the ox.

"Here I am, Papa!" She threw her arms around her father, nearly knocking him off his crutches.

"Whoa, Mercy! You'll break my other leg!"

Darby stopped the ox and the others got down and gathered around them and watched their greeting with interest. It was little Didi who spoke first.

"Mama Mer*th*y, i*th* thi*th* your pa?"

Delaney saw Mr. Crane's eyebrows shoot up, but before he could question his daughter, Mercy stepped back, and with a glint in her eye, she made the introductions.

"Papa, these are *my* children. This is Delaney and the baby is Dylan, that's Darby, here's Daphne, and this one is Didi. Children, say hello to your new grandpa. I'll go see to the ox now." Delaney saw her hide a grin behind her hand as she stepped away.

Mr. Crane leaned on his crutches and looked from face to face. "Well now, I knew Mercy was bringing home some visitors, but I didn't know she'd gone off and had a bunch of babies who grew up mighty fast into two young ladies and three little boys."

Delaney smiled and the others started giggling.

"We're not boy*th*! We're girl*th*, ex*th*ept for Dylan." Didi stated firmly. "*Th*ee! We're wearing *th*kirt*th*." She pointed down and swirled her skirt for him.

"And mighty pretty little girls you are too! I'll get to the bottom of those names soon, but for now I bet you'd like to get some supper. Let's go to the house." He lifted his crutch and pointed with it.

The girls began unloading their belongings from the wagon, and Mercy hurried from the barn to join them. An older man walked beside her.

"Girls, this is Jemison, our hired man and good friend. He'll help with the heavier things." She pointed out each child to him as she gave him their names. He nodded and grinned but didn't say anything.

Delaney clung to Dylan and watched with motherly concern as her sisters eyed their new surroundings. Didi and Daphne were distracted with the friendly dog, and she had to nudge them to take the bags that Mercy was lifting down from the wagon to them. She saw Mr. Crane make his way up the steps on his crutches and struggle to hold the door open and maneuver his crutches through the doorway. She was curious. It appeared that Mr. Crane didn't know too much about their situation. He called them visitors. Would he let them stay?

She managed to carry one bag along with carrying Dylan and followed the others up the steps. They entered a large kitchen and found Mr. Crane at the woodstove. He turned on his crutches as they entered.

"Here, let me sit down. I'll take the little one while you give Mercy a hand with the other bags." Mr. Crane set his crutches aside and held out his arms for Dylan.

Delaney hesitated.

"It's okay, young lady. I'm his *grandpa* after all." He grinned at her and she shyly smiled back.

Supper was simple. Mr. Crane had put together a pot of stew, and Mercy swept back into the role of woman of the house as easily as she had at the Dunn household. The children were visibly drooping by the end of the meal and Delaney wondered where they would all sleep.

"The upstairs has five bedrooms," Mercy explained as she let Didi's head drop to her shoulder. "We used to rent it out, but Papa and I liked it better when it was empty and just the two of us, so we haven't used it in a long time." She turned to her father. "Papa, are the beds ready?"

"Of course." He appeared offended by the question, but Delaney caught the wink he aimed at his daughter. "And I'll have you know that you owe me, young lady. That meddlesome Mrs. Ketchler took it upon herself to clean the house for me when she heard that you were coming with guests. I had to put up with her chatter for a whole afternoon, and since she was upstairs and I was down here, she *chattered* at the top of her lungs."

Delaney hid a smile. She liked Mr. Crane.

It was a short night. Mercy had them tucked into soft beds with warm quilts in no time, and the exhausted girls didn't wake again until a rooster announced that morning had arrived. Delaney couldn't remember where she was but when she heard Dylan begin to wake, she sat up and saw his makeshift bed across the room from hers. She padded across the floor and picked him up and wondered how to go about getting his breakfast.

"Delaney?" Mercy knocked softly and entered the room. She stroked Dylan's head as she smiled at him. "I have some goat's milk heating for Dylan. Do you want me to take him or are you ready to come downstairs?"

"I'm ready. Where are the girls?"

Mercy laughed. "They're waking up, but from the way they are snuggled into their blankets, I think they will prefer to stay in bed."

"No, we wouldn't!" Daphne exclaimed as she ran into the room, followed by Darby and Didi. "We want to see the farm!"

"Then you shall." Mercy laughed.

The farm was a wonder to the children. Delaney was amazed at all the space. There were fields waiting to be planted, a big barn, a milk house, an icehouse, a chicken coop, a summer kitchen, and a big area designated as the garden. Down the hill was the river. The girls were delighted.

Grandpa Crane, as he soon came to be called, took them in as his own grandchildren. Delaney wondered what he thought about his daughter marrying her father and instantly becoming the mother of five, but no matter what his thoughts were, he went along with it and Delaney felt relieved to know that he was in agreement that the children needed protecting. His crutches limited his mobility so little that it was easy to forget that he had a broken leg. He moved all around the farm, working alongside the hired hand. He couldn't do a lot out in the fields, but he drove the horses and the wagon and helped milk the goats every day.

Mercy took over the kitchen and house duties along with the girls' help and also got them involved in the outdoor chores. Delaney soon discovered the joy of gathering eggs even though she was a little squeamish about nudging some of the more persnickety birds out of the way. The warm spring allowed them to plant the garden, and they waited in anticipation for the first sign of sprouts. Jemison had his hands full trying to plant the fields, so the chores he couldn't do were left to Mercy and the girls.

"When will the cows arrive, Mama Mercy?" Daphne asked as she pet Sugar and ruffled her fur.

Mercy looked up from plucking weeds in the garden. "Grandpa says they should be here any day now. It's quite exciting to start raising cattle. We're one of the first in the area, and I know we'll be getting orders for milk and beef as soon as we build up the herd."

"Wish I was ready to handle it." Grandpa Crane stepped out on the porch now using only a cane for assistance, but still limping. "I'm afraid I'm going to have to make milkmaids out of you girls."

The girls laughed. They were getting used to their new grandpa's teasing ways.

His brow creased as he looked at his daughter. "I'm sorry to put so much on you, but I've been waiting a long time to start on the cattle and I don't want to miss the opportunity to get them here."

"I already told you I'm happy to help, Papa. Don't you worry about a thing. We can do it. Right, girls?" Mercy came up on the porch and washed her hands before she collapsed into a chair. "I forgot how much work this farm is, Papa. But as much work as it is, I really missed it!"

"Then you shouldn't have left. Elwood didn't waste any time getting over you."

"Papa!" Mercy's eyes warned her father.

Delaney watched with interest the look that passed between father and daughter. What did Mercy not want them to know?

15

Grand Rapids

DANIEL COULD FEEL the frustration and anger building within him again. When would the nightmare days and nights living in this small jail cell end? He learned from experience that pacing the tiny room wasn't going to give him relief. He dropped to the floor and began a series of push-ups then he ran in place and again dropped to do sit-ups until he was panting for air. He was not a man to sit and read all day. He was used to hard physical labor and the torture of being encased in a box was taking its toll on his body and his mind.

The worst of it was that he wasn't even guilty of the crimes!

He wrestled it over and over in his head. Who killed Murdock? Who had motive? Who would set *him* up? And why?

He sat down on the bed and stared at the opposite wall. The hardest part was feeling that he had failed his family. What would Dee think of the situation he was in? Her last words to him had been to take care of the children. His head hung forward in shame. He had run out on the children. If it weren't for that schoolteacher taking them in, where would they be now? In an orphanage? He shuddered as the thought tormented him.

His anger at Mercy Crane diminished when he realized the enormity of what she was doing, yet there were times when her timid face would flash through his mind and he found himself blaming her for taking the children from him. He knew he was being irrational but he couldn't help it. She was alive and enjoying his family while their mother was dead and he was trapped behind bars.

The door to the jailhouse opened and Daniel's head shot up. He cocked his head to listen if the sheriff had returned or if it was that weasel of a deputy. A shrill squeak from the sheriff's chair told Daniel that the large man was the one who sat down in it. He had become thoroughly familiar with the sounds and smells and goings on of the jail and for that matter, the town. Night after night he listened and watched what he could from the miniscule window in his cell.

The sheriff was gruff but he was a good man. Whether he thought Daniel guilty or innocent he never revealed. He just did his job. The deputy was a different story. Elwood used any opportunity he had to privately torment Daniel from "accidentally" dropping his tray of food to actually sitting down when the sheriff wasn't around and eating

Daniel's food in front of him, leaving the imprisoned man to go hungry.

Daniel could complain to Sheriff Talbot, but he was not one to have someone else fight his battles for him. He didn't know how, he didn't know when, but he would have his day with the deputy. He promised himself that.

The door opened again and Daniel heard the sheriff's chair squeak and slam forward. *Someone's in trouble for waking him up,* Daniel guessed. Then the door to the cells banged open.

"The preacher's here, Dunn."

Daniel stood as Pastor Sam approached him. Unconsciously, he shook his head in wonderment. The man had been to see Daniel as often as he could. That he believed in Daniel's innocence was still evident and Daniel appreciated that, but he also knew that as with every other visit, the preacher had sermonizing in mind. And he was slowly wearing down Daniel's resistance.

"I have some good news," Pastor Sam started without preamble. "There's been another robbery in town."

"That's good news?"

"Sure it is. Think about it. If they think you're the one who's been robbing the stores, then who robbed them while you were in jail? There has to be someone else, not you." The preacher grinned.

Daniel nodded while he thought about that. "Or they'll just think someone has taken up where they think I left off." Discouragement was in his voice as he sat down again. "Any news about when that judge is coming? I've got to get out of here before I lose what's left of my mind."

Pastor Sam pulled up the chair he left there for his visits.

"I haven't heard anything new about that. What concerns me right now is how you will handle it if the judge, when he comes, elects to keep you here or send you to the state prison."

Daniel leapt to his feet again. "He can't do that! I've done nothing—"

"I know. I know. Calm down, Daniel, I just think you need to be prepared for any outcome and there's only one way I know to prepare you." He reached for the Bible he had set on the floor beside him.

Daniel stared hard at the man on the other side of the bars. He rubbed the knot at the back of his neck while he returned to sitting on the side of his bunk. He watched as the preacher leafed through the pages and he made a decision. In a calmer tone, he spoke, "I've been thinking about what you said last time…and the time before that, and the one before that."

Both men grinned and the tension eased out of Daniel.

"You said that God paid the way to heaven for me, that heaven isn't something I can earn by myself. There's got to be something I have to do, some rules or something to follow like the Ten Commandments or something."

Pastor Sam smiled as he turned a few more pages until he reached the passage he sought. He turned the Bible toward Daniel. "Take a look for yourself. Read it out loud, will you?"

Daniel's callused finger followed the words that the preacher pointed out in the book of Ephesians. "For by grace are ye saved through faith; and that not of yourselves: it is the gift of God; Not of works, lest any man should boast." He nodded as he looked at Pastor Sam again.

"Okay. It says that I don't have to work in these verses, but aren't there others that say that I do have to do something?" he persisted.

"Yes. There are many verses that give us commands and instructions on how to live, but they are referring to after we are saved, after we have become God's child. But our salvation, Daniel, is a gift and gifts can't be earned. They are free. That's what grace means—undeserved favor. You see, Jesus was willing to go to the cross to die for our sins even though it cost him everything and even though he knew that most of us would reject his gift, still he paid the price of our sins with his death, the death we should have experienced. He was buried and he rose from the dead. Now, we simply place our faith in that message and heaven becomes ours."

He stopped and looked into Daniel's eyes, seeing the longing there. "Accept the gift, Daniel. Accept Jesus Christ as your Savior, your way to heaven."

"I want to. I don't understand why he would do this for me, but I want his salvation. I'm just scared that my faith won't be strong enough."

"You're still not getting it. You simply make the decision to accept his offer of salvation and it's *his* faithfulness that sustains and seals you. You're still trying to depend on your own strength. Look at this verse in Galatians 2:16, 'Knowing that a man is not justified by the works of the law, but by *the faith of Jesus Christ*, even we have believed in Jesus Christ, that we might be justified by *the faith of Christ*, and not by the works of the law: for by the works of the law shall no flesh be justified.' We can depend on the faithfulness of the Lord Jesus. Not only did he fulfill the Father's wishes in coming to die for us, but he also remains faithful to us who trust him."

Pastor Sam stopped when he saw the emotion on his friend's face.

Daniel swallowed and when he spoke, his voice broke, "Dee believed this. She tried to explain it to me, but I thought I knew all about God already and that as long as I didn't do anything too bad, I was going to go to heaven. I see it now. I accept God's gift and I trust the Lord Jesus as my savior." He wiped at his eyes and smiled sheepishly at the pastor. "So what's next, preacher?"

Under his breath, Pastor Sam breathed, "Praise the Lord! What's next? How about we thank the Lord right now and then if you don't mind, I'd like to share more Scriptures with you."

"Yeah, I'd like that. It's funny how I resented you yakking at me for weeks but now I want to hear more."

The men sat in deep conversation until the sheriff stepped into the hallway and interrupted them.

"Just got word that the judge will be here tomorrow sometime."

Daniel didn't sleep. His mind was full of awe as he reflected on the things he and Pastor Sam discussed. Knowing that he was saved and assured of heaven gave him a peace he had never felt before. Even in the middle of the trouble he was in, he had calm in his soul. The preacher explained that just because he was now a child of God didn't mean that all his troubles would miraculously vanish, but his problems seemed smaller with God on his side.

The jail door banged and Daniel heard the squeal of the sheriff's chair as he rose to his feet. He waited and it wasn't long before the sheriff headed toward his cell, the keys dangling in his hand.

"Judge is here."

"Good. Let's get this over with."

"Settle down. He just wants to talk with you before he hears testimonies."

Daniel stopped his rapid stride down the hall and turned back to face the sheriff. "Testimonies? What is there to testify? Who has anything to testify?"

The sheriff's expression hardly changed, but Daniel caught a hint of apology in the man's eyes.

"That deputy?"

"Let's start with the judge. Move along."

Daniel brushed down his shirt before he entered the sheriff's office. He wished he looked more presentable to face the judge who would determine his future. He rounded the sheriff's desk and faced the man sitting in the sheriff's chair. He looked back at the sheriff in puzzlement then at the seated man again.

The man studying the papers laid out before him on the desk was not how Daniel expected a judge to look. In fact, he looked more like one of the loggers straight from the camp. While he stared at the man wearing rugged bib overalls and a checkered shirt, he was astonished to see the man spit tobacco on the sheriff's floor. Daniel rubbed a hand over his mouth to hide a grin. Anyone else who tried that in the sheriff's office would be locked up in a minute. Out of the corner of his eye, he saw the burly sheriff scowl.

The judge finally peered over the top of his wire-rimmed spectacles at Daniel. Slowly, he pulled them off his nose and bit at the bow while he leaned back in the creaky chair. Daniel found that he was holding his breath and although no words formed in his mind, he knew he was praying, asking for wisdom for the next few moments.

"What was yer job at the camp?"

The question was unexpected, but Daniel answered it and many others dealing with his job and that of the other loggers. Before he knew it, the judge nodded to the sheriff and he was being escorted back to his cell.

"What was that?" Daniel demanded of the sheriff. "He didn't ask me anything about the reason I'm in here."

The big man just shrugged. "All I know is that he's one of the best."

Daniel leaned against the bars and watched the sheriff retreat to his office. *God, I've trusted you with my life after death, but I'm not sure how to trust you to get me through this life.* He sank to the bunk. Dee knew how to trust God, he recalled. Little things paraded through his memory—how she prayed with the children and read the Scriptures to them, how she sang hymns around the house, and how she reminded him that God always knew best.

I never understood her relationship with you, God. I knew it was there and I guess I appreciated it about her, but I knew I wasn't a part of it. I need to learn to trust you like she did so I can have the peace she had.

He stood and walked to the little window that lent him a view from the side of the building. Suddenly he straightened. *What is that schoolteacher doing here? She's supposed to be watching my children!*

16

Grand Rapids

MERCY WAS FLUSTERED. Why did the judge send for her to meet him at the jailhouse? She had nothing to do with Daniel Dunn other than taking guardianship of his children. *And being married to him*, she reminded herself. But she had nothing to testify as to his guilt or innocence. She prayed that he would be exonerated of all guilt and be free to take charge of his children again; they missed him so much, but at the same time, she didn't want to give up the children. She loved them and as each day passed, she loved them more. And little Dylan was like her own little baby.

At least he didn't tell me to bring the children.

She shook her head to free it of her thoughts. She had no right to the children. As soon as Mr. Dunn was released, their marriage would be annulled and the children would leave with their father. She knew that was what should happen, but the empty feeling it gave her hurt. It was one thing to determine not to ever get involved with a man again, and quite another to face a future of aloneness after experiencing the joy of having a family.

She lifted her skirts to climb the steps to the jail and found Jefferson Elwood blocking her path. Seeing him again unnerved her, and she backed down a step but then held her ground. She had to ignore the feeling. The judge was waiting for her.

"Excuse me, please." She put her foot back on the top step.

Jefferson moved in front of Mercy and forced her to step back again, his arms crossed in front of him. "You were supposed to wait for me." He grabbed the post and leaned toward her. "I came back and found not only were you gone, but you had decided to get involved in a fake marriage with that criminal. What were you thinking?"

Mercy fought the anger building in her. *How dare he!* "I have nothing to say to you." She grabbed her skirts and made to step around Jefferson, but again he sidestepped and blocked her way.

"Jefferson, so help me if you don't get out of my way… I'll….I'll…I'm going to kick you!" She raised her eyes to his. "And you know I mean it."

"Do I have to remind you, *Mrs. Dunn*, that I am now an officer of the law? You have to do as I say." He reached for her arm.

Mercy had enough. She pushed his arm away and took the final step onto the porch entrance of the jailhouse.

When she felt him grip her upper arm as she tried to pass, she swung fully around and kicked at his shin. Hard.

"Why, you little beast!" He grabbed her arm and twisted it behind her back. "Let's see how you like being in jail." He pushed her in front of him as he limped the short way to the door. Mercy was outraged, but she grit her teeth to keep silent. She could see a few people stop in their tracks to stare at them. She would never live this down in the town.

"Stop it!"

The deputy swung around at the voice and Mercy saw Guntar run toward them.

Oh, no!

Her former student jumped the steps two at a time and charged at Elwood. Mercy stumbled away as the younger man flew at them, forcing the deputy to release his hold on her. She caught herself from falling and turned swiftly to try to stop Guntar from getting hurt.

"That's enough! Elwood, get up!" Jon Talbot took hold of Guntar by the neck of his shirt and pulled him off the deputy. "Take it easy, young man." He stepped between Guntar and Elwood, and Mercy overheard the muttered words the sheriff spoke to the boy.

"Can't say that I blame you, but make yourself scarce. Now."

Guntar looked past the sheriff at Mercy and when she nodded at him and smiled, he nodded back and moved away down the steps.

Elwood stood to his feet. "Sheriff, don't let him go. He should be arrested for assault."

"And the lady?"

The deputy eyed the sheriff with suspicion. "You saw then? Clearly you could see that she made an attack against me."

The sheriff gave Elwood a shove toward the door to the jailhouse. "You don't want to know what I think right now." He turned to Mercy and motioned for her to go ahead of him. "After you, ma'am, and my apologies for the deputy's behavior."

Mercy studied the sheriff, trying to read what was in his thoughts, but his face remained impassive. She entered the jailhouse ahead of him and found a man sitting at the sheriff's desk.

The judge?

The man was in faded bib overalls. On closer inspection, she found that they were clean and being curious and a schoolteacher, she noted that his hands were also clean and the nails free of dirt. He obviously dressed to appear as a working man and not as an authoritative figure and she wondered why. She glanced around the room and saw that Jefferson was standing in the corner with his arms across his chest, obviously still fuming. She looked away from him with an unconscious shake of her head. In contrast to the judge's demeanor, the deputy's attempt to appear intimidating looked ridiculous.

Sheriff Talbot closed the door behind him and walked to the other corner of the room to watch the proceedings. Somehow his presence soothed Mercy's nerves. She straightened her shoulders as she waited for the man at the desk to look up.

"You may be seated, Mrs. Dunn."

Mercy was startled at the use of her married name. She glanced at the sheriff and he nodded to the chair behind her.

The judge peered over his spectacles at Mercy for several moments. Then he leaned back in the sheriff's squeaky chair and formed a steeple with his fingers across his chest.

"Yer aware that I represent the law?"

"Yes, sir."

"And yer aware that this is officially a court of law?"

Mercy swallowed and stared at the desk and the man behind it. "Uh, yes."

The judge sat up straight, and Mercy flinched at the screech the chair made.

"This court does not take lightly the matter of dishonesty, Mrs. Dunn."

"Dis...dishonesty?"

"You entered fraudulently into a marriage contract with Daniel Dunn, did you not?"

Although Mercy couldn't see Jefferson Elwood directly, she heard his boot scrape on the floor as if he stood up straighter and the sheriff, who never seemed to display his feelings, actually raised his eyebrows. And in the back of her mind, she noted that the judge's grammar had suddenly improved.

"I…we…you see, the children—"

"Bring in the prisoner." The judge kept his eyes on Mercy as he gave his command to the deputy. She flinched when he spat on the floor.

Mercy watched Jefferson reach for the jail keys and disappear through the door to the cells. She turned to the sheriff for help but found his face impassive again. She stood and approached the desk.

"You see—"

"Please remain seated, *Mrs. Dunn.*" The odd way the judge emphasized her name caused Mercy's mouth to go dry. Would he dissolve the marriage and take the children? *He can't do that! Or can he?* She gripped her hands in her lap and barely sat on the edge of the chair as she watched for some sign of what the judge was about to do, but she couldn't even guess what was in the strange man's thoughts.

Jefferson shoved Daniel through the doorway ahead of him. From Daniel's disheveled appearance, it was obvious that the deputy had not been gentle with him. The prisoner stumbled the last few steps to the desk, and although Mercy could see his jaw tighten as he watched the deputy return to his corner, she also realized that he was visibly in control of his temper.

Something was different.

She rose to her feet again to stand beside him as he faced the judge and for a moment she forgot where she was and what was happening as she studied the man who was now her husband. His expression was serious with just a touch of apprehension in it, but there was none of the anger that she saw in him the first time they met.

Mercy shook her head. Daniel had turned to her with a question in his eyes and the sheriff and judge were watching her closely. She licked her lips and folded her hands demurely in front of her and studied a spot on the floor with great interest. She jumped as the judge leaned forward with another screech of his chair.

"Mr. Dunn, I have come to a decision in your case."

Daniel straightened.

The judge reached for his revolver, which startled everyone in the room. "Not guilty," he declared and soundly smacked the desk with the butt end of the gun. "But!" He raised his hand before anyone could speak. "There are conditions to your release."

Although there was instant reaction from everyone except the sheriff at the judge's words, as one they stilled to hear what the judge would say next.

"Even though I believe you are innocent of the crimes charged to you, as yet we still have no other suspect. You may be the key to finding out who is guilty of the murder if not also the thefts. You were obviously set up to appear guilty."

"Yes, sir." Daniel's relief in being believed was evident in those two words.

The judge looked between Daniel and Mercy. "As to the two of you."

Mercy found she was holding her breath.

"You will remain married for a period of at least one year and then you will appear before this court again." He turned to Daniel. "You will join Mrs. Dunn at her father's farm and work the land and take care of your children during this time."

He again held up his hand to forestall Daniel's attempt to interrupt. "You will not return to the lumber camp until the murderer has been caught. Do you understand these instructions?" His bushy eyebrows wiggled upward as he looked to Daniel and awaited his inevitable outburst.

"But…if you believe me innocent…look, I know what you're trying to do—you know—keeping me married to Miss Crane and all." Daniel rubbed his whiskered face. "It's not going to work. Even a year won't make it work, sir." His voice dropped as he leaned toward the judge, but Mercy heard the anguish in it. "I just lost my wife."

"Your wife is standing beside you, Mr. Dunn. You will stay with her day and night for one year. You will not leave to work elsewhere. You will not take the children and live elsewhere. You will live as husband and wife for one year. Sheriff!"

The only movement the sheriff made was to turn his eyes to the official.

"I require you to make periodic checks on the Dunn household to assure that they are following my orders. If they are not compliant, Mr. Dunn is to be incarcerated again."

"Yes, sir."

The judge returned his attention to the papers on the desk. Without looking up, he said, "Dismissed."

Mercy looked uncertainly at Daniel, wondering what to do. He was staring at the judge in frustration. Finally he turned to the sheriff.

"May I get my things?"

Mercy stepped to the door to wait for his return, and as soon as she moved, Jefferson started for her, but the judge intervened.

"Deputy."

"Sir?" Jefferson looked over his shoulder.

Daniel came back, holding a few items and headed for the door. He opened it for Mercy and motioned for her to go ahead of him. Mercy could see that he was aware of the deputy's attempt to speak to her, and she felt like a pawn in a game being played between the two of them. She walked out the door with her husband behind her.

The judge waited patiently for the scowling deputy to finally turn from watching the couple leave to approach the desk. The sheriff stayed where he had been the entire time, but the judge knew the man was interested in what he had to say to his deputy.

"Please, be seated."

"Why? I haven't done anything."

The judge raised one eyebrow and eyed the man over his spectacles.

Elwood sat.

The chair squealed as the judge leaned back to study the man before him. That the man was unfit to be an officer of the law was evident in his attitude and his actions. The judge had heard the tussle on the boardwalk out front and wanted to fire the man on the spot, but he had an idea—a better idea.

"I have an assignment for you."

The judge watched Elwood perk up. Underneath that belligerent attitude was a vein of fear after all. He sat forward again as if to speak to the man confidentially.

"It will require giving up your badge for a time, but that's necessary if you're to do what I need you to do."

The deputy scowled.

Doesn't want to give up his authority, it seems.

"I'm sending you into the lumber camp again, but this time you join the men as one of them. Tell them you were fired, make some friends, nose around a little, and see what you can find out about this murder. But do so discreetly. Work the log drive and report back here with what you learn."

Elwood's brows dipped low as his scowl deepened. "What if I don't want this assignment? What if I just check in at the camp and ask some questions? I don't see any need for me to have to join the crew."

"You do this job, you keep your badge. You refuse and I take the badge now."

The deputy jumped to his feet. "Can he do that?" he questioned the sheriff.

The big man in the corner nodded. "He can do that and a lot more. Mind your manners or you'll find out what the other side of those bars look like. Now hand over the badge and go get your gear. You can head to the camp in the morning."

Elwood fumbled with the badge and finally slapped it on the desktop. He mumbled a few more things before he stomped out of the room, slamming the door behind him.

The sheriff walked to the desk and took one of the chairs across from the judge. He smiled.

"I got to hand it to you, Clarence. You get more devious the older you get."

The judge grinned back as the chair squeaked out his change in position. "He'll get kicked around a bit at the camp and they'll work the daylights out of him. Just what the hothead needs. Knock some sense into him."

"I didn't just mean the kid there. I'm talking about the Dunns. Do you really think you can matchmake now?

They don't appear to cotton to each other, and the man is grieving the loss of his wife."

"We'll see. Time will tell if it will work or not, but if I hadn't intervened, they'd never take the chance to find out and I'm tired of seeing children grow up without both parents." He stood to his feet and gathered his papers. "We'll see," he repeated.

"Staying at the house with us tonight, Clarence?"

"Of course! When else do I get to see Betty? You were one lucky dog to win my sister's hand, and don't forget, you have me to thank for it too. I'd say I am a pretty good hand at matchmaking after all, wouldn't you?"

The two men headed for the door, but the judge stopped and pointed at the sheriff's chair. "Don't ever oil that chair, Jon. The noise it makes gets me better results than my most fearsome stare."

17

Grand Rapids

MERCY AND DANIEL were silent as they walked away from the jailhouse. Mercy wondered what the released man was thinking about the judge's orders. She was in too much of a state of shock to know what to think herself. She couldn't help but be happy that Daniel had been declared not guilty and freed, but to be sentenced to a year of living as his wife was perplexing and disturbing. She felt an overwhelming relief that the children would still be hers for a time, but having their father around was a different matter altogether. What *was* that judge thinking?

Suddenly Daniel stopped and Mercy nearly collided with him as he turned to face her. She watched his face as he seemed to be trying to form his thoughts into words.

"Look, I'm sorry about all this. I guess even though they believe me innocent, they must still not trust me, making me live at your farm for a year and all. I don't know what to say." He shook his head and Mercy could tell he was struggling to make a decision. "I need to find work near your farm to take care of my family and to pay you back for what you've done. I don't know if I'll ever see my pay from the logging camp."

They stood in front of the mercantile and Mercy was aware that Mrs. Bedloe was watching them from the window. Mercy's earlier confrontation with Jefferson probably had spread all through the town by now and as she glanced about she was aware of the curious stares of others at seeing her with this man. She bit her lower lip as she saw Mr. Crenshaw open the door to his leather shop and glare at them.

"Perhaps we should discuss this somewhere more private," she suggested. She was unprepared for the hostile reaction her words caused in the man in front of her.

"I assure you, *Miss* Crane, that I have no intention of being alone in any private setting with you. I intend to make our annulment go through without anybody accusing me of anything improper."

Mercy stared dumbfounded at Daniel. "Are you serious? Do you mean to imply that I was trying to…trying to… *entrap* you somehow?" she sputtered the words, oblivious now to the onlookers as her anger increased. "After all I've done! I can't believe—"

Daniel took her arm and she would have pulled away except that he kept his grasp firm. She saw him look at their surroundings and surmised that he finally realized that they were making a scene. She allowed him to pull her around the side of the mercantile away from prying eyes.

He took a deep breath then looked her in the eye. "I guess I have to apologize again. I didn't mean to offend you, it's just that…I've been holed up in that jail with all kinds of thoughts going through my head and now that I'm out…I'm making a mess of things." He released her arm and she rubbed at the spot he had gripped. "Can we start this whole thing over?"

Mercy was about to answer when Guntar rounded the corner then stopped abruptly when he saw the two of them.

"Guntar!"

He pointed at the arm Mercy was rubbing.

"Did he hurt you?" He demanded. His hands balled into fists at his sides.

Mercy stepped in front of Daniel as she spoke quietly to Guntar. "No, of course not, Guntar. This is Daniel Dunn, my…uh…my husband."

Her words seem to pain the boy and he muttered, "Don't matter if you're married or not. He better not hurt you."

"No, of course not. I'm fine, Guntar. And thank you for helping me out earlier today. I hope you continue to work hard in school this year with a new teacher."

"Not going to school. I gotta go to the lumber camps now that…that…we just need the money." He finished hastily.

"No, Guntar! You were doing so well. What happened?"

"Ask him." Guntar nodded at Daniel then walked away.

Mercy turned back to speak to Daniel and found him staring after the boy. "Isn't that Murdock's kid?" he asked her.

"Murdock? The man who was murdered?" Mercy shook her head. "He can't be. His name is Guntar Strahle, not Murdock."

"No, that's him. Murdock married his mother." Daniel stepped forward as if to go after Guntar, but the boy had disappeared. He looked at Mercy. "I had forgotten about Murdock marrying the widow Strahle. There was some talk that he wasn't too good to her and the kid."

"Guntar's mother…I ran into her one day in town and I remember it being a rather warm day and she had a shawl about her head." She cringed as she spoke the next words. "You don't suppose she was hiding bruises, do you?" *Maybe that's why Guntar is so protective of me.*

Suddenly Mercy's lips tightened and she motioned for Daniel to look where she pointed. A woman's skirts were swept by a slight breeze around the corner of the building. "It's that Mrs. Bedloe trying to hear us," she whispered to him.

Daniel scowled. Then he grabbed her hand. "Come on."

He guided her around the back side of the building and kept her walking until they came to the back of the hotel. Mercy was confused by his changing moods. First he was angry at her then he was conspiring with her. Even now he grinned as he released her hand.

"Wonder how long she'll keep standing there."

Mercy smiled at the thought of the nosey woman wasting time as she listened in vain for them.

"Well, what next? Do we head out to your farm now?"

"We can if you're up to it, but…" Mercy hesitated. "Please don't be offended, but I think your children would be less likely to be frightened if you had a chance to clean up before seeing them…and…we'll need a meal before we go."

Daniel shook his head. "I don't have any money, not even a coin on me."

"Mr. Dunn." Mercy hesitated not knowing how to broach her suggestion to him. "I can get you a room and give you a chance to prepare yourself."

"I can't have a woman pay for me."

"Then here." Mercy quickly pulled some money out of her handbag. "No one has to know it was my money."

"That's not exactly what I meant. I don't like taking your money whether people see me do it or not." His words were laced with frustration.

"It's for the children, Mr. Dunn, and like you said, you'll pay me back. Consider it only a loan if you must, but take it before someone else comes to spy on us. I feel like a criminal standing behind this building."

He capitulated but not before she heard him mutter, "You have no idea what feeling like a criminal is like."

Daniel ignored the curious stare of the hotel clerk as he asked for a room and ordered a hot bath. He knew he looked a sight. Even though he bathed daily in the water the sheriff or deputy brought him, he never felt fully clean in the jail.

He shaved as he waited for the hot water to arrive and was surprised at how quickly it was ready when he heard a knock on his door, but it wasn't the water. It was the hotel clerk with a package for him. Curious, he opened the package and found new clothes inside.

That Miss Crane has been busy. Bet the Bedloe woman peppered her with questions when she went for these.

He wondered about the woman who had taken on the care of his children. Did her family have money that she could afford to pay for all this? Were his children going to be reluctant to leave their life of leisure to go back to scraping out a living as they had been doing all these years?

He shrugged and nearly cut himself as he continued shaving. He needed to remember to be thankful for all that had transpired in the last hours and not to borrow more trouble, but he was uncertain about the judge's ruling. He knew the man was trying to put him and the Crane woman together for the good of the children, but the old man shouldn't be meddling in people's personal lives. He'd "do his time" as it were and then he and the children would be on their way. No one was going to take Dee's place in his life. And he was going to make that clear to the woman whether it offended her or not.

His thoughts went to Murdock's murder and Guntar's face flashed through his mind. If Murdock had roughed up the boy's mother a time or two, maybe the kid was the one who finally put an end to it. He wondered if the sheriff knew of the connection.

The bath was just what he needed to feel like a new man and as he scrubbed at his skin, he felt he was removing the unjust label of criminal from his body. He chafed at the delay in seeing his children, but the woman's advice was sound and he was in no position to argue. As was becoming his custom, he turned his thoughts into prayer and asked for guidance not to mess up what the Lord had provided.

Mercy was already waiting in the dining room when he arrived. Looking at her across the room, he wondered what her thoughts were about their arrangement. *She better not get any ideas about this becoming permanent.* He was determined to make it clear to her as he crossed the room, but as he reached the table she stood.

"There you are, Mr. Dunn. I've already eaten, so I hope you have a good meal. I have some shopping to do at the mercantile so I'll meet you there when you are through and we'll be on our way. Is that satisfactory with you?"

Her words were crisp and seemed rehearsed to him. She avoided making eye contact and moved away after he gave her a quick nod. He sat down slowly as he watched her walk away.

Maybe she won't be a problem after all.

18

Grand Rapids

Mercy exited the mercantile to find her wagon being loaded and Daniel Dunn standing beside it talking to the sheriff.

He's anxious to be with the children.

She didn't blame him and she was pleased that he had taken charge in seeing that they were ready to go. The men had their backs to her, and as she approached she heard Daniel say, "Just check into it. That's all I'm asking. Maybe I'm wrong."

He's talking about Guntar. She shook her head at the thought. *Guntar would never hurt anyone.* But even as the thought came to her she remembered how gruff he had been toward Mr. Crenshaw and how he had tackled Jefferson.

The men turned.

"Mrs. Dunn," the sheriff tipped his hat.

She nodded in reply and smiled. Turning to Daniel she said, "Thank you for helping to load the wagon."

There was more to Daniel than she realized. She looked to the quiet man beside him. "Good-bye, Sheriff."

"I'll be out some time for a visit."

"That's right." She frowned. "Is that really necessary?"

"You heard the judge, ma'am."

She nodded in resignation. "I'll just be a minute. I need to settle my bill at the livery."

"Livery is taken care of." Daniel's words were curt.

Mercy was about to question him then stopped when understanding hit her. "Uh, excuse me a moment while I get my bag."

Daniel nodded without expression.

Mercy headed to the hotel kitchen and returned shortly with her bag and a package under her arm. The sheriff was striding down the street back to the jailhouse, and Daniel was holding onto the ox's head. She took his hand as he helped her onto the wagon seat.

It was clear to Mercy that Daniel was enjoying his walk. She studied his back as he guided the lumbering animal along and realized that he was reacquainting himself with freedom. His eyes continually roamed the forests around them and the sky above. Occasionally, he looked back for direction when the trail took two different paths. At one point, Mercy jumped down and walked on the other side of the wagon. Walking was better than the bumpy ride over stumps and rocks on the uneven trail. She reached back for the package she had brought and handed it over to Daniel.

"What's this?"

"Supper. You apparently gave it up to pay for the wagon and some of the supplies."

"Hmm."

"What?"

"Nothing. Thank you."

Mercy watched as he opened the wrapping and took a bite of the roast beef sandwich inside.

"Want some?" His voice was muffled around the food in his mouth and Mercy laughed.

"I knew it. You were hungry, but you weren't going to say anything."

Daniel swallowed and grinned. "Got anything to drink in there?"

Mercy pulled out the water jug and handed it over. "The river is right alongside and we have a spot here where we always stop to water the ox and rest." She hardly needed to guide the animal who seemed to know where to go.

They sat on rocks beside the running water, and Mercy waited for Daniel to finish his meal. She nibbled on some beef until he was ready to talk.

"What were you and the sheriff talking about?" she finally asked.

Daniel corked the water jug and handed it to her. "That Strahle boy. I'm not saying it was him that did the murder, but I think the sheriff should look into it, don't you?"

Mercy stared at the river before she answered. "I can't picture Guntar doing anything like that. I pray it isn't him."

"Maybe it isn't. Someone tried to set me up as the killer, so it could be one of the men in the camp. I just don't know who or why."

"Does it matter now that you're free?"

He leaned back to stretch. "I just spent one of the longest months of my life in a tiny cell because of that person. I lost my home and my children during that time. Yes, it matters to me."

Mercy was quiet as she thought on his words. *Yes, he deserves to know.* She was aware that Daniel was studying her and she tensed as he sat up, a determined expression on his face.

"I think there's something we need to get cleared up between us before we go any further. I have no intention—"

"—of not annulling our marriage. That's what you were going to say, right?" Mercy almost laughed at the surprise on his face. "Believe me, Mr. Dunn, I have no intention of allowing it to continue even an extra minute after the judge gives us both the freedom to annul it. Were you worried that I was going to fall in love with you and make it impossible for you to be around me?"

She hesitated a moment when she saw his frown. "Forgive me for being so blunt, but that is what you were thinking, wasn't it? After all, who would want a 'skinny scarecrow with big eyes'?" She smiled as his head jerked up.

"You heard that?" An embarrassed grin appeared on his face. "You have to understand the circumstances—"

"I do. Please don't be embarrassed. I've been called worse. I don't expect to ever marry, and I have to admit that having your children around has been an experience I had never expected to have. It will be difficult to let them leave with you at the end of the year, but I promise not to cause any trouble about it. Just, please, let them write to me so that I know how their lives turn out. That's all I ask."

His stunned expression told her that he hadn't expected her to understand. That he thought he would have trouble with her was clear, and she felt empowered at having taken the upper hand in the discussion to relieve them both from the embarrassment of having him tell her to keep her distance, although it pricked her pride just a bit.

"Can we be friends for the sake of the children without all this awkward notion that one of us might fall into deeper emotions?"

She should have been offended by his look of utter relief, but she had thick skin. Jefferson Elwood was to thank for that.

As if he read her thoughts, his next question pierced her newly acquired confidence. "What did that Elwood fellow do to you anyway?"

She winced. She couldn't help it. Standing to her feet, she pointed the ox toward the trail. "I trust we'll never mention his name again," was all she said.

She missed the narrowing of Daniel's eyes as he watched her walk away.

As if the children had been watching out the window for them, all four girls came tearing down the road when they saw the wagon approaching. Mercy noticed them first and felt tears spring to her eyes as she saw them realize that their father was with her.

"It's Pa! It's Pa! He's here!"

Daniel dropped the lead rope and ran forward to his daughters. Tears were in his eyes and more ran down Mercy's face as she witnessed the reunion. He truly loved his children.

She guided the ox and wagon around them and let them talk and get reacquainted. She had missed them all even just for the day she had been away; she couldn't imagine what it was like for their father. They would have a year together and then she would be saying good-bye. Some of the tears that wet her cheeks were for herself as well as for the reunited family.

"Mama Mer*th*y! Pa i*th* here! He'*th* here!"

Mercy allowed herself to be tackled by Didi on the way back from the barn. She saw the raised eyebrows on Daniel's face at the little girl calling her *mama*, but at the moment she didn't care. She reached down and swung the girl around and then hugged her. The other girls swarmed around her for a moment and then hurried back to their pa, clearly divided about which one to hug. Mercy laughed and headed to the house. Her papa waited patiently with Dylan and she eagerly took him from his arms and cuddled the little boy. She could hardly wait to see Daniel's face when he saw how much his son had grown.

Daniel approached the house slowly. He took in Mercy's father, the large white farmhouse, buildings and lands, and seemed to look at everything but Dylan. Mercy's heart started pounding as she realized that something was not right. Daniel should be reaching for the boy, but instead he stopped and held out his hand to Papa.

"Mr. Crane, sir. Thank you for taking my family in and caring for them. I would surely welcome the opportunity to return the favor by helping out on your farm." He pointed to the cane. "You've had a bit of bad luck, I see."

"We'll talk more about that later. Say hello to your son first. I imagine he's changed quite a bit since you saw him last."

Daniel glanced at the boy in Mercy's arms and then looked away. "That he has. This is a nice place you've got here. Mind if the girls give me a tour?"

Mercy watched her father's brows gather and put a hand on his arm to stop whatever he was about to say to the man. "Delaney, you and the girls show your pa around while Grandpa and I get supper. We'll call you when it's ready."

They watched as Daniel swung Didi onto his shoulders and took two of the others' hands. Delaney held his sleeve as she guided him toward the barn, and they all seemed to be talking and laughing at once.

"What was that all about?"

Mercy bit her lip at her father's words. She cuddled little Dylan closer. "He must blame him for his wife's death. I had no idea." Tears of sorrow now washed a path over the earlier tears of joy that had flooded her face. She bent her head to her father's shoulder as he comforted her. "I had no idea."

19

Crane Farm

THE LAST DAYS of August were proving to be the hottest of the summer months, as usual. Delaney felt her dress sticking to her as she hung the wash on the line. She loved living on the farm and even enjoyed all the chores there were to do. She looked around in delight at the fields of hay and alfalfa where her father was working. She peeked around the clothes at Mercy on the porch with Didi and Dylan snapping beans. She sighed in contentment. There were days when she was completely happy, like this one, and then there were others where she saw the tension between Pa and Mercy and watched Pa ignore Dylan and she wondered if something would happen that would cause Pa to want to just take them all and leave.

But we can't leave. The judge says we have to stay the whole year.

It was hard to feel at home when she knew they weren't staying for good. Deep in her heart she never wanted to leave. She finally had found a place where she felt she belonged. A home.

"Laney!"

Darby and Daphne ran across the green lawn, and both started talking to their older sister at once while they reached in the basket and helped her hang the wash.

"Mama says we can go swimming today as soon as you finish hanging the clothes. Come on, hurry up! I can hardly wait to jump in the river."

"I'm going to swim out to the big rock and jump from there!" Daphne declared as a challenge to the other two. The girls continued to chatter while they worked, and Delaney only half listened.

Daphne has slimmed down with all the exercise she gets here. Daphne used to always be looking for something to eat, but with Mercy's hearty meals, everyone was getting enough to eat and even Daphne was satisfied. Another reason life was perfect here.

Delaney followed the others to get ready for their swim. Mercy had kept her promise to teach them, and they had spent many joyous hours in the nearby river. Mercy was so patient and good in teaching them things. And that reminded Delaney that she had something she needed to discuss with her stepmother. Maybe today she'd have a chance to ask Mercy some questions.

The water felt cold compared to the hot air, but they were soon used to it and jumped in and out and ran to the blanket Mercy laid out on the ground where they dried off and let the sun warm their skin again. Then they were up and racing each other to see who could get to the water and go under first. Mercy carried Dylan down to the water and brought him in with her, letting him float and splash in her arms. When she felt Dylan had enough, she brought him back to the blanket and dried him off, just leaving him in a light nightshirt and propping up a blanket to protect him from the sun and let him nap while the others played. Delaney joined them, reclining on the blanket and allowing the sun to dry her off. Her modest swimming outfit, like that of her sisters, was made for her by Mercy and its long skirt, just below the knees dripped water liberally all about her.

It was time to tell her news.

"Mercy? I mean Mama."

Mercy patted Delaney's arm. "You don't have to call me Mama if you don't feel comfortable, Laney. With your father here now, I don't think we have to convince anyone that you children belong here."

"No, I don't mind calling you mama." Delaney turned on her side and fiddled with a blade of grass. "In fact, that's one of the things I wanted to talk to you about."

"Yes, dear?" Mercy divided her attention between the young girl beside her and the three other children playing in the water.

"I don't ever want to leave here!" Delaney blurted out. "I want you and Pa to stay married so we can live here always."

A shadow crossed Mercy's face and she didn't look at Delaney as she answered. "I'm sorry, honey. I wish things could be different, but we just have to trust that the Lord is going to work everything out for your father and for you children. I love you all so much and want you to stay here, but it's really out of my hands."

Delaney bit her lip. "There's something else…something I wanted to tell you."

Mercy sat up straighter and called out to the girls in the water, "Didi, not so far out! Remember you can't go past the big rock." She settled back again. "What is it?"

Delaney ripped the grass blade into strips while she stole glances at Mercy. "I did it. I accepted Jesus as my savior, Mama."

"Delaney!"

Delaney smiled at the happy response she received. "You made it so clear last night when you told us about when you got saved."

Mercy reached across Dylan and hugged Delaney. "Tell me about it."

"Well, you said you knew all the verses, but they didn't make sense to you until you were alone in the dark and scared."

Mercy smiled. "My imagination used to cause me more trouble! Go on."

"I realized that I was just like you. I knew verses that told about Jesus dying on the cross for my sins, being buried, and rising from the dead, but I hadn't really believed them yet. I was kind of mad at God for taking Ma away, and then Pa was in jail and everything seemed to be going wrong. I didn't want to hear about God and his love, like you told us in the Bible stories and read to us every day. Then last night after we went to bed, I started thinking of the verses again, like you did, and this time I wanted what God was offering to me. I had always believed that Jesus died for me, but last night I decided I wanted his salvation for myself. I want to go to heaven, and I want to have God with me through whatever happens next in our lives."

Mercy had tears in her eyes now as she again hugged Delaney. "I couldn't be happier. Have you told your father yet? Have you told the girls?"

"I wanted to tell you first. Maybe tonight at supper I can tell them, if that's okay?"

"Oh, yes! And I'm going to make something special for dessert to celebrate."

"Mama, look!"

Mercy and Delaney watched as Daphne made a huge splash jumping from the big rock. Mercy clapped her hands when Daphne surfaced again.

"Mama, do you like Pa?" Delaney could see that she surprised Mercy with her question, but she had to know.

"Now, Delaney, of course I like your father, but that isn't going to change what happens—"

"No, I know that. I was just wondering because there's this boy…"

Mercy pulled her watchful gaze away from the swimmers for a moment to stare at Delaney. "Yes?"

Now that she had started, Delaney felt embarrassed, but she went on anyway. "I met him back in Grand Rapids and I haven't forgotten him. He…he…winked at me and he said if he lived here I would be his girl."

"And? Would you like that?"

She shrugged and felt her face grow pink. "How do you know who you should like or love or whatever?"

Mercy bit her lip and Delaney wondered if she was thinking of her pa or if she was thinking of that deputy that she almost married. Maybe she shouldn't have brought the subject up, but she couldn't seem to get Ben Blackmore out of her mind.

"Delaney, there is no easy answer to a question like that, but there is someone who can help you when it's time for you to make the decision about who you will love and marry. You have Jesus Christ as your savior now, and you can go to him and ask him anything and tell him anything. And I'll show you some verses that will help you. You see, God doesn't talk to us directly today like he used to, but he does speak to us in his Word, and it's there that you can find answers to any questions life throws at you."

"Thanks, Mama. I'll probably never see him again, but I just wanted to know. I like being able to talk to you."

"I like it too. You can talk to me anytime, honey. Well, we better get started back. Girls! Time to dress! Why don't you go first, Delaney."

Mercy always set up a *changing room* for the girls so they could get into dry clothes before going back to the house. That way their wet things could be hung on the line right away instead of being drug all through the house, making a big mess. Two blankets made a triangular-shaped room when attached to the trees. Delaney made haste getting out of her wet things. Her skin still felt cool from the dip in the river as she slipped into her work dress. They would all sleep well tonight having been refreshed by the cool swim.

It took longer for Darby, Daphne, and Didi because they were really wet, but while Delaney and Mercy waited for them, Mercy decided to take another swim.

"I've been sitting in the sun too long and I'm hot. Will one of you stay with Dylan until I'm done? I won't be long."

The water was refreshing and Mercy made the most of the time to stretch, take long strokes, and just float while the girls finished dressing. Her swim costume filled with water and slapped against her legs making it difficult to move through the water gracefully, but getting cooled off was her goal and she accomplished that.

"Mama!"

Mercy turned toward shore.

"We're all ready and Dylan woke up. Should we take him and go or wait for you?"

"Go on!" she called. "I'll be right up."

She watched as the girls gathered the wet things and trudged up the hill toward the house then she laid her head back and floated a little longer. The summer days were almost over and this pleasure would end as well.

They're going to love sliding and learning to skate this winter.

Mercy couldn't help thinking of all the things she wanted to do with the children. She had to make the most of the time she had with them, and she refused to let the sadness of the eventual parting dim any part of it. She thought again of Delaney's wonderful news and thanked the Lord for the girl's salvation.

Delaney's question about love had flustered her for a moment. Who was she to be able to give that kind of advice? She hadn't done anything right yet when it came to knowing about love.

She turned over and swam toward shore. She had supper to start and a hungry family to feed, so she best get at it. She grabbed up her dry clothes and tossed them on the bush by the makeshift changing room. Pulling off wet, soggy clothing was difficult and she was struggling with it when she heard someone coming down the path. The girls must have forgotten something.

"I'll be right along," she called from behind the blanket. She poked her head up to see which one it was and found herself staring into Daniel's wide eyes.

"Oh!" She let out a squeal and grabbed for her clothes, but in her haste she tripped on the blanket, and as it started to fall she grabbed it and held it in front of her, pulling it around her the best she could.

"Oh, I'm sorry! This is so embarrassing—" Her words were cut off as Daniel spun around on his heel and headed back up the path away from her.

She stood stock-still with her wet hair dripping down her back and soaking into the blanket around her.

As if things aren't awkward enough between us!

20

Logging Camp

FALL WEATHER WAS upon the area and work was starting at some of the camps. The larger logging camps only worked the winter months when they could ice the roads and cut grooves in them for the sleighs full of logs to be pulled easier. But in the small camps work often kept going through the summer, and felled logs waited to be moved when the weather became cold. Men now began thronging in, some willingly as there was no other work available to them, but some unwillingly, tricked into being left out in the wilderness with nowhere else to go. Two men stood on the hill looking down into the camp. One for the former reason and the other for reasons of his own.

Guntar Strahle bore the responsibility of providing for his mother now that Murdock was dead. In many ways, Guntar was relieved to have the man absent from their small log cabin. He had been a steady drinker and was abusive in both speech and action toward the family. Why his mother married the man was something Guntar felt he would never understand. He shrugged unconsciously as his thoughts took him back to a day he overheard his stepfather bragging to some men.

"I got me a woman and a kid to do my work for me. All I gotta do is bring home some money onc't in a while. If they give me any lip, I let 'em have it!" Then he had laughed his all-too-familiar drunken laugh.

And he was good to his word. Guntar had stood between the man and his mother many a time to prevent her from a beating and had taken the brunt of the man's anger on himself. There was little he could do to protect his mother though when he wasn't home and he burned inside each time he saw a fresh bruise appear on her face.

What he didn't understand was why his mother stayed. After Murdock stumbled home from the log drive, there was barely enough money to sustain the family. The man usually lost it all in drink or gaming before he made it home. If they didn't garden and barter their produce and eggs, they would have starved long ago. They were better off without the man.

Guntar stayed in the shadows as he watched the other man on the hill. He knew him. It was that deputy who had grabbed Miss Crane's arm—Elwood. Guntar's eyes narrowed as he studied the deputy. No badge in sight, but he could still be here to question men about Murdock's murder. The pack on his back was curious. *He must be planning to stay a bit.*

Guntar stayed hidden as the man began the descent to the camp. He'd wait and go in later; he didn't want to cross paths with the deputy the first day on his new job.

Jefferson Elwood took in the scene before him with disgust. He had been to the logging camps on official business and he made it a point to leave as quickly as possible. The men who worked in the woods were a filthy lot, rarely bathing, growing vermin-infested beards, and generally living like animals. He had come across a few who gave hygiene an attempt, but once a man slept with the fleas, bedbugs, and mites in their bunks, it just seemed like a losing battle to even try to keep clean.

And the smell! Jefferson shook his head as he adjusted his pack and headed down the hill. How he was going to stand a season living here was beyond him. He should have given that judge a piece of his mind, but remembering the sheriff's threat to lock him up silenced him. He could have refused to do this job altogether but it would have cost him his status as deputy and he kind of liked having some authority over the people in town. Besides, there was a certain thrill in doing an undercover assignment like this one. He'd show that judge and that sheriff a thing or two! He would prove Dunn was guilty of Murdock's murder. The judge should never have released Dunn and definitely shouldn't have sentenced Mercy to a year of marriage to the man, but now that he was here at the camp, he would find the extra proof needed to put the man behind bars again and this time for good.

And Mercy. Jefferson grabbed a young tree trunk and held on as he caught his breath. He and Mercy were supposed to get married and he was the one who broke it off. He shouldn't be all that surprised that she despised him. He could see it in her expression. But Gloria, the dark-haired Gypsy beauty, who came traveling through town with that snake oil salesman was too much for him to resist. He was bedazzled and he left town with her and the salesman with the promise of seeing the country, the cities, and gaining riches in the process. Then he woke one morning in a ditch with only the clothes on his back and all the money he had taken with him gone.

He decided then that he would stay away and not let anyone know what had happened. He joined up with an old prospector for a time and found enough gold to get back on his feet. He took the job of deputy in a small town because it looked easy enough and before long he came to like the authority it gave him. He moved around until the office in Grand Rapids came open and he figured he could go back and take up with Mercy again. She wasn't much to look at, but her father had a good farm, one that would bring a healthy price if he could one day get his hands on it. And then there was that notice he had found one day while snooping through one of the jailhouse offices. He knew something about Mercy Crane that even she didn't know.

This phony marriage the judge was making Mercy take part in might turn out in his favor. Mercy was bound to feel foolish after the annulment when all the people were wondering what happened to her marriage. She'd probably jump at the chance to marry him again. Better still, if he could find a way to prove Dunn's guilt sooner, Mercy would be sure to see him as her hero, rescuing her from living with a murderer.

Jefferson straightened his shoulders as he strode into the camp. This assignment was going to change his life.

Guntar watched the camp foreman bark out orders to the men as they left the cookhouse. He got in line behind some others and listened to where he was supposed to go, following closely on their heels. So far, he hadn't said anything to anyone and he hadn't been questioned, but he had seen the foreman eyeing him up and knew his time would come. He watched what the men did and tried his best to duplicate their actions. He was strong, but this work was backbreaking, never ending, all day labor that left him almost sleeping over his evening meal and certainly dead to the world once his head hit his bunk. Morning came too early and he wondered if he were going to make it through another day, but slowly his muscles adapted and he became better at the jobs given him. The men nicknamed him

Gunny, and because he was hard working and willing to do whatever he was asked, he soon became a favorite.

A few knew he was Murdock's stepson, but they didn't talk of it. The foreman questioned him once about his age and having just turned sixteen, Guntar was simply given a nod. He guessed that the foreman knew about the family needing the money.

It was a couple of weeks into the job that the deputy crossed his path. Up to that time, the man had all he could do to keep pace with the others. It seemed he had never done manual work of this nature in his life by the way he stumbled around and got in the others' way. The men rode him hard once they heard that he had been fired as a deputy, but Guntar was unsure of how true that was. Elwood still was asking questions and for that reason as well as because he had tackled the man once, Guntar stayed away from him.

Guntar carried a long crosscut saw and headed to the next giant white pine the foreman wanted taken down. His partner for the day hadn't shown up yet so he stood by the tree to wait. The trees around him were of amazing height and girth and it hurt Guntar inside to see them fall, yet he knew their value in lumber and he knew if he didn't do it, someone else would. What bothered him the most was all the waste the logging companies left behind them. With the abundance of trees, they took what was easiest and most profitable for them and left the huge stumps. The branches and small stuff got mashed into the ground as they rolled the big logs over them, and the area was a tangled mess when they moved on, leaving new growth more difficult to start.

Guntar sighed. He heard stories from some of the seasoned loggers about forest fires sweeping through areas like this because of the dried dead debris left behind. It was a shame to destroy the massive forest, but what could he do?

"Hey, kid!"

Guntar's eyes narrowed as Elwood approached. The once-flamboyant deputy now looked haggard and thin. He limped as he came toward Guntar.

"This the next one?" He pointed at the tree.

Guntar nodded.

"Well, let's get to it. I'm your partner for the day."

Guntar hesitated. "What happened to Shorty?" he ventured to ask.

"Sick. Must be some of that slop the cook feeds us finally got to him."

Slop? The food in the cookshack was the best Guntar had ever eaten and there was plenty of it.

Elwood grabbed the other end of the saw. "These things are tricky, so just follow me, got it, kid?"

Inwardly Guntar groaned. He had seen the way Elwood fought the saw when working with other men. The men on either end of the saw had to be in perfect balance with each other, never pushing, only pulling on their end. If someone pushed, the saw would catch and bend, usually knocking the other man off balance. Guntar had heard plenty of cussing from the men who trained in the new guys and a lot of it due to Elwood and his take-charge attitude about everything. He just wouldn't listen well to directions.

"Now keep in rhythm with me or this thing's going to buckle. The jacks here can't seem to get it right."

Guntar raised his end of the saw level with Elwood's and allowed him the first pull. Sure enough, instead of letting Guntar pull back, Elwood pushed and the saw bent and nearly went flying.

"You stupid kid! I told you what to do!"

"Elwood!"

They turned at the voice of Ralston coming toward them. "Foreman wants you on axe over to the north. I'll take over here with Gunny."

Elwood's hands went to his hips. "Then why did he send me over here?" He muttered a few more words then suddenly looked hard at Guntar. "Gunny? Guntar? Aren't you that kid who knocked me down in town?" He took a step toward Guntar. "Why, I ought to—"

"Settle down, Elwood. Gunny's been through enough lately having his dad get murdered and all." Ralston's words made both men turn to him. Guntar glared at the man for revealing the news to the deputy, and Elwood's expression was simply confusion.

"What do you mean? Murdock was the kid's father?"

"No!" The word burst from Guntar. "He was married to my ma, that's all."

The deputy eyed Guntar with an interest that Guntar didn't want to see. It was clear he was about to ask more questions when Ralston intervened.

"What do you care about Murdock's death, Elwood? You were fired as deputy, right? Unless you're here for reasons other than working, I suggest you get over to the north side before the foreman kicks your backside clear to town."

Tension crackled in the air between the two men until Elwood turned to Guntar. "I have a matter to settle with you, kid." Then he stomped off.

Ralston grinned and spit tobacco juice before he picked up the other end of the saw. "I couldn't let you suffer with that bum all day, Gunny. Now let's see if you're as good as your pa was on this thing."

"He wasn't my pa."

Ralston straightened. "I know that. I also know a few more things about him that you're not telling."

Guntar's eyes narrowed. "Like what?"

"Like who provided him with his booze out here in the middle of nowhere." Guntar's jaw tightened and Ralston grinned.

"You see, Gunny, Murdock used to share his stash with me and now that he's gone, my supply is about gone. So…" He dragged out the word. "I could let that nosey deputy know about his supplier or I could keep quiet about it if, say, a jug were to appear in the usual spot a couple of nights from now."

"I got nothin' to hide."

Ralston positioned the saw in place again. "Maybe you don't, but I bet your poor, widowed ma might." He nodded his head for Guntar to take his place.

Guntar grabbed the saw and pulled with a vengeance.

"Settle down, Gunny," Ralston said soothingly. "Everything will be just fine, just back and forth, nice and easy now."

The saw sang in rhythm as the two men took their turns, but Guntar's heart was pounding with fear.

He knows about ma.

21

Crane Farm

LIFE FELL INTO a routine of sorts for the Dunn family, as much as could be possible under the circumstances. Delaney felt she could be happy if only Pa would take an interest in Dylan. Then there was that tension between him and Mercy. Delaney sighed. Would anything ever feel right again?

Not that she was complaining. Pa was out of jail and was innocent and that burden was gone from her young shoulders, but she could see the anger in Pa about what had happened to him. Yet there was a peace about him that had never been there before. She was confused.

She snuggled down under the warm quilt. The mornings were cold in the big farmhouse until Mercy or Pa got the fire going in the kitchen stove. She dreaded that first dive out of bed and touching the icy floor with her bare feet, but she had to do it soon because Dylan was making noises, and he could already climb out of his little bed. She had to catch him before he got to the long staircase in the hall.

She poked her head out and saw Dylan's face right in front of her.

"You little troublemaker!" She laughed as she tried to pull the chubby boy into bed with her, but he squirmed and would have none of it.

"Oh, all right! I'm getting up. You just sit here in my warm bed until I get some clothes on, young man. Life was a lot easier until you learned to crawl around." She hastened to get into her wool stockings and pulled a winter dress over her head. Grabbing a shawl, she wrapped Dylan in it. She picked up some garments for him and headed for the staircase.

"Let's get you down where there's some heat and I'll get you dressed there. Brrr! It's a cold morning."

Her sisters were still sleeping. Being a Saturday, there would be no schooltime with Mercy, and they deserved a little extra rest, but Delaney never got to enjoy that extra sweet sleep of a day off. Dylan didn't understand Saturdays and kept to his early-morning schedule regardless.

Delaney knew she could let Mercy take over his care. She was getting better at sharing him though and surprisingly it was the only thing that Pa had really commented on about his son, and Delaney found that out accidentally when she overheard him talking to Mercy.

"Laney seems to spend all her free time with the boy. That's not too healthy, is it?"

Delaney had been even more surprised by Mercy's sharp reply, "Someone needs to. He is a part of this family."

Delaney shook her head. She didn't understand Pa.

The bottom steps were already warmer than the upper ones, and Delaney hurried Dylan down them to the kitchen and stood before the stove, turning and warming each angle of their bodies. Delicious odors were emanating from the covered pots and pans on the stove top and Delaney even enjoyed the smell of the strong, black coffee Mercy prepared for Grandpa Crane and Pa.

"There you are! I thought I heard some footsteps coming downstairs. Here, let me have Dylan while you make your trip outdoors." Delaney frowned at the thought of going out in the cold, but she slipped into some boots by the door and wrapped herself in the nearest coat on the hooks.

"Be back soon," she called over her shoulder.

On the way back to the house, Delaney met up with her Pa. The cows had arrived and he enjoyed the job of milking them. He carried two pails of milk and didn't seem bothered by the cold at all.

"Mornin', Pa."

"Mornin', sweetheart. Did you sleep well?"

"Yes, Pa. You?"

"I sleep better here than I have anywhere on earth," he surprised her by saying. He stopped and breathed deeply the frosty air, letting out a cloud of steam from his warm breath. Delaney bounced on one foot then the other trying to stay warm.

"Aren't you cold, Pa?"

"Sure I am, but I love being outdoors so much that I don't let it bother me. Here, let's get you inside where it's warm. I bet your sisters are still sleeping." He chuckled. "Mercy will have to bang the pots and pans louder this morning than she did to get them up for school yesterday."

Delaney giggled. "That got them up! Mercy is so funny sometimes."

Her father merely nodded and let her go ahead of him to open the door so he could carry the pails through. Mercy was at the stove busily preparing breakfast with Dylan on her hip. She didn't even turn around. She just said, "Wipe your feet, you two. I'll not be mopping melted snow in my kitchen all day." Then she glanced over her shoulder and smiled at Delaney.

The young girl noticed that she didn't look at Pa.

"Is Grandpa coming in? Breakfast is almost ready."

"He wanted to put away a few things first, but he should be any minute. Something smells good. Should I get the girls up?"

"No, we'll let them sleep a bit longer." Mercy handed Dylan back to Delaney who put him in a special chair. Then she scooped some warm porridge into a bowl and handed it to Delaney who added some maple syrup and milk and stirred and blew on the concoction until it was ready to feed the little boy who was now banging his fists on his little tray as he eagerly awaited his first mouthful.

Out of the corner of her eye, Delaney watched as Pa and Mercy moved about the kitchen, never really looking at each other and always being careful to stay out of each other's way. She sighed. At first it seemed that the two of them were going to be friends and make the best of the situation that judge put them in, but somewhere along the way, a coldness had stilted their relationship and as Delaney scooped more porridge into Dylan's mouth, she thought she could guess the reason why. Pa hadn't given his young son so much as a glance since they came in.

The door swung open with a chilly blast and Grandpa Crane stomped his feet on the threshold before entering. Delaney shivered and tried to block the cold air from Dylan, and Mercy ran to shut the door and scold her father.

"Papa! The baby will get chilled. Why can't you stomp your feet before you open the door? I think you've developed bad habits living alone."

"Nonsense! This winter air will make a man out of him! Won't it, champ?" He tousled Dylan's soft black hair and quickly pulled his hand away, making a wry face. "Laney, aren't you supposed to put that stuff in his mouth, what's it doing in his hair?" He grabbed a kitchen towel and wiped at his hand.

Delaney tried to muffle a laugh but a *snort* from Mercy made her giggle out loud.

"Serves you right, Papa! Good boy, Dylan!"

Delaney saw Pa actually smile at the antics of the others. His good humor continued as he questioned Grandpa."

"What's on the agenda today, sir?"

Grandpa Crane lowered himself to a chair near Dylan and took over the spooning process from Delaney.

"Daniel, you're going to have to pace yourself. The winter months are slow around the farm. We mostly care for the animals, do repairs, and keep firewood supplied for the house. It's the spring planting and the harvest time that will have you dropping exhausted into your bed at night as you've already seen. You need to relax now, son, while you've got the chance."

"I'd just as soon keep busy, helps pass the time."

Delaney saw Mercy's hand still for a moment over the pot she had been stirring.

Pa's comment made it sound like he is still in jail.

"Well, you could run the trap line with me and we'll do some ice fishing. We need to harvest some ice for the icehouse too."

"Sure, sure, anything."

Grandpa crossed his legs as he scooped out the final bit of cereal for Dylan and then made sweeping motions as he guided the spoon into the boy's mouth. His own mouth opened and shut along with Dylan's, and Delaney had to turn away so that she didn't start laughing again.

"Quit laughing at me, Laney. I seen you do it too," he spoke as if he were grouchy.

Both girls at the stove laughed again.

Soon the others were up and breakfast was served. Everyone had chores for the day, and Delaney's thoughts were pleasant as she swept the kitchen floor. Life was good. All the responsibilities she had been burdened with had been lifted and she felt, even with Ma gone, that she was beginning to enjoy life again. Yet in the back of her mind loomed the knowledge that this would all one day end. The calendar counted down the days to when they would leave the Crane farm and all the joy that Grandpa Crane and Mama Mercy gave them. That thought darkened her mood so she shook it off. Maybe if she didn't think about it, it wouldn't happen.

Of course Pa and Mercy could…No. Pa still grieved over Ma and he made it clear to them all that when the year was over, they would be leaving.

A sound outside caused Delaney to go to the window. A big man in what looked like a buffalo robe was talking to Pa and Grandpa Crane.

"Mercy! Mama Mercy! Someone's here!"

Mercy lightly ran down the steps and followed Delaney to the window.

"Oh, it's the sheriff, come to make sure we're still together, I suppose." She barely muttered the words, but Delaney heard them.

"The sheriff? Again? He's not coming for Pa, is he?"

Mercy pulled Delaney into her arms. "No, darling. He's here for another visit, so we must get busy and prepare a meal. It's early enough in the day that I doubt he'll stay the night again, but we better be prepared in case he does. Let's see, I'll hunt up the extra quilts in the house to put down in the parlor for him. He can share the room with your pa. Why don't you go in there and see what needs to be done to fix it up, will you?"

Delaney watched Mercy hurry up the stairs on her mission before she turned to the parlor. It had been decided that the room would become a bedroom for Pa. Grandpa Crane had a room on the main floor, but Mercy and the children were all upstairs, and even though the children could have doubled up to make a room available for their pa, Mercy had proposed the parlor as a solution. But the funny thing was that Mercy wanted to take the parlor as a room for herself, leaving Pa to have space near his children, but Pa had insisted on letting her keep her own room. Delaney frowned as she recalled the argument the two of them had. Pa even threatened to sleep out in the barn if Mercy made any more fuss about it, so Mercy gave in but not before Delaney heard her mutter something about the man being afraid of his own children.

Pa's bed was neatly made, but the room needed to be dusted and have a few things put away. Delaney quickly set it to rights and took the quilts Mercy handed to her at the doorway to make a bed for the sheriff. She saw Mercy glance in the room and then look away. It seemed clear that she wanted nothing to do with Pa.

"Have you learned any more about Murdock's murder? Did you check out that kid I told you about—his stepson? I was thinking—"

"Hold on."

The sheriff put up a hand to stop Daniel's questions. They were in the barn where they could talk freely without the children hearing. The sheriff glanced over at Mr. Crane who was leaning against one of the posts, causing him to straighten his stance.

"I can go in if you need to talk to Daniel alone." He started for the door.

"No need, sir." Daniel insisted. "I want you to hear what Jon came to say as well. I have no secrets."

Mr. Crane hesitated until the sheriff nodded. "Wish you'd quit calling me *sir* all the time, Daniel. Told you my name's Stanley."

He shook hands with the big man then looked around for the milking stool. He sat down and winced as he stretched out his leg. Jon noticed.

"That leg still giving you trouble?"

Stanley nodded. "I can't tell you how grateful I am that you sent Daniel out here. The good Lord knew I needed the help." Jon glanced Daniel's way in time to see a scowl cross the man's face then disappear into a grin.

"I've been more of a burden than a help, I'm afraid. I've never worked on a farm before, and Mr. Crane has had to teach me everything. Besides that, he's been housing and feeding my family. I don't know how I'll ever repay you, sir."

"Stanley!" Stanley made the word sound grouchy but both men caught the humor behind it. He rubbed his leg as he directed his next comment to the sheriff. "Daniel's proven himself to be reliable and a hard worker, and I have no doubts about his innocence. Is there any reason that you have to keep checking up on him like this? Don't get me wrong, we enjoy the visits."

"Judge's orders, but I have another reason." He turned his attention to Daniel. "You mentioned Guntar. Seems he's working out at the camp now and from what I hear he's holding his own with the men. We've got Elwood working out there—"

"Jefferson Elwood?"

Jon waited for Stanley to explain his interruption. "You know him?"

Both men watched the struggle on Stanley's face as he decided his next words.

"Yeah, I know him," was all he replied, but the way he said it made Jon remember Elwood's treatment of Mercy Crane. He noticed Daniel's curiosity was piqued as well.

"I'm sorry, Sheriff," Daniel spoke up, "but that deputy has it in for me. If you're expecting him to try to find the real killer, I'm afraid you're in for a disappointment. All he's going to do is try to find more proof that I murdered Murdock."

"Since you're innocent that shouldn't worry you. But back to Guntar. What made you suspect him?"

Daniel hesitated. He paced in front of the cattle's stalls much as the sheriff remembered him doing in his cell for over a month. Back and forth, back and forth. He waited.

"I'm not accusing him, but I heard from Murdock himself how he roughed up his wife and her kid when they didn't do what he wanted. Murdock was a brute when he was sober, but when he drank he was even worse."

Finally, he stopped and stood before the sheriff. "And I can't help thinking that the murderer had to be someone other than a jack."

"Why?"

Daniel stared at the dirt floor before answering. "There are so many ways to hurt a man out in the woods and make it seem like an accident. If I wanted to kill someone, I could fell a tree on him, loosen a pile of logs, trip him when he's carrying his axe, or drown him on the log drive. There are hundreds of ways and no one would question them. I wouldn't have to stab him."

There was silence as the men thought.

"So someone purposely made you look guilty of the murder. Who?"

Daniel was shaking his head before the sheriff finished speaking. "I don't know! I've always gotten along well with the others except that…well…after Dee died, I didn't much care about life anymore and I started a lot of fights, and I was getting kind of reckless on the job. But I don't think I was a danger to anyone. At least not enough to make them want to get rid of me. If that were the case, they would have murdered me, not Murdock." He rubbed a hand over his chin. "I just don't get it. Why me?"

Jon could clearly see Daniel's frustration. "Any idea where Murdock got his booze?"

Daniel shook his head. "I could smell it on him. Not every day, but often enough. I don't know. The only time I went out at night was the night Murdock was murdered. Otherwise I was too tired to get up and take a walk. After working a day in the woods, I was out for the whole night."

"Then why that night?" The question came from Stanley.

Daniel looked sheepish. "I had to clear my head. I had been so angry about losing Dee and I was taking it out on everyone around me. I guess I finally came to my senses and decided to make a change. Then this all happened."

"Did the others go out at night?"

Daniel shrugged. "I don't know. Like I said, I slept hard."

"Then I think it was a case of being in the wrong place at the wrong time."

"What do you mean?"

The sheriff continued. "Someone was out that night with Murdock. He saw you. That made you the perfect scapegoat. Who knew you had been out during the night?"

Daniel thought a moment then his head popped up as he stared at the sheriff. "Elwood told me that I had been seen leaving the bunkhouse, but he didn't say who said it. Did he tell you?"

"No."

"The jacks don't tell on each other. If someone saw me leave, he wouldn't tell the deputy."

The men stared at each other and Stanley rose from his stool.

"Elwood's lying; I'll bet my life on it."

"Or Elwood was the other person out that night."

22

Crane Farm

Jon Talbot accepted the invitation to spend the night. It wasn't that long of a trip back to Grand Rapids, but the weather was questionable and knowing how swiftly a blizzard could happen, he was content to remain with the Dunn family a bit longer. Besides, he had more than the investigation of Murdock's murder to see to. He needed to evaluate the progress of Clarence's scheme with Daniel and Mercy to see if his brother-in-law was on the right track.

The dinner Mercy put on was delicious and Jon ate heartily. He gulped down the last of his coffee and accepted a refill.

"That pie was mighty good, Mrs. Dunn. I'm appreciative. My Betty won't fix me many sweets anymore. She says I need to slim down if I'm going to keep my job. The outlaws will be able to run faster than I can if I pack on any more pounds."

Mercy smiled at his comment as she picked up some of the dishes. She seemed skittish to Jon, like she was trying to do everything just right.

I suppose she feels like I'm putting her to a test.

He looked at the others around the table. The oldest girl had jumped up to help Mercy clear the table and the others were listening to a story Stanley was telling about one of the cows. Occasionally, they cast wary looks his way and Jon wondered what they were thinking. Daniel eased back in his chair and sipped at the last of his coffee as he listened too.

Looks like the perfect family. Almost.

It was obvious that Daniel and Mercy were uncomfortable with each other. They didn't communicate. They didn't even look at each other. Daniel was good with his kids, but Jon noticed immediately that he ignored the little one, the boy. That made Jon curious.

"Ahw you takin' Pa back to jail?"

The question startled everyone and Jon turned to the youngest girl who was staring wide-eyed at him.

"Didi! Hush!"

"No, it's all right." Jon wasn't used to kids, not having any of his own, but he made what he hoped was a reassuring look at the girl. "No, I'm just here to visit your pa. He's helping me solve a crime."

"He i*th*?"

"Ye*th*—*yes*, he is." Jon stammered at his blunder. The kid was so cute and her lisp was catchy. He felt his ears redden and his eyebrows raised when he heard a *snort* from the kitchen. Soon the other girls at the table were giggling and

Daniel and Stanley were grinning at him. But Didi jumped down from her place at the table and came around to stand protectively by Jon.

"It'*th* not funny. Don't laugh at him. He can't help it."

That brought more laughter and a chuckle from Jon. Apparently Didi had heard that said about her a time or two.

"Why, thank you, miss."

Daniel pulled his daughter up on his lap. "Didi, I think you've accomplished something that I've never seen before."

"What'*th* that?"

"You've made Sheriff Talbot smile. I didn't know he could."

Didi's mouth made a round O at her father's statement, and she stared at the big man next to them.

The others laughed again and Daniel pushed away from the table, setting his daughter in his chair.

"I better close up the barn for the night," he stated as he reached for his coat.

"I'll help."

Daniel nodded to the sheriff and was still chuckling as they went outside.

They worked together in silence for a while. Mostly Jon watched what Daniel was doing and lent a hand when it was needed. It was obvious the man had a nightly routine and that he enjoyed what he was doing.

"You miss logging?"

Daniel swung the creaky gate shut and latched it before he turned to the sheriff. "Miss it? Do I miss sleeping with fleas and vermin and doing backbreaking, dangerous work and being away from my children?" He grinned then looked at Jon and answered in a more serious tone. "No. I don't miss it and yes, I love this kind of work, but I know where you're headed with this."

The sheriff raised his eyebrows.

"I can't stay here and be dependent on these people. I need to take my family back to town or to a town and find work where I can be with them."

"Seems like you've found that here."

"There's strings attached to this job and you know it. That meddlesome judge thinks he can manipulate people, but he can't. He can't change how a person feels."

"She's a nice lady."

Daniel scowled. "Doesn't matter. She's not my wife."

Jon turned to go back to the house, but he threw a statement over his shoulder before he shut the door to the barn behind him.

"Actually, she is."

The next morning Jon set off for Grand Rapids with a hearty breakfast to warm him, a tasty lunch in his saddlebag, both prepared by Mercy, and a lot of questions to occupy his mind. Jefferson Elwood was first on his list.

He found time before he left and when Daniel wasn't around to question Stanley on what he knew about the man. His opinion of the deputy dropped even lower when he heard how he had run out on his engagement to Mercy Crane to chase after some gypsy woman. No wonder Mercy had made comments about never being involved with another man.

Then there was that question about who told Elwood about seeing Daniel outside that night or if it was Elwood himself who was out and about. And why would he be?

And Murdock's stepson was somehow involved too. Did the kid kill Murdock to stop him from abusing his mother? But how would he have gotten Daniel's knife? And who put the stolen articles in Daniel's bag?

That brought his thoughts back to Daniel. Jon shook his head. The guy didn't know how good he had it right there on the Crane farm. It was obvious he loved the work he was doing and was a good fit for it, but he was too stubborn to allow himself to see that Mercy would make him a good wife.

No, Clarence overstepped his authority this time. Being a judge must have gone to his head if he thought he could make two people fall in love. It couldn't be forced and it didn't look like this particular plot of his brother-in-law's was going to work.

23

Crane Farm

Mercy was relieved when the sheriff left. She had been on edge the entire time he was there, dreading that he would say something to change their present way of life. Everything was going so well. The children were happy and Daniel was smiling more and seemed to enjoy the farm work. Her father had the help he needed and he liked Daniel, she could tell.

There were only a few clouds darkening her happiness. One, Daniel still didn't acknowledge Dylan. It ached in her heart to see the little boy reach for his pa and have Daniel turn away. She held her tongue when she wanted so badly to sit Daniel down and reprimand him for his behavior like she would a spoiled child in her classroom. But it wasn't her place to remind him that he had to get over his wife's death. No, that wasn't her place.

And it was a shame because they had started out this arrangement as friends, but now since that day at the river, the atmosphere between them was awkward. She avoided looking at him and he went out of his way to stay out of her way. Her cheeks still burned when she thought of the way he stared at her then fled up the hill like a man with a bull chasing him.

I seem to have that effect on men.

She wiped the crumbs off the table as she thought about the other problems they faced. The murderer was still unknown. Until the killer was found, there would be a stigma attached to Daniel and his family. People heard that he was a suspect and had been in jail and even though he was pronounced innocent, they were wary of him. She saw it when they were in town or when they gathered with a few other families to hold a church service. Daniel didn't seem bothered by it, but when Darby and Daphne told about being ridiculed by some of the children, she saw his lips tighten. She was proud of him for how he handled it and how he talked with the girls about how to respond. Still, it shouldn't be happening and if the real killer was found, it would help take that disgrace from them.

Then there was Guntar. Mercy paused in her work while she recalled the visit she had from the boy before she and the children left Grand Rapids. Having him appear at the rental house to talk to her was disconcerting and learning the reason why was even more so. She hadn't realized that his feelings ran as deep as they did. With compassion and discretion, she told him that she was too old for him and that he would one day find the right girl to love. When he wouldn't be convinced, she told him that she had married Daniel Dunn, but his angry reaction to the news shocked her as he spun on his heel and ran. On the day that he helped her with Jefferson in front of the sheriff's office, she thought she saw an acceptance in his face but then he had nothing but anger in his voice when he as much as accused Daniel of his stepfather's murder.

Back to that again.

Mercy sighed. She paused and listened to Didi and Dylan playing in the other room. How she loved the children! And there was her other worry: how was she ever going to let the children go? She had never had so much joy in her life as now with a house full of children to care for and love. There were almost times when she wished Daniel back in prison so she could keep the children as her own.

No!

She pressed the towel she was holding against her face. *No, Lord Jesus! That was an awful thought! I don't want Daniel back in jail. I want him here with us.*

She dropped into the nearest chair with a thud.

I want him here with us.

The thought stunned her and she stared into space while she recalled how she often watched Daniel from the kitchen window as he went to and from the barn and how she listened to him play with the girls and read to them from the Bible.

He has a nice voice.

"Mama Mer*thy*?"

Mercy focused in on the little girl standing in front of her.

"Yes, Didi?"

"Dylan is twying to walk."

"He is?"

Mercy grabbed Didi's hand and ran into the next room. They were laughing and playing with the boy when the men came in the house.

"Papa! Daniel! Come see Dylan. He's walking!"

The men looked around the corner in time to see the child wobble on his pudgy legs and take a couple of steps before dropping and crawling to Mercy. She laughed and hugged him tightly while she turned and cast a dazzling smile to them. Her face froze when she saw Daniel's expression.

He turned away and marched out of the house, the door slamming behind him.

Daniel paced the dirt floor of the barn while he tried to deal with his thoughts.

I don't understand this, God. I don't want to feel anything for this woman, but she...she...

"Daniel?"

He swung around to find Stanley watching him. He expected a confrontation after his sudden departure from the house, but he wasn't prepared for the sternness in his new friend's face.

"This has to stop. He's your son, and it's time you treat him as such!"

"But it's not—" Daniel stopped. He wasn't ready to share the thoughts he was just now trying to process.

"Now, I'm going to tell you a story and you're going to sit down and listen." Stanley indicated the milk stool.

Daniel heaved a sigh and threw up his hands in defeat. He sat.

"I've never told anyone this before." Stanley leaned with both hands on his cane. "My wife died when Mercy was born."

Daniel watched Stanley's face carefully. Even though this topic wasn't what was on his mind, he was interested in hearing what the man had to say.

"I was angry, much like you are, and I struggled to find how any good thing could come from this tragedy, but I believe God's Word is true, and Romans 8:28 says that 'all things work together for good to them that love God, to them who are the called according to his purpose.' I would go into my daughter's room and stare down at her in her basket and, God help me, I would wish with all my heart that it had been she who died and not my precious wife."

Daniel stared at the man. He had done the very same thing with his son.

"But my Noreen wouldn't have wanted that. She wanted our baby with all her being and willingly gave her life to give birth. She always reminded me of our Savior's love for us and how he sacrificed all for undeserving mankind.

I wanted to rage at God for taking my love away from me, but her words would remind me that I didn't deserve the mercy God had given me in the first place. It was only by God's grace that I came to see that even though I wasn't happy with the way things were happening, I could be happy in the knowledge that God's love for me never changed and he had promised an eternal glorious home for my beloved wife and she was there in his presence. When I finally accepted that, I picked up that little baby girl and I named her Mercy. I never wanted to forget how God showed mercy to me and as a result I have been given the best gift any father could have—the love of his child.

"Daniel, I don't know why your wife was taken from you earlier than you wanted, but I know from my own experience and from God's Word that you will never find happiness unless you allow God's peace to engulf your heart. There are so many verses I could show you about being thankful *in* our circumstances, not necessarily *for* our circumstances."

Daniel was nodding before the man finished speaking. "I know, I know. Pastor Sam showed me some of those verses and I admit that I've fought against them. I *have* been angry. You talked about good things coming out of bad situations and I can tell you that one good thing that came from me being locked up in jail is that I accepted Christ as my savior there. That preacher kept after me until I was sick of him, but his words finally made sense to me.

Dee would be so pleased to know that I now have the peace that she had."

"Then why—?"

"Why do I shun my son?" Daniel hung his head as he exhaled slowly. "I have no excuse, sir. I've been wrong. I know it's not his fault that Dee is gone." There was a pause before he continued, and his voice cracked as he said, "She wanted me to have a son."

He rose to his feet and held out his hand to Stanley. "Thank you for sharing your story with me. Mercy, huh? That *is* a good reminder."

"Glad to be of help." The older man raised an eyebrow. "Anything else you'd like to talk about?"

Daniel's glance at the man was speculative. It was apparent that Stanley was seeing more than Daniel wanted him to see. "Now that you mention it, yes, there is. What do you know about Elwood?"

He watched a satisfied look cross over Stanley's features, but his own expression remained stoic.

"Elwood caused my girl a lot of pain. He came to town and wooed her like some knight in a fairy tale and Mercy fell for it. See, she never thought she would find a beau, thought she was too plain."

Daniel's lips tightened at that, but he missed Stanley hiding a grin behind his hand as he rubbed at his whiskers.

"Yep. Mercy thought Elwood was her dream come true, but it's my own personal opinion, and mind you, I'd never let on to Mercy that I thought this, but I think the man knew that this farm and all would one day go to her and if he married her, he would get it for himself. Anyway, he didn't even have the patience to wait for their wedding day. He was attracted to some traveling gypsy girl and ran off with her. I thought it would break Mercy's heart, but instead I'm afraid it just convinced her that she wasn't worthy of a man's love and she swore off of ever marrying. She took the teaching job in Grand Rapids to get away from the farm and then Elwood showed up over there."

Daniel wasn't aware that he was clenching and unclenching his fists until Stanley's silence made him realize that his thoughts were on smashing in the deputy's face with his bare knuckles.

He nodded at Stanley. "Thanks for telling me. I could tell you a few stories about the man too, but be assured that I know what he's like and I'll not let him bother her again."

He missed Stanley's raised eyebrows as he turned to go back to the house.

"Now if you don't mind, I'd like to go see my son walk."

24

Logging Camp

THE MOONLIGHT WAS bright enough to cast shadows throughout the snow-covered forest, but Guntar didn't appreciate the beauty of it. He crouched low in the brush, wishing for a cloud to block the brilliant light.

Ralston was going to be a problem. Guntar could appease the man into silence by meeting his demands or he could try to silence the man himself. He shuddered. How had it come to this? He studied the area around him for any sign that he was not alone before he moved on.

No clouds meant no fresh snow that would make his tracks more visible. That could be a help.

Being raised in the woods gave Guntar skill in how he moved through the cold night. He stayed on the well-traveled path whenever he felt he couldn't be seen for a distance and moved off it when he felt exposed, and then only when he could step over a log or bush to make his tracks less noticeable as having left the path. He had traveled this path in the night many a time and knew the route well.

A coyote howled. Guntar waited and listened. Soon others yipped and howled with it until a loud chorus of yelps rose to a crescendo and then an ominous silence followed.

They made their kill.

Guntar waited. His focus was on an area to his right, but he kept his eyes and ears opened to everything surrounding it. He didn't want to be caught out this far from the camp; he could lose his job and he needed it. He was actually enjoying some of the work and the men were treating him well, except for that deputy. And now Ralston.

A rabbit hopped out into the open. Guntar smiled as he watched the timid creature look one way and then another and hop here and there like it couldn't make up its mind.

It was time. He rose and stretched the cramp out of his legs before he moved on. The rabbit darted out of the way as Guntar stopped again and knelt down by some brush. He pushed the dead branches away and swept aside some snow to reveal a crock buried in the ground. The wooden top was frozen onto it. Looking around he grabbed a stick and pried the top off. He reached into the container and found the jug his mother had put there for Murdock.

This is what Ralston wanted.

Guntar stared at the jug a long while.

If he gave it to Ralston, he was committing himself to the blackmail Ralston was forcing upon him. If he didn't, the truth about Murdock's murder would come out and he couldn't allow that.

He tucked the jug into his coat and covered up the crock. He did what he could to wipe away the tracks he made and crept back to wait by the trail until he was sure he wasn't being watched. Then he made his way back to the camp.

Each day that passed made Guntar more uneasy. The work was going along fine but he found himself paired up with Ralston more than he wanted. The man was becoming more demanding about being supplied with the forbidden booze, and Guntar was tired of being manipulated and tired of being worried. He was just plain tired. He had been up one whole night to return home and explain the situation to his mother so that she could keep the supply of crocks filled. He knew she wasn't happy about it but she agreed. He wanted so much to quit it all, but he was more afraid of what would happen if Ralston sent the law after him.

But he couldn't go on the way he was.

He felt someone nudge his elbow and he opened his eyes. The cookshack was empty and he had fallen asleep at the table. He stumbled to his feet and joined the others and was pulled around the corner by Ralston.

"Time for another delivery, Gunny."

Guntar pulled his arm out of Ralston's grasp. Suddenly he had enough.

"No!"

"Keep your voice down, kid." Ralston grabbed the boy's arm again.

But it was too late. Elwood was approaching them and Guntar's nerves were ready to snap. He yanked free of Ralston and ran down the path into the woods. Neither man followed.

"What was that about?"

Ralston's sneer was almost hid under his bushy beard. "Looks like the kid has something to hide. You're the lawman, you figure it out." He walked away.

Elwood stood in indecision for a minute then he headed for the boss.

25

Grand Rapids

"Hey, Sheriff."

"Evening, Latham." The lawman picked up his pace but couldn't avoid the inevitable. Only a moment passed and the mercantile owner's wife poked her head out the door behind her husband.

"Oh, hello, Sheriff. Are you out for your evening rounds? I do hope you keep a close eye on our store, with all these robberies in town. I can't imagine why you haven't caught the thief yet."

"Evening, Mrs. Bedloe. Doing my best." He made a hasty retreat for the jailhouse.

Sheriff Jon Talbot would rather face an armed outlaw than the nosey woman who ran her husband and the mercantile and in that order.

Five minutes passed and Jon was about ready to leave for the night when the door burst open and a disheveled young man stumbled into the room. His face was haggard and he was panting as if he had been running.

The sheriff stood up from his chair. "Can I—"

"I did it—Sheriff—sir—*I* did it!"

The sheriff grabbed the boy as he dropped to his knees. He pulled him into a chair and patted his face.

"You okay there, kid? Wait! Aren't you—?" He studied the boy's exhausted features. A frown creased Jon's forehead as he walked around his desk and reached for the jug of water on the floor.

"Here, drink this."

The boy took several gulps and wiped his face with his sleeve. He was about to speak again when the sheriff stopped him.

"There's a cot in the cell back there. I want you to get some sleep before we talk."

"No! I need to tell you—"

The sheriff pulled the boy to his feet. "We'll talk tomorrow after you've had some sleep." His tone brooked no argument and he had no trouble getting the kid to the cot where he dropped off to sleep immediately.

The sheriff peered down at Guntar through squinted eyes.

He's going to confess to killing his stepfather.

He shook his head and walked away leaving the door to the cell open. He'd have to get word to Betty that he was spending the night at the jail.

I need a deputy.

Thoughts of Elwood brought the frown back to his face.

I don't need one that bad.

He pulled his coat on and headed for the hotel to order a meal and send a messenger to his house. On impulse, he sent another message off with one of the Chippewa men hanging around the hotel to the Dunns. He wished Clarence was due in the area, he could use the help.

The next morning after an uncomfortable night on the bed he kept in his office, the sheriff sat at his desk deep in thought as he waited for Guntar to awaken. The outside door opening caught him by surprise but his expression didn't change even when the visitor proved to be a woman and none other than Murdock's widow.

The sheriff rose. "Morning, ma'am."

She nodded and slid her shawl off her head. "Is my Guntar here? Have you put him in jail?"

"He's right back there." Jon indicated with his head. "Still sleeping. Won't you have a seat, ma'am?"

Mrs. Murdock remained on her feet forcing Jon to continue standing. She twisted her hands in her shawl and he noticed that her eyes were red from crying. She was a comely woman, probably in her forties, petite and timid. She opened her mouth to speak then closed it again.

"Ma'am?"

"My Guntar…what…what has he said?"

"Mama!"

Guntar rushed into the room and his mother clasped him to her and sobbed. "You can't do this! I won't let you!"

"Mama, don't say anything. You hear me? Don't say another word. You go on home and let me handle this. It will be all right."

"No! I will tell him the truth." She turned to the sheriff who was watching with interest. "Is Guntar a prisoner? Can he leave? What has he told you?"

Sheriff Talbot indicated the chairs. "Why don't we all sit down? I'll send for some breakfast and we'll have a talk."

"You're sure your father can handle all the children?"

Mercy shook her head at the question. She had already answered Daniel three times about her father's ability to care for the children, but she sensed that he was more concerned about how long her father would be caring for them rather than if he could do the job.

"Mrs. Ketchler will check on them, but I really don't think we need to worry. If the sheriff was arresting you again, he would have come to get you instead of sending a message asking us to come to Grand Rapids."

Daniel stopped walking and Mercy was glad because she needed to catch her breath. Daniel's pace was as brisk as it could be on the icy path and the extra layers she was wearing was making it difficult to keep up. She loosened her scarf as she leaned against a tree to rest.

"Why do you think he wants us?"

Daniel brushed snow off a rock and motioned for her to sit which she willingly did. She waited while he studied the woods around them, but instead of answering her question, he made a statement.

"I suppose we could eat our lunch now."

Mercy nodded and reached for the bag Daniel carried. She set out the food she had prepared and as she handed Daniel his share, he spoke again.

"My guess is that he's found Murdock's killer."

Mercy's sandwich was held midair as she looked at Daniel.

"But why does he need us? He could have told us next month when he comes to check up on us."

"Whatever the reason, I must be involved somehow. I don't know why he wants you to come too, unless…"

"Unless what?"

Daniel shrugged. "Maybe that judge is back." He didn't look at Mercy.

She stared at him. "Oh."

The rest of the trip was made in silence, but Mercy's thoughts were shouting within her.

Is this it? Will he leave me now?

She didn't want to admit it. She tried to deny it. As they walked side by side, she was aware of Daniel in a way she had not allowed herself to be before. These last weeks she had seen a new side of him. He finally was holding his son and playing with him. He was laughing more and every once in a while their eyes would meet and her heart would do a *thump*.

But she couldn't let Daniel know any of her thoughts or feelings because she had promised him she would be no trouble when he left. She had to remind herself about Jefferson and why she would never get involved with a man again.

But the children.

Mercy's emotions were a mess by the time they reached Grand Rapids.

"I'll get us rooms at the hotel before we head to the jail. Would you like to do your shopping now?"

Mercy nodded. "I'll give Mrs. Bedloe the order so it will be ready, and we can pick it up when we leave, and don't worry, I won't get more than we can carry."

Daniel suddenly grinned at her. "Why? Don't you think I'm strong enough?"

"I...I...no, that's not what I meant."

He touched her arm. "I was joking, Mercy. Get whatever you need. I'll get a sled if I have to. I'll meet you at the mercantile as soon as I'm done at the hotel, okay?"

Mercy nodded. She couldn't have spoken if she had to and she stared at Daniel's back as he walked away.

He smiled. He teased me. He called me by my name!

She took a deep breath and pushed open the door to the mercantile and was immediately entrapped by Mrs. Bedloe and her inquisitive personality.

Daniel slowed his steps as he turned toward the hotel. He wished he had more time to think before they met with the sheriff. And it wasn't what awaited them at the jail that was on his mind.

She's...she's...

He stared into space as he tried to formulate his thoughts. *She has beautiful eyes.*

He closed his own eyes briefly.

Dee.

"Sir, may I help you?"

Daniel blinked. He was standing at the hotel desk and the clerk was eyeing him warily. He cleared his throat.

"Two rooms, please."

The sheriff left the jailhouse window to return to his chair. He sighed as he leaned back, ignoring the accompanying squeal his weight invoked in it. The Dunns had arrived and decisions had to be made. And, frankly, he needed their help. He had never come across a situation like this in all his years as a lawman.

He stood when the door opened and Mercy was motioned in by Daniel who held the door for her. Jon kept his interest well hidden from the two as he watched her timidly smile her thanks to her husband.

"Good afternoon, Mrs. Dunn." He indicated a chair for her while he shook Daniel's hand. "Good to see you again, Daniel. Thank you both for coming."

That they were nervous was obvious and it suddenly occurred to Jon that he hadn't taken into account that his message would give them cause for concern. It could have easily meant that new evidence had been brought to light that would incriminate Daniel. It spoke well for them that they had obeyed the summons regardless.

"What's this about, Jon?" Daniel posed the question while Mercy sat stiffly watching the lawman.

"Let me put your minds at rest, folks. This isn't about you directly but you are connected in a way."

They continued to stare and Jon realized that his comment hadn't reassured them.

"I have a confession to Murdock's murder."

"What? Who?" Daniel stood as if he could get the sheriff to answer more quickly while Mercy stared at him and then at the sheriff. "Was it Ralston? I always wondered if he was the one. I mean, he was my friend but there was always something about him—"

"It wasn't Ralston. At least it wasn't Ralston who confessed, but that doesn't mean that I've ruled him out."

Now Mercy stood and approached the sheriff's desk. "I don't understand. You said you have a confession, but it sounds like you're still looking for the murderer. What's going on?"

Jon nodded to the chairs again and waited for the couple to be seated. He leaned forward in his chair. "Guntar came barreling in here last night saying he killed Murdock."

"No!" Mercy gasped and covered her mouth with her hand.

Daniel's jaw tightened.

"Then this morning his mother came in." The sheriff lowered his voice. "She knew Guntar had come here and she wanted to know why. She kept telling me that he had his reasons, as if she knew he was the guilty one."

Daniel and Mercy appeared stunned, but Daniel finally shook his head.

"And you don't believe he is."

Jon raised an eyebrow.

"Do *you*?"

But Mercy was puzzled. "I don't understand. You think Guntar is lying. But…you think Mrs. Murdock is not being truthful either."

Daniel turned to Mercy. "I think, and correct me if I'm wrong, Jon, but I think that Guntar really believes his mother killed Murdock, and he is trying to take the blame to save her."

"And," the sheriff took over, "even though Mrs. Murdock knows Guntar is innocent, she's willing to let me think he might be guilty. She's certainly not admitting to anything herself. Murdock was abusive to both of them and it could be that each one thought the other finally had enough and put an end to it. I don't care for what the woman is doing to her son, but I don't really think she did it either."

"Oh no!" Mercy stared blankly at the floor as she thought over what the men were saying then she turned to the sheriff again. "But you seem to think that it's still someone else. Is it that Ralston fellow? Where are Guntar and his mother? Why do you want us here?"

"I'm getting to that. First of all, I have both Guntar and his mother back there in the cells."

"What? But you said you didn't think they did it!"

"Hold on, Mrs. Dunn. They're back there, but the cells aren't locked. I told them they were free to go, but neither one of them would leave. They just marched back there and made themselves at home. That's where you come in." He pointed at Mercy. "You know Guntar. Talk to him and his mother and see if you can get them to tell each other the truth about that night and maybe it will shed some light on who really is responsible for the man's death. They both are hiding something, even from each other, and I need to know what it is."

Mercy licked her lips. "I'll try, but—"

"Second, if they tell us what I think they are going to tell us, I may need to take Daniel to the logging camp with me to sort this thing out once and for all. In that case, I would ask you—" He paused and pointed at Mercy again. "—to take Mrs. Murdock and Guntar to your place with you for safety."

"For safety?"

"I think they may be in danger now if word gets out that they've come to me. There's someone out there who doesn't want them to talk. And they're scared, ma'am. Guntar and his ma are scared."

"Hold on, Jon. If there's any danger associated with these two, I don't want them around Mercy and my family," Daniel spoke up.

"No one should suspect them of being at the Crane farm. I wouldn't ask if I thought so and I need to get them out of town."

The three sat in silence as they thought over the predicament. Jon wondered what was going on in the couple's minds, and he was pleasantly surprised when Daniel turned to Mercy and asked what she thought.

Mercy seemed to look to Daniel for guidance. "I guess…I think….no, I *know* that it is all right. I want to get this murder solved and I believe Guntar is innocent. I don't know what his mother is trying to do, but I will try to talk with them as the sheriff suggested. If you want me to take them to our house, should we go by their place to get their things before I take them home with me?" Her last question was for the sheriff.

"No need. First off, I don't want anyone in town knowing where they are, so I'm going to ask that you and Daniel leave for home tomorrow as you normally would do. I'll bring them with me to meet you on the trail and you can go on from there. Daniel and I will head to the camp. And second, Mrs. Murdock already packed for the two of them. I guess she thought one or both of them would be locked up. Now, I've asked Bedloe from the mercantile to watch things here in town while I'm gone. Meanwhile, the two of you continue on this evening as if you've just come to town for supplies and to check in with me. We don't want to arouse any suspicion of why you're really here."

"We'll do what we can to help. Should Mercy go back and talk with them now?"

The sheriff stood. "Ready, ma'am?"

Mercy nodded and Jon caught the surprise in her face when Daniel reached for her hand and squeezed it in encouragement.

Things seem to be going well.

Mercy waited for the sheriff to call out to the "prisoners" that they had a visitor and then she walked back to the familiar cell where Daniel had been kept. Guntar and his mother were sitting side by side on the bunk with the cell doors open. Their heads had been close together and they were whispering but stopped suddenly when Mercy stepped forward. Guntar jumped to his feet.

"Miss Crane!"

His face went red with embarrassment and he turned away from facing her as she approached.

"Hello, Guntar. Mrs. Murdock."

The widow rose to her feet and Mercy saw tears in her eyes. Her reaction was instinctive and she opened her arms and embraced her. Mrs. Murdock hesitated a moment then began to weep against Mercy.

"Mama. It's okay." Guntar patted her back and looked helplessly at his former teacher.

"There now." Mercy led the woman back to the cot and sat beside her with her arm still around her. "Why don't you tell me what's going on? I know neither of you killed that man."

Two startled faces turned to her. Guntar cast a sideways glance at his mother before he spoke.

"You're wrong, Miss Crane. I did it."

Mercy reached for Guntar with her free hand and gripped his shoulder. "No, you didn't, Guntar." She looked him straight in the eye. "And neither did your mother. Did you, Mrs. Murdock?" She turned to the distraught woman.

Mrs. Murdock's head jerked up. "No!"

"Mama." Guntar dropped to his knees before his mother. "I don't understand."

Mrs. Murdock put a hand on her son's face. "You thought *I* did it? That's why you told them you did?"

"But, Mama! I didn't kill him either. I...I thought you had, but I didn't want *you* to go to jail."

"Oh, Guntar, I'm so glad it wasn't you. I was afraid for you."

Then as if it suddenly dawned on Guntar, he said, "You thought it was me? Really?" He seemed distracted by that for a moment then asked the inevitable. "But...then... who did?"

"That's what we need to find out." Mercy waited for Guntar to pull up the only chair in the room and she had their full attention. "No more lying now. There is still something that you both are hiding, and we need to know what it is so that we can catch the murderer and stop the two of you from living in fear."

"How did you—?"

"I can see it in your faces. Something is troubling you. Deeply." She watched as the two of them looked at each other in silent communication.

"Please. Tell me what you know so that we can get to the bottom of this."

Guntar stood. "We can't. They will hurt my mother."

"No, Guntar. I am going to take you and your mother to my place until this is over. You will be safe there. Please tell me what is going on and tell me who *they* are."

"You will take my mother to safety?"

"I will take both of you."

"No, I will go back and face these men and put an end to it."

"No, Guntar!" Mrs. Murdock grabbed her son's arm as he started for the door.

"Guntar, sit down!" Mercy used her teacher's voice and walked around the boy to the cell door, grabbed it and slammed it shut, locking them in. "Now there will be no more talk of you going anywhere until I know what is going on."

Guntar stubbornly crossed his arms as he glared at Mercy.

"Guntar, that is enough. We must tell Miss Crane the truth."

"Mama—"

"No, I am done with this. That awful man is gone and can't hurt us anymore. We should have moved away before they involved us again." She turned to Mercy. "Murdock was a drunk. He couldn't go a day without his liquor, so I had to make it for him. He set up the still and taught me how to do it and I had to keep a supply in the woods for him so that he always had some on hand even when he was at the logging camp."

Mercy sat down and took the woman's hand. Mrs. Murdock had begun to tremble.

"It was wrong to let him drink when he was doing such dangerous work, but Murdock was a demanding man and if I failed to have his jug to him on time, he…he…"

Mercy squeezed her hand. "Yes, I know. Go on."

The woman took a deep breath. "That was bad enough, but then he told us that there would be deliveries made to a hollow tree on our property. We were to take the leather pouch we found there and add it to the crock where we put his liquor jug. He would pick it up and I don't know what happened to it after that."

"Who made these deliveries? What was in them?"

Guntar had been staring at the floor, but he spoke now. "We don't know. I had to check the tree every day and if I found a pouch in it, I had to get it to one of the sites in the woods where we stashed his booze or he'd…he'd beat my mother."

Mrs. Murdock reached for Guntar's hand and he gripped it.

"I'm sorry, Mama. But why didn't we just leave? Why did you let him treat you like that?" Emotion choked his voice.

Through her tears, the woman whispered, "He would have killed you if I had. He swore he would find us and kill you. I had no choice. And we had no money so that we could not leave, he made sure of that."

Mercy fought back her own tears as she embraced the widow again. "I'm so sorry. I had no idea."

Mercy stood and walked to the cell door. "Sheriff?"

Both the sheriff and Daniel appeared immediately and the sheriff had the key ready to open the door.

"We heard. Ma'am," he spoke to Mrs. Murdock, "please accept my apologies for not seeing that you were in danger. I would have helped you get away from that man." He waited until they had all reentered the office and the ladies were seated.

"I'm going to send you and your son to Mrs. Dunn's farm until this is over, but I need to ask you a few more questions. These pouches, how big were they?"

Guntar answered. "Not very big." He indicated the size with his hands.

"Did you ever look inside to see what was in them?"

Guntar's eyes darted to his mother before he answered again. "We were told not to, but I did once. There was money and jewelry. I wanted to take the money so that we could leave, but Mama told me no. It wasn't ours."

"The stolen goods from town." Daniel spoke for the first time.

Mrs. Murdock hung her head. "We are so sorry. We should have come to you, Sheriff, but we just couldn't."

"You have nothing to be sorry for, Mrs. Murdock. You were manipulated and threatened. I don't know that any of us would have done any different."

The woman wiped at her eyes and gave the sheriff a wobbly smile. "Thank you for that. I...I don't want to be called Mrs. Murdock anymore either. I will go back to my first husband's name. Please. It's Strahle. Ilsa Strahle."

"I don't blame you for that, Mrs. Strahle. Now, one more question. Do you have any idea who was making the deliveries to the tree or who Murdock was passing them on to?"

They were both shaking their heads, but Guntar spoke up. "The pouches didn't come regularly. Some days one would be there and others, not. I tried to watch the tree, but I never caught anyone there. Of course, I couldn't watch it all the time, I had school and chores and I had to make trips to the woods every other night or so. All I know is that every time I left a jug in one of the buried crocks, it would be gone and an empty one appeared in its place. I thought I was done with that until Ralston—"

"Ralston?"

"Yeah, he knew about the booze and he wanted it too. He threatened to tell about Mama…he thought it was Mama that…who killed Murdock and I couldn't let him tell on her, so I started making the deliveries of the liquor again."

The sheriff leaned forward. "Did the pouches show up in the tree again?"

Ilsa frowned. "I don't know…I…I chopped the tree down."

"You did?" Guntar knelt by his mother.

"I had to do something or it would never stop. When you came and told me that I had to continue with the liquor, I just finally reacted out of anger and I grabbed the axe and chopped it down. I should have destroyed that awful still as well."

"When did you do this?" the question came from the sheriff.

"Last night."

The sheriff leaned back again and the squeaking chair put everyone's attention on him.

"You have been very helpful. Now here's what I want you to do."

26

Grand Rapids

"Are you going to be okay with the Strahles living at your place? I mean, you've already taken on all my family and now you're being asked to take more. What will your father say?"

Daniel kept his voice low as they ate in the hotel dining room. They didn't want anyone to know where Guntar and Ilsa were because they knew someone in the town was a threat to them. Mercy couldn't help glancing around the room, suspicious of everyone.

"Be natural, Mercy. People can tell if you're nervous."

"I can't help it. To think that someone here is in on these robberies! I just can't believe it." She sipped her coffee and the cup rattled when she replaced it in the saucer.

"You really are nervous. I'm going to tell the sheriff to find another place for them to go."

"No, Daniel, no. I'm fine. It will be okay and I don't mind them coming to the farm. My father will welcome them too, so that's not a problem. I'm sure Guntar will help him with the chores while you're away." She hesitated. "I'm worried about you."

There. I said it.

Daniel made no reply but she saw his eyebrows raise in question. She better change the subject.

"Where did you go before supper? Did you and the sheriff have plans to make?" She took a bite of the apple pie they had just been served.

She saw his lips tighten and wondered what was amiss. "I'm sorry. You don't have to—"

"I visited the graveyard."

"Oh."

She mentally kicked herself. It was a year now since his wife's death. Coming to town must have brought it all back to him. Suddenly an empty, lonely feeling came over her as she realized that he would always have his wife on his mind. She set her fork down, no longer hungry.

"Dee would have liked the way you care for the children."

"Oh." The statement surprised her. He never spoke of Dee to any of them and it must have been difficult for him to tell her that. "Thank you."

He pushed back his chair. "If you'll excuse me, I think I'll take a walk before settling down for the night. I'll meet you for breakfast then?"

"Uh, yes. Good night."

"Night."

She watched him walk away and was deep in thought when a voice at her elbow startled her.

"Miss Crane?"

The dishes on the table clattered when she jumped.

"Pardon me. Didn't mean to startle you."

She had a sinking feeling as she looked up at the portly man with the waxed mustache.

Mr. Crenshaw.

He nodded toward the chair Daniel had vacated. "May I?"

"Uh, well, uh…I was just leaving."

He sat.

"Heard you was in town and over at the jail. Is it true that this phony marriage of yours is annulled now?"

"What?"

"I heard the sheriff sent you a message. Are you done with this charade? You know I have been waiting to court you myself. I'm willing to forgive all this business, you being associated with a convict, but I want to make it clear that under the circumstances of this marriage, phony or not, you won't be able to teach school any longer. You must set a good example for the children. The whole town agrees on that."

"What?"

"Of course it just makes it easier for me. I couldn't court you before when you were a teacher." He twisted his face into what Mercy assumed was a smile as he stroked at his mustache.

She stood.

"Excuse me, please."

Mr. Crenshaw stood also. "Now, now, Miss Crane, why don't you just sit and visit a bit?"

Mercy used her best teacher stance as she looked down on the short man. "The name is Mrs. Dunn, sir." She turned and left him staring after her.

Her anger didn't simmer down until she had paced in her room for a while. "He is insufferable! Approaching me like that! Who does he think he is?" Her muttering continued until she suddenly stopped.

"He owns the leather shop." She stared into space. "The leather pouches! Could he be the town thief?"

She needed to tell Daniel.

She stepped out into the hallway, closing the door softly behind her, but as she turned to go she realized that she didn't know which room was his. She couldn't very well go knocking on doors looking for her husband. Then she remembered that he said he was going out for a walk.

Quickly she entered her room again and grabbed her coat. She was careful as she went by the dining room to avoid being seen, in case Mr. Crenshaw was lingering there. She stepped outside and pulled her coat closer around her. The wind had picked up and the cold winter night was suddenly bone chilling.

He wouldn't stay out long in this.

She looked both ways for any signs of someone, but the residents of Grand Rapids were smart enough to be settled in for the night. The only light besides the homes was in the saloons and the mercantile, and Mercy had no intention of going there to be scrutinized by Mrs. Bedloe. She moved carefully along the frozen road and searched between buildings as she passed up one side of the street and then the other. No sign of him.

She was on her way back to the hotel and passing the mercantile again when she heard a noise as if something had been knocked off the counter. She peered in the frosted window to see if everything was all right but stepped quickly away when she realized she was an unwanted witness to the husband and wife's amorous embrace.

She couldn't help giggling at the thought of the prim and prissy Mrs. Bedloe being swept off her feet by her dull, prosaic husband. A vision of Latham Bedloe in shining armor on a white steed entered her head and she had to choke back a laugh, and the unavoidable snort was carried away in the wind as she headed back to the hotel.

Good for you, Mr. Bedloe!

Daniel was still nowhere in sight so Mercy retraced her steps back to her room. She had just unlocked the door and entered when a hand grabbed her arm. She let out a shriek.

"Mercy! It's me. Daniel. Where have you been?"

Mercy's heart was pounding as she stared wide-eyed at Daniel.

"What are you doing in my room?"

He released her arm. "I knocked and you didn't answer and you weren't in the dining room and I was worried. I came in to check on you."

She willed her heart to slow down, but the thudding continued. She said the first thing that came to her mind. "You have a key?"

Daniel turned away so she didn't see his face when he answered. "I asked for one at the desk."

Mercy couldn't stop. "And they gave it to you?"

"You're my wife."

She stared at his back.

Finally, he turned but his face revealed nothing to her. "I can see that you're all right. Good night then." He deliberately pulled the key out of his pocket and placed it on the bureau before opening the door and letting himself out.

Mercy let out her breath. She was acting stupidly. This meant nothing.

There was a knock on her door.

She stared at it as her heart started thumping again.

"Who is it?"

"Daniel."

Her hand went to her throat and she took a deep breath. She hesitated then reached for the door handle. He was standing there as if he hadn't moved away from the door; as if he was making up his mind about something.

She held her breath.

He reached out his hand to her. He was holding a key.

"I left the wrong one."

She couldn't help it. She burst out laughing. He just stood there with a sheepish look on his face which made her laugh harder.

Snort.

That made him crack a smile. "It could happen to anyone, you know."

Mercy took the key and retrieved the one from the bureau. "But it happened to you and that's why it's so funny. Good night, Daniel."

"Good night, Mercy."

Mercy leaned against the door after she closed it and smiled.

It was breakfast the next morning when Mercy remembered to tell Daniel her thoughts about Mr. Crenshaw.

"So since he owns the leather shop, I thought maybe he might have something to do with this."

"And why's that?"

"You know, because of the leather pouches."

Daniel's look was skeptical. "That hardly would convict him. I would imagine most of the people in town own a leather pouch."

Mercy sighed. "I suppose. I really thought I was on to something. I even went out last night to try to find you and tell you. That's why I wasn't in my room." She felt her cheeks redden as she recalled their exchange the previous evening.

"What made you think of him in the first place?"

"Well, I didn't right away, but after he spoke to me in the dining room, it just occurred to me that he—"

"He spoke to you?"

"Yes, after you left he came to the table."

"What did he want?"

"Oh…he…he just spoke to me."

"Is there something I should know? Is he bothering you?"

Mercy was flustered by the questions. "It's fine. Shouldn't we be going?"

Mrs. Bedloe had their order ready and she chattered endlessly while Mr. Bedloe and Daniel loaded the sled. Mercy fought to keep a straight face as she kept recalling her imaginary scene of Mr. Bedloe as a knight in shining armor. The Bedloes were hardly the Romeo and Juliet type. Still it made her happy to know that the couple had a loving relationship despite the prudish way they treated each other in public.

"Mr. Bedloe has been asked by the sheriff to oversee the town for a few days. You know that he is really one of the most well-respected citizens in town to be asked that. But rest assured that he is reliable and will do well. I have no idea what Sheriff Talbot is up to, but I sincerely hope that he is finally going to catch the thief who has been terrorizing us. I can't tell you how frightened I am that he will show up here to rob us sometime when Mr. Bedloe is away. You know we were robbed once already, don't you?

He took cash right out of our store. Well, I have taken care of that." She patted her ample bosom. "It's in a safe place now." She gave Mercy a knowing look.

It took great restraint for Mercy to reply in a normal tone of voice. "Quite safe." But as she moved away from the woman, the laughter built up inside her until a quiet snort escaped.

She managed to get her features under control before turning to bid the store owner good-bye.

Mrs. Bedloe eyed her curiously.

"Good-bye then, Mrs. Bedloe. I'll see you in a month or so." Mercy repeated her farewell.

"What? Oh, yes, good-bye."

Daniel and Mercy walked in silence for a while. The wind was no problem today and the cold, crisp air was actually delightful. Daniel pulled the sled with a harness around his shoulders and made it seem effortless.

"When do we meet up with them?" Mercy asked.

"Shouldn't be long now. Jon took them out of town in a roundabout way. He didn't want to attract any attention so he left before light." He stopped suddenly and sniffed the air. "Ah, a campfire. That way." He pointed.

They found the little group waiting for them with a hot cup of coffee and the fire to warm them. Ilsa was obviously worried as she kept looking into the trees around them. Guntar seemed much more relaxed having the burden off his shoulders of telling the truth.

"Time to go." The sheriff stood. "You send a message if you need me, Mrs. Dunn, although I can't see any reason why you will. I hope to have your husband back to you in about a week, maybe less if things go well." The sheriff spoke as he packed up the coffeepot and put out the fire.

Daniel stepped away and motioned for Mercy to follow. "Tell the children I'll be home soon, will you? And take care of yourself." He smiled.

"You take care as well. The children need you." She poked her toe into the snow. "I'll be praying."

"Thank you, Mercy. I appreciate that." There was a moment of awkward silence. "Well, good-bye then."

"Bye."

Mercy and her traveling companions watched the two men walk away for a few moments then Mercy spoke. "Feel like pulling a sled, Guntar?"

They chatted on their way to the farm, and Mercy felt like she found a new friend in Ilsa Strahle. She learned that the woman and her first husband had emigrated from Germany and Mr. Strahle had died of influenza the first winter in their new homeland. Ilsa and Guntar had a rough year with no income and no friends to help. Marrying Murdock seemed like a solution to all their problems, but it had only compounded them.

"How did you learn English so well?" Mercy asked as they ate the lunch she brought from the hotel. Guntar appeared to have no trouble pulling the sled and wanted to keep going, but the women convinced him that they needed the rest even if he didn't.

"A teacher from America came to our town and taught at our school when I was a girl. I speak well because of him, and it was his influence that made me want to come here to live. He told of the free land and the beauty and riches it possessed and my husband and I determined that we would live here one day too. My husband was a widower with a young son." She looked over at Guntar who was standing a distance away. "When I married, Guntar was three and I have learned to love him as my own son. When we came to America, Guntar was only ten and he has had to grow up too fast." She put her hand over Mercy's. "You have helped him so much. He loved going to school and learning because of you."

Mercy swallowed. Guntar's schoolboy crush seemed to be over, but she wondered if his mother knew about it.

Ilsa seemed to read her thoughts and she spoke softly. "He is a good boy and he will be a good man. He has outgrown his boyhood." She smiled at Mercy and she nodded in understanding.

It was late afternoon when they came in view of the farm. Ilsa's eyes lit up. "It is like my father's farm. How did you ever carve a place out of all these woods to plow this land? My husband was so disappointed when we arrived and found trees instead of fields. He was a farmer too."

Mercy laughed. "It isn't easy farming here. Now if you had settled farther west or south you would have found great farm country, but this is the north woods and not best suited for raising crops. We were fortunate to find grassland, but we only grow enough crops to feed our cattle and enough garden produce to feed ourselves. Still, we love it and I will always love having the forest as my home. Oh, look! Here come the girls."

They were soon surrounded by the Dunn girls who had exuberant hugs for Mercy and endless questions about their father and the Strahles. Mercy smiled over their heads to her father who was watching from the doorway with Dylan in his arms.

Thank goodness for an understanding father.

27

Grand Rapids

"Jon, what do you know about Crenshaw?" Daniel raised the question when they paused on their journey for rest and refreshment. He explained to the sheriff about Mercy's concerns.

The lawman chewed his sandwich in silence for a moment. "Crenshaw likes to be in charge. He's on the school board and the town board, and I think he would like to be the mayor of the town if someone would elect him, but he doesn't have the smarts for it. He's wily in his business dealings and charges high prices for his goods, yet he's cheap, a penny-pincher. He sure put up a fuss about Miss Crane being married to you because he was trying to court her himself. He came to me to find out when the annulment would take place."

"The annulment? How does he know anything about that?"

"Everyone seems to know. My guess is that Elwood did some talking before we sent him up to the logging camp.

Elwood." The sheriff shook his head. "Now there's a sorry piece of work."

Daniel was still trying to get his head around the news that the leather store owner wanted to court Mercy, but having Elwood's name brought up provoked another question.

"What's his story?"

The sheriff began packing up their belongings as he answered. "The man showed up at my office one day wearing a badge and handed me a paper that said he was sent to work with me by some judge I never heard of. The paper looked legitimate and I needed a deputy, so I took him on, but I tell you, he's been nothing but trouble since the first day."

"What do you mean?"

They started walking again.

"He's insubordinate, rude to the townspeople, too bossy for his own good. I only sent him to the logging camp that first time just to get him out of my hair for a few days. I had no idea he would get in the middle of a murder and then throw his weight around like he has."

He stopped and grinned at Daniel.

"You must have really gotten under his skin. He doesn't like you."

"The feeling is mutual."

"Anyway," the sheriff continued, "Clarence had a good idea when he sent him back to work at the camp. Maybe the jacks will knock some of that chip off his shoulder."

"Clarence?"

"The judge."

"The judge's name is Clarence? You must know him pretty well."

"Uh-huh." The sheriff pointed ahead on the trail. "This here's Murdock's place. Let's take a look around."

Daniel watched the sheriff move ahead, but he was remembering when he was back in jail and the sheriff commented that he heard that the judge was one of the best. *He heard? Seems like the sheriff knows more than he's telling me.*

They walked around the clearing where the log house sat, and Daniel tapped the sheriff's shoulder and pointed to the felled tree not far into the woods. They studied the area around it and realized that it wasn't visible from the house, so it would be easy for someone to come and go without being seen. A pouch was there, buried under the debris from the fallen tree.

"There's jewelry in here. You recognize any of this stuff, Jon?"

Jon looked through the items taken out of the pouch, picking up a necklace, then a ring, and some pieces of gold. "I've seen some of these pieces in the glass counter at the mercantile. Looks like the Bedloes been hit again. And that necklace looks like the one Mrs. Hamilton wears."

"Hamilton?"

"The banker's wife. Our thief has been making the rounds." He pocketed the pouch.

Further investigation revealed the still and the sheriff picked up a heavy stick and was about to smash it when Daniel grabbed his arm to stop him.

"Maybe we shouldn't. If Ralston's booze supply is dried up, maybe he'll come looking for some more. What do you think?"

The sheriff lowered the stick. "You're right. He must be getting desperate for some any day now. I'm willing to stake out the area."

"Guntar's been with you for two or three days. I'd predict that Ralston could show up here tonight or tomorrow."

The sheriff pulled off his hat and smoothed down his hair before repositioning it more comfortably. He frowned. "I wonder."

"What?"

"Mrs. Strahle said she chopped down the tree night before last. Maybe whoever makes the deliveries doesn't know yet and will show up again. I kept Guntar and his mother's presence quiet, so no one should know they aren't still out here. I suggest that one of us watches the still and the other the tree."

"Sounds good."

The men found their hiding places and settled in for a long wait. Daniel opted for the still. He would dearly love to get his hands on Ralston and find out if he was the one who had set him up as Murdock's murderer. Revenge would be sweet.

"Vengeance is mine; I will repay saith the Lord."

Daniel grimaced as he recalled the verse from Romans. Pastor Sam's endless teaching had yielded in him finally accepting the Lord Jesus Christ as his savior, but he still had much to learn about living for the Lord. Now when he would like to wreak vengeance on an enemy, he had to go and remember some of the other things the preacher had taught him. Things like, "If your enemy hunger, feed him; if he thirst, give him drink."

I don't think this is the kind of drink you were talking about, Lord. Daniel's thoughts made him smile, but as he lay there on the snow-covered ground, he recalled more of what the talkative preacher said. Things about being kind and forgiving.

Is there ever a time to stand up and fight, Lord?

Daniel had been in his share of brawls and fights, and he knew the satisfying sound and feel of a fist rightly placed in another's jaw. It was exactly the feeling he'd like to have when he got the opportunity to knock Ralston off his feet.

But that's not my place.

No, Ralston's punishment would be up to the judge, not up to Daniel. However, if the man resisted, Daniel would be only too happy to subdue him.

The darkness descended early as it did in the winter months. Daniel knew that work at the logging camp ended when the light did and that Ralston would wait until after the evening meal to make his disappearance. Once the weary loggers hit their bunks for the night, they were usually dead to the world until morning, and Ralston could leave undetected.

The Murdock place was one of the farthest from the town of Grand Rapids, making it closer to the logging camp. Still, it would take Ralston a couple of hours to make the trek, if indeed, he were to come tonight.

Which left Daniel more time for his thoughts to wander, and he allowed himself to think through his situation. Visiting Dee's grave had been good for him. He missed her terribly, but he finally felt as if he were healing from the wound her passing had left within him. Seeing the wooden cross with her name carved into it made it all so final.

He talked to her as he stood over her grave. He told her about the children and about how wrong he had been to ignore their son. He told her about Mercy and Stanley taking them in and caring for them. He told her about Pastor Sam showing him the way of salvation and how he knew now that he would see her again in heaven.

He said his good-byes.

He knew she wasn't there listening to him. He knew she was in the Lord's presence and enjoying her heavenly home, yet it comforted him to verbalize his thoughts to her. Most of the time he realized he was actually praying and that the comfort he sought was coming from the Lord.

Then there was Mercy.

Daniel closed his eyes. He had an instant picture in his mind of how she looked with her long wet hair dripping all over the blanket she clutched around her. He shook his head. Now was not the time to try to figure out what he was feeling in regard to her. Their relationship was too complicated and he needed to focus his attention back on solving the mystery of Murdock's murder.

His muscles were getting sore from lying on the ground for so long and the snow beneath him had packed down from the heat of his body so that it was molded to his shape. He wondered how the sheriff was doing, and he hoped the older man didn't fall asleep as he waited. He remembered from being in the jail cell how loudly the lawman could snore.

He caught a movement out of the corner of his eye. The moon hadn't shown itself yet and the night was dark but his eyes were adjusted well to the darkness. There was a man coming down the path at a rapid pace and he didn't appear to be concerned about being seen. He was the right height and build to be Ralston.

Daniel kept very quiet as he watched. He didn't know if he should make his presence known yet because they were still waiting to see if anyone else would show up, and he knew the sheriff couldn't see what was happening from where he was hidden. The man approached the still and started rummaging through the jugs that were scattered around it, shaking one and then another until he found a full one. It was Ralston and he was not being careful about the noise he made nor was he looking about him, so Daniel eased his way to his feet, cringing as the pain woke his muscles, and stepped carefully and quietly to the man who now was guzzling from one of the jugs.

It was an easy matter to slip an arm around the unsuspecting man and clamp a hand over his mouth. Or so Daniel thought. Ralston reacted like a wildcat. He swung the jug he had in his hand around to smash it on Daniel's head but Daniel saw it coming and dodged. The jug caught him on the shoulder and caused him to lose his grip on Ralston. Daniel dove for him and they began wrestling and rolling in the snow. Daniel avoided Ralston's fist and landed a punch of his own to Ralston's jaw that made an audible *crack* in the quiet night. Ralston responded with a fist in Daniel's stomach that caused the air to whoosh right out of him. While he was doubled over, Ralston grabbed a stick and was about to club Daniel when the sheriff smacked the man on the back of his head with the butt of his pistol. Ralston crumbled to the ground.

Daniel was breathing heavily as he dropped to one knee. "'Bout time…you…showed up."

Jon grinned. "I kinda hated to interrupt, but I thought it might be best if we got back into hiding in case we get another visitor. You okay to walk?"

Daniel weaved a bit when he stood up, but he nodded. He held a hand over his stomach as he bent to pick up his hat.

"I take it this is Ralston then?" The sheriff looked down at the fallen man. "I'll get him trussed up and gagged so he can't alert anyone."

Together they dragged Ralston to Jon's hiding place and Daniel shared his thoughts with the sheriff while he watched him tie the unconscious man.

"He didn't seem concerned that anyone would be here at the cabin the way he was tromping down the path at full speed like he was. He just made a beeline for the booze."

The sheriff finished his task and rolled Ralston onto his side. "Either the need for a drink was so strong that he didn't care if anyone heard him or he already knew that the widow wouldn't be here. Or maybe he didn't consider her a threat so he didn't care if she knew he was here. He went straight for the still though. That could mean he didn't know about the tree or he was going to go there next."

"Oh." Daniel looked up. "I hadn't thought about that. Sorry. I guess I should have given him more time before I grabbed him. I just didn't want him to get away."

"No problem. We'll just keep fishing and see what else we can catch tonight."

The men settled down in silence to wait.

The morning light awakened Daniel and he blinked and looked around him before moving. The sheriff was gone and Ralston was still tied up beside him with his eyes closed, either in sleep or from unconsciousness, Daniel didn't know which and didn't much care. He turned his head slowly to locate the sheriff and found him kneeling near the fallen tree.

The sheriff looked up when Daniel approached.

"Did anyone show up? Sorry about falling asleep."

"I didn't see anyone." He stood and scratched his head. "Well, let's move on. I think we need to take a trip to the camp."

"And Ralston?"

"He's coming too. We may learn something from him that will help piece this mystery together. But first I'll smash that still once and for all."

Ralston's complaints reverberated through the forest until the sheriff finally threatened to gag him again. There were no real legal grounds to arrest the man, but because he could be considered a suspect in Murdock's murder, the sheriff chose to use jail time as another threat, anything to have some quiet.

And Daniel needed the quiet as well. Quiet so he could think. He was trying to recall each moment of the night Murdock was murdered. Seeing Ralston again brought back the frustrations and anger he had gone through during the time right after Dee's death that led up to his fistfight with the man. He never had animosity toward any of the jacks he worked with even though he had demonstrated rage in his careless behavior on the job. Now as they entered the camp in the dark of night, he was overcome with the memory of the decision he made that night to change his life. Little did he know at that time that it wasn't that decision that changed him but rather the one he made later on to give his life to the Lord Jesus that made the difference.

"We can stay in the cookshack." Daniel pointed out the building. "There won't be bunks, but frankly I don't want to pick up all the vermin from the bunkhouse if I can help it."

The sheriff nodded and tugged Ralston along with him when the man turned toward the bunkhouse. "You're staying where I can keep an eye on you."

Ralston's steps were lagging and he was jittery from not getting enough of the alcohol he so desperately wanted. He followed Daniel into the cookshack with the sheriff behind him. The cook was roused and told why they were there and they settled in for the remainder of the night. By morning, they were up and having coffee when the men began to arrive.

"Sheriff Talbot!" Jefferson Elwood stopped abruptly in the doorway and the unmindful man behind him smacked into his back. The cook glared at Elwood, a warning that talking wasn't allowed in his cookshack, but the sheriff wasn't cowed by the cook and motioned to Elwood.

"Sit here, Elwood. I need to talk to you."

Daniel stifled a laugh when he saw the cook's glowering visage. The man was already put out that he had been awakened in the middle of the night and if his temper didn't improve, Daniel knew the food would be affected. He turned when he felt a tap on his back.

Shorty grinned and held out his hand. Daniel shook his friend's hand but they didn't speak. He motioned with his head that he would meet him outside after breakfast then they sat down and proceeded to devour their breakfast in silence except for the murmuring of the sheriff and his former deputy. Daniel felt Elwood glance his way but he ignored the man for the time being. He didn't care for him, especially after he learned of his treatment of Mercy, and right now he wanted to do his own detective work and look over the men for clues.

As he made eye contact with his old coworkers, he nodded greetings, and it occurred to him that he did not miss the lifestyle and work of the logging camp. He wasn't afraid of the hard work, but the conditions were less than ideal and the more he looked around him, the more he realized how much he enjoyed being at the Crane farm. He liked the satisfaction of working with the animals and he looked forward to farming the land again in the spring. And he liked being with his children.

Boots scraped on the wooden floor as the men stood and began to exit the building. Since the meal was over, Shorty spoke out loud to Daniel.

"You back to work?"

"No." He tilted his head toward the sheriff and deputy. "I'm here on another matter."

Shorty scratched at the beginning of whiskers on his face. Of all the loggers, Shorty was one of the few who tried to keep clean-shaven. "Ah. They still think you murdered ol' Murdock, is that it? You ask me, they shouldn't have to look much farther than right there." He indicated Ralston who was staring into the depths of his coffee cup at a table across the room from them.

"Ralston?" Daniel lowered his voice. "What do you know?"

"Think about it. His bunk was next to yours. He could easily get ahold of your knife and plant those stolen items in your stuff."

"But why? Why kill Murdock? And how did he get those stolen things?"

Shorty shrugged as he got up to leave. "Why not Murdock? The man was hated by everyone here. As far as the booty, he'd been working in cahoots with Murdock on that. If you want to know more, you'd do well to check with Murdock's kid. He was in on something with him."

The foreman stepped into the room and scowled at Shorty.

"I gotta get to work, Daniel." He patted his friend on the shoulder. "I hope I've been able to help."

Daniel nodded and watched the two men leave. Shorty seemed to know a lot more than he ought to know, so why didn't he come out and tell what he knew when Daniel was being accused? Why did he let him be taken off to jail? No, something was not right.

Jon motioned for Daniel to join them.

Daniel picked up his coffee cup and slid down the bench beside Jon and got his first good look at Elwood—the logger—who was now directly across from him. Daniel brought his cup to his mouth to try to hide the grin he couldn't contain when he saw the bedraggled, bearded, haggard face staring at him. Working in the logging camp seemed to have taken some of the starch out of the arrogant deputy.

"Elwood thinks it was Ralston," the sheriff stated without preamble. His sideways glance at Daniel told him he was not impressed with his deputy's deductions.

Daniel's eyebrows raised.

Ralston again.

"So you're not accusing *me* anymore?" His gaze didn't falter from Elwood's and he bristled at the dislike he saw in the other's eyes.

"I mean to prove that you still had something to do with it," growled Elwood. "But like I told the sheriff, Ralston would sneak out at night and so would that kid. They were in on something. I just haven't figured out what yet."

"What they were in on, *detective,* was a forbidden booze run. Murdock's wife made the brew and the kid delivered it for Murdock to find and apparently he shared his bounty with Ralston. When Murdock was killed, Ralston made the kid keep on delivering to him."

"So Ralston must have killed Murdock to get all the booze for himself." Elwood sat up straighter and glared at

Ralston who still slouched over his breakfast, not paying them any mind.

"Seems to be settled then." The sheriff waited for Elwood's attention to return to him. "Oh, I forgot. What about the thievery in town and how did the goods get out here and why? And why frame Daniel? And why didn't you look into that further before you left the scene and hauled Daniel into town? Or could it be that *you* were in on it too?"

"What?" Elwood stood so suddenly the bench flipped over and crashed onto the floor. Ralston jumped, then held his head as if the noise hurt it.

"Sit down, Elwood!" The sheriff barked the order then waited as the deputy righted the bench and sat down. Elwood's face was red and his fists were balled in anger.

"You were just as likely a suspect as Daniel as were any of the men in the camp. Sure, Daniel's knife was used and stolen items were found in his bunk. Any killer would cast the blame elsewhere, but he wouldn't blatantly point the finger at himself." The sheriff took a deep breath and Daniel guessed he'd been wanting to knock some sense into his deputy's head with that bit of news for quite some time. "But you took the easy way out and grabbed the first man you could and made off for town like some hero. You very nearly ruined this man's life and destroyed his family. If you're going to continue as my deputy, you need to start using your head, man!"

The scolding didn't appear to sit well with Elwood. He glared at both men but he remained at his seat. Daniel had to at least give him credit for not marching off in anger as he had done in the past.

The sheriff continued in a quieter tone. "Now what else have you learned from being out here?"

Elwood's lips were tight and he hesitated before admitting, "Nothing. That's it."

The sheriff shook his head then he turned to Daniel. "How about you? That big fellow you were talking to have anything interesting?"

Daniel glanced at Elwood then at the sheriff. At Jon's nod, he spoke. "Shorty thinks it was Ralston too and for all the same reasons. He was in on the booze run with Murdock and my bunk was next to his which made me an easy plant as the suspect. But…I don't know why, but I don't think it was Ralston."

"Shorty goes to town a lot."

Elwood's statement caused both men to turn to him again.

"What do you mean?"

"I don't know if I mean anything. You asked if there was anything else suspicious and that's the only thing out of the ordinary around here. He always volunteers to go for supplies and he's been injured and had to be pulled out of here."

"Injured?" Daniel leaned forward.

"He hurt his foot."

"Did you see it happen? Did anyone see it happen?"

Elwood's brows creased. "I didn't. I don't—wait! He was alone. I remember that he said he kept calling for help and no one heard him."

"When was this?"

"Uh...just this week. He got back yesterday."

Daniel turned to Jon. "Shorty was the injured man Ralston and I brought to town when Dee—that's when my wife passed away."

"He was sick a few weeks ago too and went to town."

The sheriff and Daniel stood as one.

"Bring him in for a talk."

"Yes, sir."

Daniel located the foreman and together they went in search of Shorty, but he was nowhere to be found. They talked to other men but none could tell where he went.

Daniel hurried back to the cookshack and explained to the sheriff.

"Elwood, grab your gear. You're coming with us. And you." He pointed at Ralston who still sat alone. "Go with him and get your things too. We aren't done with you." He motioned to Daniel. "Let's take a look around."

The logging foreman wasn't too happy about losing two more men and offered no help to the sheriff and Daniel as they asked questions and scouted the area where Shorty was sent to work for the day. No telltale prints indicated where he had taken off into the woods as he could have done so from any of the well-traveled paths the men used.

"We need to get back to town. I have my doubts he's gone there, but it's a place to start and we need to do something with Ralston. I don't think he's done talking yet."

"I'd like to think that the Strahles are safe out at the farm, but I have an uneasy feeling that Shorty will figure out where they are and take out after them. If he is the one thieving from town, he might think they could testify against him." Daniel relayed his worries.

"Stanley's there."

"He walks with a cane, Jon."

The more Daniel thought about the danger his family may be in, the more he pushed the men as they moved through the forest paths to town. The sheriff had all he could do to make him rest during the darkest part of the night.

They arrived at the jailhouse the following day, exhausted and hungry. Mr. Bedloe was at the sheriff's desk but rose as the men trudged into the room.

"Sheriff! I didn't expect you back so soon." He looked over the group curiously but asked no questions.

"Evening, Latham. Could you rustle us up some food?"

"Sure, Jon. I'll have some sent over from the hotel. I need to get back to my store anyway since the missus is gone."

"Gone?"

"She decided to go visit her sister. Of all times to go when I was busy doing your job! But once Hedda makes up her mind about something, there's no stopping her. I don't have to tell you!"

"Things quiet in town?"

"Sure. Except for those robberies, you know nothing much happens around here. I'll be going now and I'll send you some food."

"Thanks, Latham."

The men dropped into the chairs and began pulling off their heavy outerwear except for Daniel.

"Sheriff, I'm going to the hotel for a hot bath and meal and a warm bed, then first light I'm headed for home. I need to make sure everyone is okay there and with Shorty on the loose, I just don't have a good feeling about it."

"Let me take care of Ralston and stop by my house for a few hours and I'll join you."

"I won't wait."

Jon nodded.

After Daniel left, the sheriff took Ralston's arm and led him to a cot in one of the cells where the weary man willingly stretched out.

"I'm not arresting you. See, the door's open and you're free. I just want to get you some help." The sheriff turned to go.

"He's got a woman."

The sheriff stopped. "What?"

Ralston's arm was over his face as he spoke again. "Shorty's got a woman in town. That's why he finds excuses to leave the camp."

"Who?"

The man on the cot shook his head. "No one knows who it is, but we all know…he sees…someone." His voice drifted off.

The sheriff stood in thought until he heard snoring from Ralston, then he headed back to his office and found Elwood still sitting there, dozing off in the chair. Irritation crossed the lawman's face.

"Did you know Shorty had a woman in town?"

Elwood's head jerked up. "What?"

"Did you know Shorty had a woman in town?"

"He did? He does?"

The sheriff shook his head in disgust. "You were sent there to find out the truth. It seems all you wanted was to try to make Daniel guilty."

There was a knock on the door and a boy from the hotel delivered their meals. The sheriff wolfed his food down then stood and shrugged into his coat.

"See to it that Ralston gets his food when he wakes up which may not be until breakfast time. The man is not a prisoner, but I'd like him to go see the doc. If he won't go, have the doctor come here. Keep an eye on things while I'm gone."

The sheriff left. Elwood stared long at the closed door before getting up and heading for the cot in the back room. On the way he caught a glimpse of himself in the mirror the sheriff kept there for shaving after an overnight stay. Elwood stared at his whiskered face.

"She can't see me like this," he murmured as he rummaged through the items on the table until he found the razor.

28

Crane Farm

Mercy knew the Strahles felt uncomfortable about moving in with the family, so she did her best to make them feel welcome. The older Dunn girls were shy about having Guntar around, but Daphne, Didi, and Dylan in their innocent ways soon had Guntar and Ilsa talking and laughing at their antics. Grandpa Crane included Guntar in the chores and Mercy gave Ilsa kitchen jobs to make them feel a part of the family. She didn't know how long they would be staying with them, but it helped to make them feel that they were contributing to the workload and not just guests.

Mercy couldn't get used to the fact that Guntar was not Ilsa's real child. The mother and son seemed so close especially after the trials they had faced together living with an abusive husband and father. Mercy looked lovingly at the five children gathered around the breakfast table. They weren't her flesh and blood either, but she understood the love a mother could have for her children. Again she felt the pain in her heart at the thought of being separated from them.

"Why don't you have to go to *th*chool?" Didi asked Guntar the question as she struggled to lift the bowl of potatoes to pass to him.

Guntar smiled kindly at Didi as he reached for the tippy bowl, and Mercy was pleased to see how well he handled the many questions put to him by the inquisitive child.

"It's because I'm already so smart," he teased.

"Weally? Awe you *th*marter than Delaney and Darby?"

Guntar glanced at the two mentioned. "No, but I'm older so I don't have to go now."

"Oh."

Didi thought about that while the others smiled. Mercy saw a blush creep over the older girls' faces. She also noticed that they had taken care to brush and fix their hair before coming to the table. Having a young man in the house was making the girls primp more and Mercy could only imagine the young romantic thoughts going through their heads. As a teacher, she had dealt with boy-girl relationships and could easily recall her own silly, girlish crushes.

Grandpa Crane pushed back his chair. "Thank you, ladies, for another fine meal. I better get to my chores or the cows will be bellowing louder than old Mrs. Ketchler."

"Papa!" Mercy scolded as the girls giggled.

"I'll help you, sir." Guntar rose to follow him out.

Mercy and Ilsa started on dishes as the older children went to get ready for school and Didi took Dylan to play in the next room.

"I thought there was no school in LaPrairie." Ilsa's look was puzzled as the girls prepared to leave.

"There wasn't until just recently the town arranged to have classes above the jail. I've been teaching the girls up to now, but I thought it might be good for them to get out and meet the other children in the area even though it's a rather long walk for them. I still teach them at home when the weather is bad."

Ilsa nodded in understanding.

"Guntar is so good with everyone," Mercy commented.

Ilsa smiled. She dried the dishes as she watched the three older girls walk down the road. "Are the girls in school for a full day today?"

"Yes. They get home just before the daylight is gone. I do long for spring when the days are longer, don't you?"

Ilsa didn't answer right away and Mercy looked over her shoulder to find the woman staring out the window.

She must have much on her mind.

"You know you are welcome to stay here as long as you need to."

"Oh!" Ilsa turned away and picked up another dish. "I don't know how to thank you for all you're doing for Guntar and me. I don't know what we will do now, but it's nice to know I have friends."

Abruptly Ilsa set the cloth down. "I know it's a little early for Dylan's nap, but I would dearly love to rock him for a while. Would you mind?"

Mercy stopped what she was doing and turned in time to see Ilsa wipe at her eye. "Of course not. Go on, I'll finish up here."

Ilsa nodded and hurried off.

Mercy was deep in thought and prayer for the needs of the distraught woman when she heard the backdoor to the kitchen open. It was odd for Papa to use that door as it was the farthest from the barn, but maybe it was Guntar. She reached for a towel to dry her hands and was startled when she turned to find herself face-to-face with Mrs. Bedloe.

Mercy let out a shriek as the woman grabbed her arm.

"Quiet!" Mrs. Bedloe commanded. "Are you alone?"

Mercy just stared openmouthed at her.

"Are you alone?" The woman insisted.

"Wha—? What are you doing here?" Mercy was too shocked at finding the store owner from Grand Rapids in her kitchen to pull her arm free from her grasp and let herself be tugged toward the door.

"I have to talk to you." Mrs. Bedloe pulled Mercy out the door to stand alongside the house.

"What is it?" Mercy could barely contain her astonishment at having the woman appear in her house and it didn't register with her that they were now standing outdoors. That Mrs. Bedloe was agitated was clear and Mercy could see she was tired from her long walk to the farm on this cold winter day.

"You saw us! You saw us, didn't you?"

"What do you mean? What are you talking about?"

Mrs. Bedloe gripped Mercy by both arms. "I heard you laugh that night, so I know you were outside the mercantile. You saw!"

The woman is insane!

"What—oh!" The night she caught the Bedloes in a passionate embrace! *Is that what this is about?*

"See! You know what I'm talking about. Who have you told? No one can know!"

Mercy was puzzled and she pulled free of the woman's grasp only to have Mrs. Bedloe grab her arms again.

"Mrs. Bedloe," she spoke in a no-nonsense voice. "Let go of me, please, and we'll discuss this. In fact, it's cold out here. Let's go inside and I'll make us some coffee."

Mrs. Bedloe wavered then shook her head. "I can't risk anyone overhearing. I have to know if you've told anyone else what you saw that night."

Now Mercy was exasperated. "Really, Mrs. Bedloe, why would I tell anyone that I saw you and your husband kissing? What you and Mr. Bedloe do is your business."

She saw surprise cross the woman's face.

"I just happened to walk by the store and saw you. I'm sorry that it has upset you so badly."

Mrs. Bedloe dropped her hands from Mercy's arms and took a step backward. She frowned. "Why did you laugh?"

"My goodness! Are you upset with me because you heard me laugh? Believe me, I was not laughing at you. It was just at a…a thought I had." Mercy was more perplexed than ever at the strange actions of the woman. "Won't you please come in and warm up now? You must be cold."

Mrs. Bedloe allowed Mercy to lead her back into the house and to a chair. She seemed stunned and Mercy hurried about to heat some coffee, all the while chatting about inconsequential things in hopes of bringing some normalcy to the situation. The woman must have been up at dawn to reach the farm by this time. To her, this was very serious, and Mercy just didn't understand.

"It wasn't Mr. Bedloe."

Mercy turned from the stove to find Mrs. Bedloe staring at the floor.

Oh! In a flash Mercy understood.

She hurried over and put her arm around the woman. "I didn't know. Mrs. Bedloe, I honestly thought you were with your husband."

The woman quietly began to sob and Mercy gently held her, praying for the right words as she waited. It finally made some sense to her why the woman was so distraught and wanted to be sure that Mercy hadn't told anyone. But was she upset over the infidelity or over being caught in it?

When Mrs. Bedloe had settled down somewhat she wiped her eyes with her hankie and took the coffee Mercy offered her. They sat in silence for a few moments and Mercy was thankful that Ilsa had the children upstairs so that they could talk in private.

"I never meant for it to happen. I care for my husband; you have to believe me, but when Cordell came into the store, he would look at me in a way that my husband never had. It took my breath away." The talkative storekeeper seemed at a loss for words as she stared past Mercy, deep in her thoughts. "He came only when Mr. Bedloe wasn't there and we would…talk. He was interested in me. He looked at me. He really saw me…and…I fell in love with him." Another tear rolled down her cheek.

"But…" Mercy was at a loss to know what to say. She wanted to scream out, *It's wrong!* But as she patted Mrs. Bedloe on the arm, she could tell by the tears and the conflict on her face that the woman knew it already. This was a battle Mrs. Bedloe would have to fight on her own.

They both turned as they heard footsteps coming down the stairs.

"You're not alone? Oh, dear!" Mrs. Bedloe swiped the hankie briskly across her face and rose to leave.

Ilsa came into the kitchen and stopped in the doorway. There was an amused expression on her face as she put one hand on her hip and commanded, "Sit down!"

Mercy frowned as she stood and Mrs. Bedloe stopped in half-stride and stared in astonishment.

"Mrs. Murdock? Why are *you* here?"

"I said sit down." Ilsa pulled her other hand from behind her and revealed a pistol that she pointed directly at the storekeeper.

"Ilsa! What are you doing?" Mercy headed toward her, but Ilsa waved the gun her way.

"You sit down too."

Mercy stopped in shock but the look on Ilsa's face convinced her that she was serious. She sat down slowly and stared at the gun. Ilsa waited until both women returned to their chairs and then she went to the window and waved to someone to come to the house.

"Ilsa! I don't understand. What are you doing?" Suddenly Mercy jumped to her feet again. "Where are the children?"

"Sit!" The pistol faced Mercy again. "The children are fine. They won't bother us."

"What does that mean? What have you done to them?" Mercy stepped forward but halted when the backdoor opened and a tall man entered. He took in the scene and pulled a revolver from his waistband.

"Hi, darlin'. I'll cover them while you get your things."

Mercy took a step back as the man approached. He was calm and smiling and never took his eyes from her as he reached for Ilsa and pulled her to his side. He kissed the top of her head and then grinned at the women again. Mercy opened her mouth to speak but Mrs. Bedloe was suddenly beside her, her hands balled into fists at her sides.

"Cordell!"

The man's grin faltered when he recognized the woman, but he quickly regained his composure. "Well, if it isn't my old friend Hedda. What are you doing so far from home, darlin'?" His arm remained around Ilsa, and Ilsa smirked at Mrs. Bedloe.

Mercy could feel the trembling of the woman beside her, but whether it was from fear or rage, she couldn't tell. She took her arm and led her back to a chair then she turned again and faced the couple.

"I'm going to check on my children."

The gun followed her movements.

"You can threaten to shoot me all you want, but…but…I know you won't. Now get out of my way!"

The man pulled the hammer back on the revolver and chuckled. "It don't matter to me if I kill you too. You can only hang once no matter how many people you kill."

Mercy stopped. The grin was still on the man's face, but she could now see his eyes weren't smiling. They were cold and hard. The man was a killer.

"You killed Murdock."

The man threw his head back and laughed again. "I wish I could take credit for that one, but it wasn't me. Have you asked Ilsa?" He hugged Ilsa closer to his side.

Mercy scowled at Ilsa.

Ilsa's returning look was amused. "Sorry, it wasn't me, but I wouldn't put it past Guntar. He hated Murdock."

"You said you believed Guntar was innocent."

Ilsa shrugged as if it didn't matter.

Mercy's voice shook. "Get out of my way! My children need me!"

Ilsa laughed as she blocked the doorway. "Quit your worrying. They're just sleeping. A few drops of chloroform and they'll sleep all day."

"You *drugged* my children? Ilsa! Why are you doing this? Why?"

"Git your things, Ilsa! We have to git goin'."

"Sure, Shorty." Ilsa left the room.

"You!" He pointed at Mercy. "Sit back down."

Mrs. Bedloe's head shot up. "Shorty?"

Shorty laughed as he lounged against the counter. "What's the matter, Hedda? Didn't you know my nickname? I bet you didn't know why I was comin' to see you all the time either, my sweet love."

"Don't call me that!"

"Now, darlin', you didn't mind me callin' you that the other night." He smirked as he crossed his arms, keeping the gun pointed in their direction. "Bet you didn't know I was robbin' you blind either."

"What?"

Shorty laughed again. "You missin' anything from thet precious store of yours?"

"*You're* the thief?"

He laughed again. "I'm one of them. Why else did you think I was sparkin' you? Ilsa is pretty good at thievin' herself. She and I had a good thing goin' until Murdock caught on to it."

Suddenly he straightened and stepped away from the window.

"Who's the old man with the cane?"

Mercy's heart thundered in her ears. "That's my father. He...he doesn't come back to the house until lunch. Leave him alone. Just go! Just go and leave all of us alone!"

Shorty watched the window a few more moments. "You must be tellin' the truth, he's gone back in the barn. Anyone else out there?"

Silence.

"I said is anyone else out there?"

Mercy glanced at Mrs. Bedloe then back at Shorty, but she still didn't answer. He took a step toward her, but Ilsa stopped him by answering him as she came back to the kitchen.

"Guntar's out there with the old man. Come on, let's go before he sees us."

Mercy gaped at her. "You're leaving Guntar?"

Ilsa didn't meet her eyes.

Mercy turned to Shorty again. "How did you know to come here? No one knew where the Strahles were."

Shorty reached for Ilsa again and pressed her against his side. "I was in town when Ilsa and the kid were at the jail. Easy enough to talk to her through the window when the kid was asleep. Enough of this. Tie and gag them."

Ilsa looked around the kitchen and picked up the towels they had been using for drying the dishes. She efficiently ripped them into strips and used them to tie Mrs. Bedloe to her chair first while Mercy shook her head at her. Anger was boiling up inside Mercy and she tried to get ahold of her emotions. *Father, help! What can I do to stop this? Please, please let Didi and Dylan be okay!*

Everyone stopped where they were when they heard a *thump* from upstairs.

"Ilsa, go see what that was," Shorty commanded.

Ilsa listened intently for a moment. "It was just one of the children. Nothing to worry about."

"What do you mean *one of the children*? Did they fall? Are they hurt?" Mercy pushed against Ilsa as the woman was trying to restrain her to the chair. "I have to see to them! Let me go!"

Ilsa grabbed at her arm, but Mercy was determined. All the mother instinct that comes from loving a child came out in her and she swung her fist with all her might and connected with the smaller woman's jaw. Ilsa dropped to the floor.

Mercy ran for the doorway, but Shorty was there ahead of her. He grabbed her arm and twisted it behind her back.

"That wasn't too smart, sweetheart. You give me anymore trouble and I'll knock you senseless, you understand?"

Out of the corner of her eye, Mercy saw a man creeping down the stairway. She didn't know who it was, but it meant help was on the way and she needed to do something to get the advantage over Shorty. The pain in her arm was piercing, but she had to act. With her other elbow, she jabbed at Shorty's ribs. He grunted but it didn't loosen his grip one bit. On the contrary, he pulled her arm higher and she cried out in pain.

But Mercy wasn't about to give up. She stomped with all her might on Shorty's foot. For just a moment his hold slackened and she took advantage of it. She bent forward and sunk her teeth into the hand holding the gun.

"Yeow!" He cursed and pushed her to the floor.

Mercy stumbled and fell hard on Ilsa who was just starting to get up. She heard a noise behind her and turned to see Daniel leap on Shorty's back.

Daniel?

Then there was chaos. Sheriff Talbot burst through the backdoor and Grandpa Crane rushed through the front door so fast no one would believe he used a cane. But there was no time for relief. Shorty and Daniel were in a wrestling match and Shorty still had his gun. Ilsa struck out at Mercy, catching her on the side of the head and making her see stars.

"Ma!"

Guntar stood transfixed behind Grandpa Crane, staring at the scene before him and at his mother in particular, but Mercy couldn't afford time to sympathize with him. Grandpa Crane grabbed Ilsa and held onto her while the sheriff barreled into the fight between Daniel and Shorty. Daniel had Shorty's gun hand in a death grip and veins were bulging in his temples. Shorty was actually the taller man and had the advantage, but Daniel had the determination and the help of Sheriff Talbot who bashed the butt of his pistol on Shorty's head. The man tumbled to the floor like a fallen tree. And Daniel dropped to his knees gasping for air.

"Daniel!" Mercy scrambled across the kitchen floor to him. "Daniel, the children! Ilsa drugged them!"

"What? Where are they?"

Mercy led the way as they raced for the stairs. She could feel Daniel right behind her as she searched for Didi and Dylan. Ilsa had the children in a room together and Mercy gasped as she saw them lying still. She rushed to the bed.

"Didi! Dylan!" She felt for Dylan's heartbeat as Daniel reached for Didi.

"They're alive." Daniel was panting as he gently lay Didi back down on the bed. "Thank God!" Mercy knelt down and stroked Didi's hair while she held onto Dylan's hand. Her eyes closed in silent thanks and when she opened them, she found Daniel watching her.

"Are you all right?" he whispered. He brushed hair from her forehead. "You have a lump forming."

Mercy's eyes closed briefly at his touch. The voices from downstairs were muffled and the even breathing of the sleeping children helped to settle her nerves. "I'm okay now, but I was so worried about Didi and Dylan." Her breath caught. She kept her voice to a whisper too. "I can't believe Ilsa was involved in this. Who is that man?"

"That's Shorty. We think he's the thief."

"He is. He admitted it and he said Ilsa was as good at it as he was. He also said something about Murdock, but he said he didn't kill him. Do you think he did?"

"I'd bet on it." He looked at the children again. "Do you think they'll be all right?"

Mercy sighed. "I don't know much about chloroform, but I will stay with them until they're awake. The sheriff might need you."

"Yes." He rose. "Thank you, Mercy. Thank you for how you care about my children." He looked like he wanted to say more but he turned to the door then stopped. "Why is Mrs. Bedloe here?"

Before Mercy had to answer, the sheriff called. "Daniel!"

He looked once more at her and the children before he hurried from the room.

Mercy stayed with Didi and Dylan the rest of the day. She didn't know what was happening downstairs, but she knew it wasn't as important as the two little lives she cherished right in this room, and it was several hours before either of the children stirred and she was able to hold and cuddle them as they awoke.

Daniel hurried down the stairs and took in the scene before him. Shorty was still out cold on the floor, but the sheriff was taking no chances and was busy tying the man's hands behind his back. Stanley held Ilsa in front of him with both his arms wrapped around her, yet she still squirmed and kicked and screamed obscenities at all of them. Guntar stood motionless, watching his mother in shock and disbelief. Daniel hurried to relieve Stanley and together they managed to bind Ilsa's hands and Stanley even tied a towel around her mouth.

"We've heard enough out of you," he told her. Then he took out his handkerchief and mopped his brow. "I'm too old for this, Daniel."

His touch of humor made Daniel smile but he kept an eye on Guntar, wondering what the young man was thinking and wondering which way he would choose to go. Would he suddenly decide to rush in and save his mother? It was then that he noticed Mrs. Bedloe. She was still sitting, tied to her chair, with a towel around her mouth. The woman was beet red but she wasn't struggling or demanding attention in any way. Daniel was about to go to her when Guntar turned to the woman as if aware of her for the first time.

"Mrs. Bedloe!" He hurried to her and undid the towel around her mouth.

Mrs. Bedloe gasped for air and in a hoarse voice said, "Thank you. I need…water…please…water."

Guntar turned, but Daniel motioned for him to stay as he went for the water himself. Guntar worked on untying Mrs. Bedloe's hands.

"Thank you, young man."

She reached for the water glass, but her hands were shaking, so Guntar took the glass and held it to her lips and she drank. She rubbed her hands together then held them out to look at them.

"My goodness, I can't seem to stop shaking." She cleared her throat and tried to pat down her wayward hair.

Daniel was amazed when Guntar placed his arm around the trembling woman. "It's okay, Mrs. Bedloe."

Then Guntar turned to his mother. She was glaring at everyone, but when Guntar made eye contact with her, she faltered and her gaze dropped.

"I don't understand, Ma. What have you done?" He kept his arm around Mrs. Bedloe and Daniel didn't know if it was to comfort the woman or to give himself some form of strength to go on. "First, I thought you killed Murdock, then I believed you when you said you didn't kill him, now I find out you're a thief. I don't understand," he repeated. "Did you kill him?"

Ilsa was shaking her head and since she had calmed down, Daniel released her mouth to speak.

"I didn't kill Murdock! I really thought you had. The man deserved it. He found out about Shorty and me, and I suppose Shorty did it."

Daniel saw that, like him, the others were astonished at her nonchalance.

"Why were you stealing?"

Daniel, Stanley, and the sheriff stood back and watched the exchange between Ilsa and Guntar with interest. They were as much in the dark as he was and since the woman was willing to talk to her son, they hoped to get the truth out of her.

"I had to! I had to get money to get away from Murdock, don't you see? You knew how he was, what he did to us. I couldn't live like that anymore. When Shorty came around, we decided to work together and get enough to leave this area for good. He got friendly with her." She indicated Mrs. Bedloe with her chin and the storekeeper covered her face with her hands. "That's how he was able to get so much from the store."

"I didn't know," Mrs. Bedloe spoke through tears. "I didn't know he was stealing from me." Guntar patted her shoulder.

"I found ways to pick up things here and there, and I sent them on to Shorty at the camp. He had a buyer and when we got enough cash, we were going to leave."

Daniel was watching Guntar closely for any sign that he knew and was in on the thievery, but the boy's face was changing from shock to anger.

"And me? What was going to happen to me?"

Ilsa must have missed the underlying hardness in his tone because she bent forward with an imploring look at her son. "You would come with us, of course. Haven't I always taken care of you?"

"No!" Mrs. Bedloe shook her finger at the woman. "You said you wanted to get out of here before Guntar saw you. That's what she said, Guntar! She was going to leave you here."

Guntar regarded Mrs. Bedloe a moment, scowled at his mother then nodded. "Yes, she was. Excuse me." He got up and left the house. Daniel nodded to Stanley and he stepped out the door behind Guntar.

"You didn't have to tell him that!" Ilsa hissed at Mrs. Bedloe.

"Someone has to start telling that boy the truth. Living a lie doesn't do anyone any good. I found that out the hard way and now I need to go home and tell my husband the truth. I only hope he accepts my apology." She started to rise then as if something just occurred to her, she sat down again. "Sheriff? What will happen to Guntar?"

The sheriff thought a moment. "Well, I don't know if he's old enough to be on his own. He was out at the lumber camp, but I don't think that's the place for him. I don't know."

Mrs. Bedloe stood. "That is a fine young man, Sheriff. If Mr. Bedloe forgives me and if he's willing, I would like to offer Guntar a job and a place to stay with us." She stepped around Ilsa who was glaring at her, but a little of the storekeeper's spitfire was coming back to her. "Now I'm going upstairs to see how Mrs. Dunn and the children are doing. Excuse me." She headed for the doorway and paused as she had to step over Shorty who was still prone on the floor. "Hmpf." She sniffed and raised her chin and walked on.

Stanley opened the door. "Hey, Jon. The road looks pretty good right now. Would you like to take the sleigh back to town? It would save you a lot of time."

"That would help a lot. Let me come and give you a hand getting it ready. You okay to keep an eye on these two, Daniel?"

"Yeah. I can handle it. I'll see what I can put together for a lunch for us and I'll ride along to help out. I imagine Mrs. Bedloe could use the ride too."

It wasn't long before Mrs. Bedloe returned to the kitchen and upon hearing of the arrangements took over the meal preparation and had them ready and on their way in no time. Daniel was amazed at the change in the woman. Her judgmental way and gossipy conversation were gone. In its place was still a strong, spirited woman, but with a much more humble attitude.

Guntar stepped out of the barn as the sleigh was about to leave and Daniel saw him make eye contact with his mother. Ilsa was the first to drop her gaze. Guntar's shoulders sagged, but Stanley was right there with a pat on his back and together they returned to the barn.

The trip back to Grand Rapids went without mishap. Shorty and Ilsa were kept bound and at one point when Shorty let out a string of curses, the sheriff put the handkerchief back over his mouth. That was enough to keep Ilsa quiet though she glared her hatred at all of them.

"I spoke with Mercy before we left," Daniel said quietly to the sheriff who was sitting right behind him as he drove the horses. "She said Ilsa told her that Guntar isn't her real child. He belonged to her first husband."

"That should make things easier for the boy to feel free to do as he wishes." The sheriff patted the bag filled with leather pouches of cash and stolen items. "The townspeople are going to be relieved to get some of their things back. But there's still one thing that concerns me."

"The murder?"

"Yep. Neither one admits to it but they're both willing to blame the other. I'll tell you, I'm ready to convict them both as co-conspirators, but the judge will have to make that decision."

Daniel nodded and kept the sleigh moving toward town. The road had been used enough to pack down the snow, making it easier for the horses to get through, but should a snowstorm hit before he got back to the farm, he would be stuck in town until the horses could get through again. He studied the sky.

29

Crane Farm

MERCY KEPT A close eye on Didi and Dylan the rest of the day. After they had been awake for a while, she allowed them to get up and they seemed to have no ill effects from the drug.

Thank you, Lord Jesus! She repeated her thanks many times as she relived the events and couldn't help but imagine what worse things could have happened but didn't. She let her mind dwell on the few tender moments she had with Daniel. *Could it be that he is starting to feel something for me too?*

The older girls came home from school and were told the basics of what had occurred that day without going into too much detail. Mercy could tell from how they stole glances at Guntar throughout supper that they were concerned about him. Guntar was very quiet, and Mercy could only imagine what was going through his mind. Her father found a private moment to tell her that he had explained to Guntar that he was welcome to stay as long as he wanted. She agreed.

It took longer than usual to get everyone settled down for the night. The children had so many questions, and Mercy could sense that they were fearful. She stayed with them until they fell asleep then she headed back to the kitchen to await Daniel's return. Guntar and Grandpa Crane were closing up the barn for the night and, knowing her father, probably still having a discussion about what happened. Since she knew none of them were likely to sleep well anyway, she put on a pot of coffee and began slicing some bread to go with it.

She had a lot to think about.

She was stunned beyond belief to find that the woman she had offered her home and protection to had turned out to be a criminal and had actually held a gun on her. Guntar appeared confused and betrayed, and she didn't know what was to happen to him, although Mrs. Bedloe told her when she came upstairs to check on the children that she would like to take Guntar to live with them at the store. And then there was Mrs. Bedloe herself and her astonishing admission of unfaithfulness to her husband. Finding out who the thieves were was a relief, but there was still the question of who killed Murdock, and could anyone now trust the two prisoners to tell the truth? And there was Daniel. And the children.

Mercy slid into a chair and pulled her father's Bible toward her. The concerns and questions were building up within her, and she knew she could find solace and answers in God's Word. No matter how difficult life situations were, she always had the Lord Jesus to guide her through them.

She opened to Ephesians and let her eyes roam through the verses, picking out especially the ones that were underlined.

"And be renewed in the spirit of your mind." She smiled. *Yes, I need renewing daily, Lord.*

She followed her finger down the next verses in chapter 4 until she came to verse 28, "Let him that stole steal no more; but rather let him labour, working with his hands the thing which is good, that he may have to give to him that needeth." She thought of Ilsa and how stealing had landed her in jail. *How can I help her? I need to tell her of you, Lord Jesus, and how you can free her of the sin that has ensnared her and caused so many so much pain.*

Chapter 5 brought tears to her eyes as she read about the relationship between a husband and a wife and as she thought of Daniel, her heart cried out to God for his will in her life.

She closed the book after reading about the Christian's armor in chapter 6 and how as a believer she needed to stand fully prepared by God and his Word to face the challenges ahead, and that she should face each situation with prayer.

Mercy bowed her head and poured out her needs to her savior. She felt refreshed and strengthened by her time spent with the Lord. As she wiped another tear, she heard the jingle of the horses' harnesses and she ran to the window. Daniel was home.

Mercy watched as the men in the barn came out to help Daniel with the team and put the sleigh away. Her heart overflowed with thankfulness that they were all safe and all back together again. She quickly set about getting cups and plates ready for the men, although she knew they would probably talk for a while before they came in.

The door opened and she turned, surprised that they were done so soon, but it was not who she expected standing there.

"Jefferson!"

"Hello, Mercy."

He was clean-shaven and dressed in a suit that sported his deputy's badge. His gun was holstered in a belt that bulged on his hip. He smiled as he pulled off his hat and stepped into the kitchen.

"Coffee smells good. Could I have a cup?"

Mercy was uneasy. Something wasn't right. He shouldn't be there at this time of the night. She glanced out the window and saw the light in the barn. The men were still out there. She took a deep breath to calm down and faced him again.

"Why are you here? Has something happened? Did you come with Daniel?"

A brief irritation crossed his face, but he masked it as he walked over and poured himself a cup of coffee. Mercy didn't like his being there, making himself at home in the kitchen.

"Relax, nothing's wrong. Sheriff Talbot asked me to come and tie up loose ends."

"Tonight?"

"Dunn stayed in town to help the sheriff with the prisoners. I bet he's pretty pleased with himself now that he's off the hook for Murdock's murder." He took a sip then made a sour face. "You used to make better coffee than this."

He doesn't know Daniel is here.

"It wasn't ready yet." She tapped her fingers on the counter while she thought. "Did one of them confess to the murder then?"

"Huh?"

"You said Daniel would be pleased to be off the hook for the murder. Does that mean one of them confessed? Because they denied it while they were here."

Jefferson carefully set the cup down. "Just what did they say?"

Mercy frowned. "Didn't the sheriff fill you in?"

"We didn't have a lot of time to talk. He wanted me to get back here and—look, Mercy, let's quit pretending. I'm here for you."

Mercy felt her mouth go dry. *Not this again! Not now!*

Jefferson smiled. "I have some great news. You're free! I found the marriage papers the preacher made you fill out along with the annulment papers. Everything's been destroyed and you're free now, Mercy. Free to finally marry me." He reached for her hand. "Now that Dunn is cleared, he can take his kids and go. I know how much you liked the children, but you and I can start our own family now. Think of it, Mercy. Your own children!"

Jefferson's voice rose and Mercy was immediately concerned about the children upstairs waking up. She felt sickened by the look on his face and tried to pull her hand free, but he kept a firm grip on it.

"I'm not...I'm not marrying you, Jefferson!"

He tugged her over to a chair and sat down with her. His voice was cajoling but there was no tenderness in his eyes. "I hurt you once, I know that and I'm sorry. But you have to know that I still love you."

"Stop it!" Mercy pulled away and stood to her feet. She kept her voice to a fierce whisper. "You are lying just like you did the first time. You don't love me and you know I don't love you. I want you to leave. Now! You can talk to the men in the morning."

Jefferson eased to his feet, all tenderness gone.

"No." He took her arm again. "I can see that sweeping you off your feet isn't going to work, so we'll do this the easy way." He pulled a folded paper from inside his coat. "I took the liberty of filling out a marriage form for us and I had it signed by a judge who owed me a favor. We're legally married."

Mercy's anger turned to puzzlement. "I don't understand. Why? Why are you so insistent on this?"

"I have a lot to gain here."

"The farm? You want this farm?"

He threw his head back and laughed, making Mercy cringe.

The children!

"Oh, I wanted the farm once because it will bring a good price, but I have no interest to live on it. It's nothing but a lot of work and that's not for me."

Mercy was terrified. She knew he didn't want her for a wife, but he wanted something she had. What?

"If not the farm, then what do you want? We're not wealthy."

He laughed again. "You really don't know, do you?"

"No, I don't understand."

"Didn't your pa ever tell you about your ma?"

"My mother?" Mercy couldn't be more surprised at his answer.

"I don't know when he planned to tell you, but you are her sole heir."

"Heir? Of what?" She was incredulous.

Jefferson's face came alive with excitement. "She was from a wealthy family back East and their solicitor has been looking for you to pass on the inheritance."

Mercy shook her head in disbelief. "How do you know this?"

"The notice is being sent to towns around the area, and I happened on it at one of the jail offices. There's a lawyer looking for any descendants of your mother—her maiden name was Lewis, right?—and that would be you."

Still, Mercy didn't understand. "But you didn't know about this when you first courted me."

Either unwittingly or uncaringly, the man responded. "I knew you'd get the Crane farm and land then, and as your husband it would go to me."

Her disgust for the man should have protected her from the sting of his words, but she couldn't help feeling the rebuff. "I see. So now in order to get this so-called "inheritance," you have to annul my marriage to Daniel Dunn, marry me yourself, and then kill me." She stated it plain and simple.

Jefferson's smile disappeared. "Now, Mercy, it doesn't have to go that way. We can be married and live happily ever after just like the fairy tale stories. I'll be a good husband to you."

Mercy caught his smirk as he turned away. She chose not to say anything more as she needed to think about how she was going to get out of her predicament without anyone getting hurt, especially her family.

Jefferson was unstable. That was clear. The other thing that Mercy knew for a fact was that she wasn't about to inherit anything like Jefferson thought. If there was any possibility of such a thing, her father would have told her. But she didn't dare let Jefferson know the truth because she didn't know what he would do then.

"Get your coat." All semblance of humor left him as he pulled her arm to the coat pegs. "Put it on. We're leaving now."

Mercy was in a quandary. She wanted with all her being to fight Jefferson tooth and nail, but if she made a fuss, the children would wake up, and she didn't know what the man might do to the children in his present state. And she didn't want to put the men in the barn in any danger.

She knew what she had to do. She had to leave with him and get as far away from the farm and the children and all the people she loved as she could. And she had to do it before there was trouble. The gun on Jefferson's hip was all the convincing she needed.

She pulled her coat on and grabbed a scarf and mittens. She slipped out of her shoes and put on a pair of heavy boots she kept near the door. She didn't know where they were going or how long she would be outdoors, but she was going to be prepared.

"I need to move the coffeepot off the stove." She made the statement as matter-of-fact as she could and was relieved when Jefferson nodded. She felt his eyes on her as she moved to the stove and pulled the pot away.

"Do you want some bread along?"

He frowned slightly then as if glad of her willingness, he smiled and nodded again. Out of the corner of her eye, she kept aware of his gaze until for just a moment he looked out the doorway. She hastily swept the knife she had used to slice bread in her coat pocket. She grabbed up the bread and a flour sack bag and stuffed the bread inside.

"I'm ready." She walked over to him.

He didn't move as he looked down at her and Mercy held her breath, wondering if he knew what she had done.

"I know why you're going along with this so willingly," he whispered, and she felt his breath on her face. "You don't want those children upstairs to wake up."

She didn't move as she stared at him.

"Just remember, my dear, they won't get hurt as long as you cooperate."

Mercy's anger at him nearly boiled over, but she kept her control and moved to the front door. He took her arm and pulled her instead to the kitchen door where the men in the barn had no chance of seeing them. He chuckled softly then pulled her to a sudden stop and this time when he spoke into her face it wasn't done softly or with a chuckle in his voice.

"And don't try to leave any sign so that someone can follow us, even if they would. I've killed one man for you already. I won't hesitate to kill another."

Mercy's mouth dropped open. "You? You…killed Murdock?"

At his quick nod, she stuttered, "For…*me*? What…what do you mean…for me?"

He pulled her outside and was moving her along with him at a fast pace behind the house and over the fence to a trail often used by the cows. Snow had started and their tracks would soon be gone. "It's not what I planned at first, but I caught Murdock that night with some of the stolen goods, and he fought me in his drunken stupor and drew his knife on me. I stabbed him with his own knife in self-defense. Since I had seen Dunn leave the bunkhouse, I went in and found his knife and replaced Murdock's with his. I knew then that if Dunn was in jail for murder, his children would have to go into an orphanage, and you would be free to marry me. It all fell into place." He took her arm to lead her but she pulled back. His astounding statement made no sense.

"But you didn't know I would keep the children. I didn't even know what was going to happen."

"I know you, Mercy Crane. You were too ashamed after I left you to marry anyone, but you would jump at the chance to be a mother to those children. How was I to know you would be stupid enough to marry a murderer just to keep them? Well, I'm not losing out."

They were moving into the woods by now but Mercy couldn't stop asking questions. Jefferson made no sense. He must have been in Grand Rapids long enough to find out that she was taking care of the Dunn children before he went to the logging camp and arrested Daniel. Did he really think his plan was going to work?

And what now? He claims he has papers to prove we are legally married, so all he has to do is—all he has to do is kill me to inherit! He really is going to kill me. "Oh Lord God, protect my family from this madman."

30

Crane Farm

"Neither of them will admit to killing Murdock. Jon seems to believe them but I don't know. They certainly had motive. Murdock found out about their affair and their thieving and I know how angry he could get. They could probably even claim self-defense, but they deny any part of the murder."

Daniel finished updating the other two about the happenings in Grand Rapids. He was glad for Stanley and Guntar's help with the horses. He was tired. It was his third trip to or from the town today and he was looking forward to a good night's sleep. He was aware of how quiet Guntar had been when he told about putting his mother in jail, and he wondered what the boy was thinking about that. He also wondered about something else.

"Guntar, your mother mentioned that you were three or so when she married your father. Did you know she isn't your real mother?"

A quick nod gave Daniel the answer. He turned to head for the house, but Guntar spoke.

"She didn't like my father to talk about my real mother, so he only told me things about her when we were alone. Ilsa's the only mother I've known. I hated it when she married Murdock, but she wouldn't listen to me. I don't know why she stayed with him when he treated her so badly."

"Why did you try to protect her and say that you had murdered Murdock?" Daniel questioned.

Guntar shrugged and tried unsuccessfully to hide his emotions from the other two men. "She was my mother."

Daniel patted the young man's back. "I'm sorry things turned out this way, Guntar. You know you're welcome to stay on with us." He looked to Stanley for confirmation and received a nod. "But something for you to think about is that the Bedloes would like to have you live with them and they'd give you a job in the store so you could earn some money. The sheriff said that the judge would have to look over the situation, but it could be that the Murdock place will go to you if you want it. If not, you could sell it."

Guntar sniffed and nodded.

Stanley stood. "Well, we don't have to make any decisions tonight. I see Mercy has a lamp lit in the kitchen for us and I'd bet she's got something out to eat too. Why don't we—?"

"Grandpa!"

Delaney pushed open the door and burst into the barn. "Delaney! What's wrong?"

She was breathing heavily as she tried to answer. "Oh, Pa! I'm glad you're back! That man was in the house and he took Mama with him!"

"What man?"

"She…called him…Jefferson."

Daniel was holding Delaney by both arms. "What do you mean he took her? What did you see? What did you hear?"

"They didn't see me, but I was on the stairs and he told her…he said they were married! Pa, he said he destroyed the papers that made *you* married to Mama! He said they could get her inheritance from her mother."

"What?" Stanley tried to keep up as the others ran for the house. Daniel was still questioning his daughter and trying to figure out if Mercy went with Elwood willingly or was taken.

"Did she want to go with him?"

"I don't know. I couldn't hear everything, but I know she asked him if she should bring bread along."

Daniel hurried to the house and looked around the kitchen. Everything was in place, no evidence of struggle. The coffee was off the fire. He turned to Stanley.

"Would she go with him?"

"No!" Stanley looked around too. "But…she might have gone along to protect us."

"That's what I'm thinking. I'll get my rifle and go after them."

"I'm coming—"

"No! I need you to stay and take care of the children. I'll get her back, I promise."

Stanley gave him a quick nod. "I'd just slow you down. Be careful, Daniel. I'll be praying."

"I appreciate it. Delaney, did you see which way they went?" As he listened to his daughter, Daniel felt a slow burning inside of him. He was afraid for Mercy. He knew from personal experience what kind of man Jefferson Elwood was. But there was more to his emotion than that.

"I'm coming too. You might need help."

Daniel paused for only a second before agreeing to Guntar's statement. "Let's get going then."

They found the cattle path Delaney pointed out and began their search. The snow was light so the tracks were still visible, meaning the couple didn't have too much of a head start on them. Delaney said she ran to the barn as soon as they were out of sight. Daniel took the lead and moved forward at a run. Every so often, he would signal to Guntar to stop and they would listen. As they progressed they stopped more frequently. If Elwood suspected he was being followed, he could wait and ambush them, but Daniel surmised that the man was too self-confident to believe anyone could catch up to him. Still he was careful.

Another stop. Daniel grabbed Guntar's shoulder and pushed him down, motioning for quiet. They listened and Daniel heard again the sound that had made him crouch to the ground. It was a voice. Mercy's voice. The wind made it difficult to hear what she was saying, but they were close now. He pointed ahead and waved Guntar to follow, staying low to the ground. The snow falling was fluffy and the ground beneath well trampled, so there was no crunching sound to announce their presence.

Daniel stopped again. Elwood and Mercy were standing in the middle of the trail and she was talking. Elwood grabbed her arm and moved forward, but she pulled back and this time her voice was clearer to the listeners.

"You might as well kill me here and now! I will not live as your wife!"

"You'll do as I say! The longer we're together, the less likely the papers can be questioned in court. If I need proof that we were living as man and wife before you died, then I will have it. We're going to live together and make sure there are others who can testify to it if necessary. Once you're dead, there will be no need for inquiry as to the validity of our marriage. I intend to get the full inheritance. Now come along!"

That was all Daniel needed to hear. He pulled his pistol out of his waistband and handed his rifle over to Guntar.

"Stay here in case he runs this way. Don't shoot at him. Just fire a warning shot if necessary. And don't shoot Mercy! Got it?"

Guntar nodded.

Daniel knew the boy was an excellent shot as he said he had been providing meat for his family for years, but he didn't want him involved in shooting at a human being and certainly not at him. He inched forward and to the side of the trail to get a better view of Elwood. He had to keep the man from using Mercy as a shield. If he could get Mercy to see him, maybe he could motion her out of the way.

Elwood was still threatening. "Don't make this harder on yourself! You know there's no way out now, so quit fighting. I can always go back there and take one of those children as an incentive for you."

"No! You leave those children alone, Jefferson! I told you I'll go along with you. Just leave them and Daniel and my father alone."

They started moving forward again, but Daniel heard Elwood laugh. "Your father? He'll be fine as long as he doesn't interfere with the inheritance. That's why you're going to write him a nice long letter telling him how happy you are to finally be married to your one true love."

Mercy said something, but Daniel couldn't make it out. He stopped moving when they did and nearly jumped to his feet when Elwood backhanded Mercy across the face.

"I don't ever want to hear Dunn's name again, you hear me?"

Mercy fell to her knees and it was the opportunity Daniel needed. He raised the pistol.

"Put your hands up, Elwood. Do it now!"

But Elwood reacted with lightning speed and pulled his gun out of its holster. He aimed it at Daniel while he grabbed Mercy and held her up in front of him, which was just what Daniel feared.

"Leave her out of this, Elwood!"

"You want me, Dunn? Or do you want my wife? You've got no claim on her anymore. I destroyed it all. Now walk away. She doesn't want anything to do with you. Tell him, Mercy."

Mercy's eyes were huge as she stared at Daniel.

"Too late, Elwood. I heard you say you were going to kill her. You'll never get that inheritance with my testimony against you. So you're going to have to kill me too, I guess. But what are your chances with my gun on you? Think about that."

Daniel took a step closer to them. "Or you can drop your gun and we'll all go back to town together and explain this to the sheriff. Don't make it worse than it has to be."

But Elwood was laughing before Daniel finished speaking. "Make it worse? Tell him, Mercy. Tell him why it can't get any worse for me."

Daniel's gun never wavered from Elwood as he wondered what the man was talking about. Mercy was squirming in the man's grip, making it difficult for Daniel to dare take a shot.

"He killed Murdock. Daniel, please go away! He'll kill you too."

"I can't do that, Mercy. Put the gun down. Now!"

Suddenly Mercy jerked and Elwood doubled over, releasing her. He fired a shot as he fell forward and Daniel returned fire at almost the same instant. He rushed forward.

"Mercy! Are you all right?" He pulled her away from Elwood. "Stay here, away from him."

Guntar came running with his rifle at the ready, but he stopped when he saw the fallen man. Daniel checked Elwood.

"He's still breathing. My shot got him in the shoulder, but there's blood here on his side."

Mercy began sobbing and Daniel reached for her and held her close, cherishing the opportunity to finally hold her despite the circumstances. He didn't know how long he held her, but he became aware of Guntar waiting nearby and he eased away from her.

"Are you hurt?" He held her arms and looked at her tearstained face and the red mark from Elwood's hand.

She shook her head and he saw a blush steal over her.

"What made him fall forward like that? What did you do?"

Mercy pulled free from Daniel and reached into her pocket. It was then that he noticed a dark stain on her coat. He was even more surprised when he saw the knife she now held in her hands.

"I took…I took the knife…I was cutting bread…it was in my pocket." She began to tremble.

Daniel took the knife from her and pulled her close again. "You stabbed him right through your coat."

He felt her nod against him. "And that's why he fell forward. Mercy Dunn, you are one brave woman."

Her trembling ceased and he felt her arms tighten around him. He knew then that he never wanted to let her go.

But Guntar was waiting.

He pulled back and she immediately dropped her arms to her sides. "We better get you home. Your father is terribly worried."

"How…how did you know…where I was?"

"Delaney was on the stairs and heard some of what you and Elwood were saying, but she didn't know exactly what was going on. She just knew that she should stay quiet and not let him know she was there."

Mercy's hand flew to her mouth. "Is she all right? She didn't think I was leaving them, did she?"

"She's fine. No, she knew you would never do that." He smiled down at her and she looked away, apparently confused.

No wonder. You're not exactly sure yourself what you're doing. Daniel scolded himself.

"Guntar, let's make a travois and drag him back to the farm. We'll wrap up these wounds and take him to the doctor in Grand Rapids tomorrow." As the men set to work, Daniel questioned Mercy more on what happened when Elwood appeared in her kitchen.

"So he admitted to killing Murdock? Is there any way we can prove that?"

"He said he used Murdock's knife in self-defense because Murdock started the fight, and then he found your knife and replaced it."

"It should be enough to convince the judge," Daniel announced. "Would both of you be willing to come to town tomorrow when I tell the sheriff? I don't want this hanging over my head any longer."

The night was nearly over by the time they returned to the farm and were able to tell Stanley their story. Delaney had fallen asleep on Daniel's bed in the parlor, but Stanley had spent the night watching, praying, and waiting for the return of his daughter and the others. Daniel felt his emotions stir when he saw Stanley's tears as he hugged Mercy.

Elwood's wounds weren't life-threatening, so they did what they could for him and put together a makeshift bed on the kitchen floor. Daniel tied the man's hands together and tied one ankle to the leg of the kitchen stove. He wouldn't be going anywhere. Then he made a bed for himself across the room from Elwood so he could keep an eye on him.

He didn't get an opportunity to talk with Mercy alone after that. They were exhausted and everyone went to bed for a few hours' rest before the new day dawned. Daniel's mind was too full to allow himself the pleasure of sleep.

I almost lost her tonight, Lord God. Thank you for the protection for her and for all the family. Thank you for giving me this new opportunity to love again.

There. He said it. Love. He stared at the ceiling while his mind journeyed over the events of the past months. He had grown through them. He had learned through them. He had become a child of God and would see his Dee someday again, but he could let her go now. He would always love her, he knew that, but there was room in his heart for more love to come.

He rolled over on his side and smiled. He could hardly wait to tell Mercy that he loved her. Would she agree to become his wife for real?

Suddenly he sat up. Or would she think he was after this inheritance that Elwood found out about?

31

Grand Rapids

IT WAS A quiet trip to Grand Rapids the next day. The new snow wasn't deep and its freshness made the sleigh glide with ease over the usually rutted road. Daniel drove the team and Mercy sat alongside him. Guntar sat in the back with Elwood wrapped in a blanket at his feet.

Mercy found Daniel to be more quiet than usual and on top of that he was acting so strangely. The night before when they had embraced, she almost believed that he cared for her. Certainly his concern was genuine. But today he seemed to avoid her eyes although she had caught him staring at her once or twice. He quickly looked away when he was aware of it.

And Guntar was quiet but for good reason, Mercy supposed. His life had been turned upside down with his stepmother now in jail for stealing. He was on the verge of manhood, but not quite ready to face life completely on his own. He hadn't given them a decision yet on where he wanted to stay, with them or with the Bedloes. Perhaps today would help him make up his mind. She wondered if his infatuation with her was now an embarrassment to him after seeing her and Daniel in each other's arms the night before.

Mercy's silence was due to her father's announcement that her mother indeed had come from a wealthy family, but that she had been disinherited when she married him. The news that her family was now seeking an heir was causing them both some anxiety, but as Mercy said to her father in an effort to reassure him, maybe Elwood was misleading them about that as well. Her father never talked about there even being living relatives on her mother's side and she was curious to know what her mother's life had been like.

Daniel brought them straight to the jailhouse and helped Mercy down from the sleigh. She wondered what he was thinking when he gently squeezed her hand and smiled at her. They entered the office and stopped short when they saw the judge sitting in the sheriff's chair. This time instead of bib overalls the man looked the part of a judge, suit and all. The sheriff came through the door leading to the cells.

"You back so soon, Daniel? What can I do for you folks?"

They quickly told the story of the night's events. Both the sheriff and the judge had questions, but by the time they were through, the lawmen were convinced that Elwood had murdered Murdock, but whether or not it was in self-defense remained to be proved. The sheriff went with Daniel out to the sleigh, and he sent Guntar to get the doctor while they walked Elwood into the jailhouse. Mercy stepped back as they brought the former deputy to a chair. He groaned in pain as he sat down before the judge.

Mercy jumped when the judge banged the butt of his revolver on the desktop.

"This court is now in session. Jefferson Elwood, you are accused of murdering the man named Murdock. How do you plead?"

Elwood sneered and then winced as he shifted his position. "Not guilty!"

Mercy gasped and would have spoken, but Daniel took her arm and gave her a negative shake of his head.

Elwood's laugh was malicious. "You've no proof. It's their word against mine."

The judge's expression remained stoic. "In the case of kidnapping this young woman, how do you plead?"

This time Elwood hesitated before blurting out, "Not guilty!"

"He's lying!" Guntar shouted out as he entered the room. Behind him the doctor peered at everyone over his wire spectacles.

"Who's the patient then?"

When Elwood was pointed out to the doctor, he requested that they lay him on the floor. "Untie his hands, please. I need a better look at that stab wound."

They watched in silence as the doctor poked, prodded, and examined his patient. Elwood made no effort to hide his pain and at one point even doubled over in apparent agony. It was Guntar who spotted the knife Elwood pulled from his boot, but his shouted warning was too late as Elwood wrapped his arm around the doctor's neck and pulled himself to his feet with the doctor held as a shield in front of him and the knife at the man's throat. His wounds didn't seem to hinder his movements in the least.

It all happened so quickly that the group in the room was stunned. But guns appeared at once. The sheriff drew his pistol, the judge picked up the revolver he had on the desk, and Guntar pointed the rifle he still carried, all at Elwood. Daniel was unarmed but he stepped in front of Mercy and kept her hidden behind him.

"That's Murdock's knife!" Guntar exclaimed.

Elwood flashed a look of hatred at the boy. "So it is. Now you gentlemen put your guns down and slide them over to me or this knife will kill again. Do it! I've got nothing to lose now."

The room was filled with tension as the men remained motionless. Elwood yanked his arm tighter around the doctor's neck, making the man gasp for air, his feet nearly lifted off the floor. "Do it, or this town won't have a doctor anymore!"

Mercy peered from behind Daniel's back. The judge placed his revolver on the floor and sent it sliding toward

Elwood with a push from his foot. The sheriff had a grim expression on his face as he slowly knelt and placed his pistol down and then gave it a shove. All that was left was Guntar's rifle, and Mercy could tell by the look on his face that he wasn't about to give in to Elwood's demands.

"Sheriff?" The door opened without warning.

Elwood turned, pulling the doctor along with him. It was just enough of a distraction to cause the sheriff to dive for his gun, but at the same time Guntar's rifle fired.

Elwood screamed out and his grip on the doctor loosened. Daniel pushed Mercy to the floor and covered her with his body. The doctor grabbed Elwood's hand and wrested the knife out of his grasp. As Elwood hit the floor and rolled over in pain, the sheriff had his pistol in hand and pointed at him. The judge retrieved his revolver and slowly they all stood. After checking that Mercy was all right, Daniel walked over to Guntar and patted him on the back.

"Good shooting, Guntar. Well done!" There was a satisfied grin on Daniel's face.

The doctor leaned over Elwood who was squirming in agony on the floor. His voice was a bit raspy from nearly being strangled, but he managed to speak. "Looks like you've been shot in the buttocks. Bet that hurts."

Mr. Bedloe stood uncertainly in the doorway. "What's going on?"

Mercy waited with Guntar and the judge while the others took Elwood to a cell and the doctor tended to his new wound. There was no doubt now that the man was at least guilty of attempted murder and it would be up to a jury to decide if he murdered Murdock in self-defense. Mercy felt nothing but relief that it was all over. The judge explained to Guntar what would happen to Ilsa.

"She'll be given a trial and then possibly taken to Stillwater. Stealing is a serious crime and in some cases punishable by death. The man they call Shorty is wanted for a couple of murders as well as the thefts. It doesn't look good for him.

"Now, let's talk about you, young man."

Just then the door opened and Mr. Bedloe returned with Mrs. Bedloe. Mercy was surprised and delighted to see Mr. Bedloe's arm around his wife.

"Excuse me, judge. We were wondering if we might have a word with Guntar." Mr. Bedloe did the talking, which was another surprise for Mercy. Hedda Bedloe stood silent at her husband's side although she beamed a smile at Mercy and Guntar.

"You the family who wants to take the young man in and give him a job?" The judge was back at the desk.

"Yes, sir, that's us. We'd be happy to give him a good home, seeing as how's we don't have children of our own. And he'd only have to work at the store if he wants to. If you want to take on a job somewhere else or just go on for more schooling, you can do what you'd like." Mr. Bedloe directed his comments to Guntar. "We'd just be happy to share our home with you, son."

Guntar stood awkwardly looking between the judge and the Bedloes.

"Well, son, do you have anything to say?" the judge inquired.

"I guess I was just wondering why they want me," he finally admitted.

Hedda looked at her husband and at his nod she stepped forward and put her hand on Guntar's arm. "We've both been victims of lying and we've both been hurt and I've hurt someone I love." She looked back at Mr. Bedloe before turning to Guntar again. "I've seen how kind you are. You're a good boy and deserve a chance to have a good life. Mr. Bedloe and I can help you and we'd love to have you. Please. Will you let us do this for you? It would mean so much to us."

Guntar watched Mrs. Bedloe's face carefully as she talked. They all waited while he made up his mind. Finally he answered, "Yes. Thank you."

Hedda couldn't seem to help herself and she threw her arms around Guntar and gave him a big hug. Mr. Bedloe held out a hand and shook Guntar's.

"You come on over when you're done here and we'll get you settled. I'll have a nice hot lunch ready for you."

They waved good-bye to Mercy and left with smiles on their faces. Guntar still stood in the same spot and seemed a bit overwhelmed.

The judge looked at him with interest. "They seem like good folks. You have an opportunity to better yourself and your life with them, but even more, I think you will bring them a great deal of happiness."

"How?" Guntar still didn't understand.

"They have no family, but with you they have someone to look after and someone who will look after them and maybe bring some joy into their lives. Think you can do that?"

Guntar nodded. He turned to Mercy. "Thank you, Miss Crane—I mean Mrs. Dunn—for all you've done. I'm really sorry about all my ma put you through."

"Guntar, you will always be welcome to come see us. I only wish the best for your life."

Mercy hugged him.

Guntar faced the judge again. "If my ma asks, will you tell her I'll be okay?"

"Would you like to see her?"

"No, sir. I don't think I would." He tipped his head at Mercy and left.

"And that brings us to you, Mrs. Dunn." The judge turned his attention on Mercy.

"Me?"

"There is this concern about an inheritance." The judge pulled some papers from a satchel on the desk. "I've come across the notice that Elwood was talking about." He scanned the document. "Could you spell out your mother's name for me? First and last, please."

Something in the judge's tone put Mercy at ease. "Her name was Noreen Lewis." She spelled it out.

The judge smiled. "I hope this won't disappoint you too greatly. The notice is about a Maureen Louis." He spelled out the name to her. "Either Elwood didn't read it right or he heard someone else read it and thought he understood it to be your mother. I'm very sorry."

"No, don't be. I didn't believe it to be true, although I have to admit it would have been nice to learn more about my mother. She died when I was born."

The judge peered at her over his spectacles. "I can see why you took in the Dunn children like you did."

She smiled and nodded at his statement.

"The other issue I'd like to clear up is this nonsense about Elwood having a marriage certificate for the two of you."

They were interrupted by the men as they returned to the room from the cells. The judge finished speaking to Mercy. "I'll get that paperwork cleared up right away and be assured there will be no legal problems associated with it."

Daniel stopped abruptly and the doctor smacked into his back.

"Ouch!" The doctor rubbed at his neck where Elwood had choked him. He stepped around Daniel and said his good-byes to the others. "I won't say it's been a pleasure, but at least I got a chuckle out of it in the end. That boy couldn't have shot him in a better spot."

There were grins and a few more chuckles as the men saw the doctor out the door. It was a delicate subject to laugh about in the presence of a lady, and Mercy knew they were trying to be polite.

Snort.

She clapped her hand over her mouth and looked at the men's surprised faces as her mirth couldn't be contained. *Snort!*

They joined in her laughter, all but Daniel who merely smiled. Mercy wondered what was wrong.

The judge startled them by rapping his gun butt on the desk again.

"Court is now in session!"

"What?" Daniel dropped to the chair beside Mercy as the sheriff raised an eyebrow at the judge.

The judge interlaced his fingers and leaned back in the sheriff's squeaky chair and studied the couple before him. "In light of what has transpired here today, that is to say the incarceration of the two town thieves and the killer of Murdock, I hereby release the two of you from your marriage contract and terminate the need for the sheriff to check up on Mr. Dunn. Court dismissed!" He slammed the gun butt once more on the desk.

Mercy and Daniel didn't move.

"You're dismissed," the judge repeated. He motioned with his hand for them to leave. "And, Miss Crane, come see me if any legal concerns arise."

Miss Crane. Mercy felt numb at hearing him call her that. She stood woodenly to her feet and followed Daniel out the door.

The sheriff turned one of the chairs around and straddled it, leaning on its back while he studied his brother-in-law.

"What are you up to, Clarence? You'd have to be blind not to see that those two don't want the marriage annulled."

The judge leaned back and grinned when the squeal of the chair made Jon wince. "They are going to have to figure out the next step on their own."

Daniel didn't speak as he helped Mercy into the sleigh, and even though he avoided looking her in the eye, he noticed that she didn't look at him either.

This isn't what I wanted. Lord God, I love her! But...

It was that inheritance! He had walked in the room just as the judge told her he would take care of some paperwork and legal issues. That had to mean that Elwood was right and Mercy was heir to her mother's wealth.

I can't ask her to marry me now. I have nothing! She'll think I'm after her money.

"I need to stop at the mercantile." Daniel's words made Mercy jump.

She must have a lot on her mind too.

"Did we forget something?" Mercy asked.

"No. I just need to talk to the Bedloes a minute." He didn't look at her. "I have to see about renting the house again."

"Oh."

He heard her sharp intake of breath as he stepped down from the sleigh and hurried into the building. He found Latham and quickly made his request. It wasn't easy to ask the man for a favor, but Daniel had to swallow his pride and think of his children.

The ride home was done mostly in silence. Daniel wanted to at least thank Mercy for all she'd done for them, but he couldn't bring himself to raise the subject. Not when his throat choked him just to think the words. He couldn't speak them. Not yet.

When the farm came into view, Mercy spoke for the first time.

"I'll get supper going right away. You must be hungry."

Hungry?

Daniel squeezed his eyes shut tight. He'd forgotten to get her lunch at the hotel. Food was the last thing on his mind. "I'm so sorry, Mercy. I meant to take you to lunch at the hotel before we started back."

Mercy didn't even turn his way. "It's okay. I didn't want lunch anyway."

He noticed that her hands were gripped tightly together in her lap. "When…when will you tell the children?" She finally asked.

He swallowed and pulled the team to a stop in front of the house. They sat in silence, but he knew the girls would come running out any moment so he had to speak. "I'll tell them in the morning. Could you help them pack their things? I think it best if we leave right away."

The door burst open and Delaney and Darby waved to them from the porch as Daphne and Didi ran to the sleigh. Mercy didn't wait for Daniel's help and stepped down from the sleigh and held her arms out to them. Daniel saw for the first time the tears that were streaming down her face as she held out her arms for the girls. He had to turn away and pretend to work on the harnesses.

"Mama Mer*th*y, awe you okay? What*th* wong?" Didi's concern was so tender it tore at Daniel's heart.

"I'm fine, Didi. Hello, Daphne! I'm just so happy to be home and see you." She hugged them both to her with her eyes tightly shut. Then she stood and took their hands. "Come on, let's get some supper ready and you can tell me all about your day."

Daniel's feet felt heavy as he led the horses to the barn. Stanley watched from the doorway.

"Did something go wrong? What's the matter?"

Daniel steeled himself against the emotions he was feeling. The sooner he got his family together and away, the better it would be for all. He loved this farm and the work, but he had no right to stay. He saw the concern in Stanley's eyes and he longed to tell him how he felt, but that would only make things more difficult, for he knew Stanley would try to convince him that he belonged here with Mercy.

Mercy.

Daniel braced himself. "Stanley, we need to talk."

Supper would have been uncomfortable if not for the antics of Dylan and Didi. The older girls seemed to sense that something was not right, but with all the turmoil of the last few days, they seemed to feel this was part of it.

Mercy didn't know how she managed to get through the meal and the evening without breaking down in front of the children. She kept busy up until bedtime and then she faced the hardest part of all—putting the children down for the night. They had gotten into the habit of gathering in one room for Mercy to read to them from the Bible and talk about the passage she read. Tonight they were finishing up the story of Esther.

"E*th*ter wa*th th*ad when *th*ee had to leave her family, but *th*ee *th*aved them all, didn't *th*ee?" Didi cuddled against Mercy.

Mercy pulled the little girl closer. "Yes, Didi, and I want you to remember that wherever God chooses to take you, you can be used by him to help others. Will you remember that, darling?"

"Ye*th*!" Didi pulled away and turned around to look Mercy in the eye. "Did God put u*th* here to help you?"

Mercy couldn't hold back the tears that streamed down her face. She pulled Didi close again and gave a wobbly smile to the other girls who were watching her with concern. "Oh, yes, he surely did! You have given me so much joy!" She choked on the words and buried her head in the little girl's hug.

"Mercy, what's wrong?" Delaney put her arm around her.

"It's been a long day, girls. I guess I'm a little emotional tonight." Mercy stood and wiped her tears away with the back of her hand. "Let's get you tucked in, shall we?" She moved to each one, hugged and kissed them, and pulled the blankets up around their shoulders. "I'll see you in the morning. Good night."

It was a relief to get to her own room and close the door so that she could let her tears fall freely. *Father, this is too hard! I can't bear to let them go. Please give me strength—*

Her prayer was interrupted by a soft tapping on her door. She wiped her face and crossed the room to stand by the door.

"Who is it?" she whispered.

"Delaney."

Mercy's eyes shut and she took a deep breath and opened the door. "Is Dylan asleep already?" She attempted to sound normal.

Delaney nodded as she studied Mercy's face. "What's wrong? Is Pa going back to jail?"

Mercy shook her head but she couldn't speak.

"Do we have to leave? Is that it?" She gripped Mercy's sleeve as she saw the answer in her eyes. "Why? Don't you want us to stay?"

Mercy pulled Delaney to her and wept. She tried to compose herself as she sat down on the side of the bed with the young girl.

"The judge…annulled our marriage, so your pa and I are no longer bound to stay together. He…your pa….he…is renting your house again from the Bedloes." Mercy smiled at Delaney. "So you won't be too far away. That means we'll be able to see each other sometimes."

The girl sat as if stunned. "But we don't want to leave! Don't you love us, Mama?"

Mercy nodded through her tears. "Of course I do. I wish you could stay too."

"So it's Pa? Don't you love Pa? Couldn't you try to love him?"

"Oh, honey, it's not that simple. Your pa would have to love me too and…he doesn't."

They sat in silence. Mercy gently rocked Delaney and let her cry. She needed to be strong for the children through this separation. She had to make their leaving as painless as possible even though it was hurting her. She would have to put aside her pain and deal with it after they were gone. She prayed for strength to do just that.

Mercy led Delaney back to her room, and as she was tucking her in, Delaney asked, "Did you get an inheritance?"

She smiled and kissed the girl's cheek. "No, it was all a misunderstanding. They were looking for someone else."

"Do you mind?"

Mercy shook her head. "Having had all of you as part of my life has made me richer than any inheritance could have. I love you, Delaney. Good night."

"I love you too, Mama."

Mercy swallowed back the tears that threatened. She blew out the lantern and returned to her own room. She doubted she would get any sleep tonight.

∞ 32 ∞

Crane Farm

THE NEXT MORNING Mercy was up early and had most of the children's things packed before she started down the stairs to work on breakfast. The men were already out the door. She had waited purposely for them to leave the house before she came down to avoid contact with Daniel. This day was going to be hard enough for her.

Her eyes were red and stung from the tears that slipped to her pillow during the long night. Twice, she had gotten up just to look at the children sleeping in their beds. Each time brought on fresh tears and she didn't know how her body could produce any more. She felt worn out from her weeping and lack of sleep, but she had splashed cold water on her face and trusted the Lord to sustain her through the hours ahead.

Breakfast was subdued. Mercy avoided looking at either of the men even though she knew her father was concerned about her. She helped the children through the meal, feeding Dylan, cutting food in smaller pieces for Didi, and tried to make light conversation with them. It was at the end of the meal that Daniel finally spoke.

"There's something I need to tell you, girls."

Grandpa Crane pushed back his chair. "Excuse me, I have work in the barn. I could use a hand, Mercy."

"Sure, Papa."

Bless you, Papa!

Daniel remained silent until Stanley and Mercy left the house. He appreciated that they wanted to give him some privacy when telling the children that they were leaving the farm. He opened his mouth to speak.

"We don't want to leave, Pa!"

Daniel turned to his oldest daughter and expected to find defiance in her face, but instead he saw fear and heartache. He felt the sting in his eyes that had been there ever since he saw Mercy's tears the day before.

This is going to be harder than I thought.

The other children, except for Dylan, were stunned by their sister's words, so that meant they hadn't heard anything yet. No doubt Delaney, in the wisdom of her nearly thirteen years, had figured it out.

"We have to leave. This isn't our home and we don't belong here. I've talked with the Bedloes and we're going back to our house in town. I'll get work—"

"No!" Darby stood. "We want to live here."

"Darby."

"I don't want to leave Mama." Daphne crossed her arms in front of her.

"Me eith*uh*!" Didi imitated her sister and crossed her arms.

Daniel reached for Dylan and held him on his knee while he looked at the mixture of defiance and worry in his daughters' faces. "None of us want to leave the Cranes. This is a wonderful place to live, but we have no right to stay and live off these kind people any longer. We'll be in town for now and you'll still be able to see Mercy and Grandpa Crane once in a while."

Delaney frowned. "What do you mean *for now?*"

"I don't know what the future holds, honey. I have to go where I can find work."

"Mama Mer*thy th*ay*th* we have to help people wherever God put*th* u*th*."

Daniel pulled the reins on his emotions a little tighter. "Mercy is right. Now, go and get your things and meet me outside. Grandpa Crane is lending us the sleigh."

Four pairs of eyes stared at him. Daniel's reserve almost cracked when he saw tears start to roll down the girls' cheeks. He turned away.

"Hurry now. We have a lot to do."

The girls shuffled away with their heads hung low. Delaney took Didi's hand and looked back over her shoulder at her pa. Daniel nodded to her.

He had just finished putting Dylan's coat on him when the girls returned with their bags. "Here, Delaney, take him, and you girls get your coats on. I'll get the sleigh and load it."

Daniel stepped out into the cold morning air and took a deep breath. The sad faces in the kitchen were more than he could handle, but he was reluctant to go out to the barn and see Mercy again. Leaving her was going to be the hardest part of all. He heard the jingle of the harnesses and looked up to see Stanley leading the team out of the barn. Mercy was nowhere in sight. He stepped off the porch and went to give him a hand.

"I could have taken care of that, Stanley. I didn't mean for you to do it."

"I know you probably want to get going."

"Yes, I do. The girls are taking it pretty hard."

"Aren't you?"

Daniel looked sideways at the man. "You know I am. But you know why I have to do this."

"If you say so."

Daniel scowled. They had talked it through last night in the barn and Stanley had accused Daniel of having too much pride.

"You're thinking that I'd just be giving you this farm," he said, "but the truth is you would work harder here than you ever did in the woods and you know I can't manage this place without you. Jemison is gone and I'll have to hire someone else. At least I didn't

have to pay you." Stanley's humor always came through even in these trying circumstances. Then he brought up Mercy, and Daniel admitted that he was in love with her, but he couldn't marry her when she had so much and he had nothing to offer.

"Truth is," Stanley told him, "you don't deserve her."

Daniel readily agreed.

"Any more than you or I deserve what God has given us through his Son. It's called his mercy toward us, a blessing we don't deserve."

Daniel had thought on the man's words all night. *His mercy.* Was Stanley right? Was his pride keeping him from the woman he had come to love? *His* Mercy?

"We're ready, Pa."

Daniel watched the children carry their belongings to the porch. He sighed. It had to be done. He loaded the wagon and tried not to watch as Stanley hugged each one of the children and told them how much he was going to miss them.

"And remember, you're coming back to visit a lot." Stanley raised an eyebrow at Daniel, daring him to contradict him.

He heard Delaney ask where Mercy was.

"She's in the barn, but she asked me to say good-bye for her. She's kind of weepy and said something about promising not to make a fuss when you left." The look he gave Daniel was challenging and caused him to flinch.

Daniel lifted the girls into the sleigh. He waited to take Dylan from Stanley and had to blink away threatening tears when the older man leaned over to kiss the boy's forehead.

"Your grandpa's going to miss you, little buddy."

Stanley handed the baby over to Daniel and stepped back. He waved until the sleigh was out of sight.

Mercy watched with tears streaming down her face as the sleigh left the yard. She knew it was cowardly to not come out and say good-bye to the children, but she couldn't do it.

"Papa."

She ran into her father's arms while she wept her grief at having lost not only her family, but the man she had come to love. Together they returned to the house.

"I could use a cup of coffee," Papa stated. "And maybe another pancake. All this crying has made me hungry."

Mercy smiled through her tears. It was good to have Papa to cheer her up. She set about fixing him some food while she finished cleaning up the remains of the others' breakfast. She needed to be busy today. Maybe she'd start her spring cleaning early this year.

She sat down with her father and sipped on coffee while he ate again. He talked about farm issues and inconsequential things, and he asked about the happenings in town the day before. Mercy told about Jefferson's attempt to escape and Guntar shooting him in the backside, which caused her father to laugh and almost choke on his coffee.

"So did you find out anything about that inheritance Elwood was ranting about?"

Mercy stood and carried the dishes to the counter. Over her shoulder she said, "It was as you expected—not true. Turns out it was for the heirs of someone named Maureen Louis."

"That's what Delaney said!"

Mercy swung around at hearing Daniel's voice. He stood panting in the doorway with a huge grin on his face.

"Daniel!"

He stepped into the room and approached her, his eyes never leaving her face. "I know I don't deserve you, Mercy Crane, whether you have an inheritance or a farm or nothing to your name. I don't deserve you because you are the kindest, most caring, and loving person I have ever met and I love you with all my heart."

He paused as she gasped and put her hand over her mouth.

"But even though I don't deserve you, I'm asking if you will be my wife. I will live here and work this farm if you want or we can move into the rental house in Grand Rapids or I will take you wherever you want to go, just say you'll be mine. Please. I can't leave here without you."

Mercy's hands were still over her mouth and she stared with wide eyes at the man before her then suddenly she threw her arms around him.

"Yes, Daniel! Yes! Yes! Yes!"

His arms encircled her and he held her tight. "I love you, Mercy."

"I love you too." Her voice was muffled against him.

"You'll marry me? For real this time?"

She pulled back and nodded up at him. "If you're sure you want a scarecrow with huge eyes."

His answer was to kiss her.

The sound of Stanley clearing his throat made Daniel raise his head, but he didn't let go of Mercy.

"May I have your daughter's hand in marriage?" he asked Stanley but kept his eyes on Mercy.

"'Bout time! Saves me the trouble of hiring help around here." Stanley slapped Daniel on the back and received a glad hug from Mercy.

"Daniel, where are the children?"

"They're coming. I ran on ahead after I learned from Delaney that you really did love me. I couldn't wait to get back here."

Mercy shook her head. "But I never told Delaney that."

"She said that you didn't think I loved you, and I knew I had to tell you so. Your father pointed out that I had too much pride in me to stay here and live on the farm, but I realized that I don't care where we live as long as we're together."

Mercy laid her head on his chest. "Me too. You've turned one of the darkest days of my life into the happiest."

"When can we get married?"

Stanley stepped to the door as they heard the jingle of the harnesses. "Well, if you want my opinion, the sleigh is already hooked up, the kids have their coats on, and that judge is still in town."

"Today? Right now?" Mercy searched Daniel's face for confirmation.

"Yes, today!"

Crane Farm
Nine Months Later

Delaney smiled at the little bundle in her arms. She swayed slowly back and forth as she brushed a finger over her new brother's peach-fuzzed cheek.

"He looks like Pa," she commented to her stepmother.

Mercy rested back on the pillows and watched Delaney with her new son. "My life couldn't be any more perfect than this." She sighed in contentment.

"Do you know what you'll name him, Mama?"

Daniel quietly came in the room as she asked the question, and he stopped to admire his son for at least the hundredth time before pulling up a chair beside the bed where Mercy lay. "We thought we might let you children help with that."

"Really, Pa? Because we have a name! We talked about it last night before he was born. If it was a girl we thought Dorcas would be nice, but if it was a boy, we all agreed on David because we love how David in the Bible wasn't afraid of Goliath and how he became the king of Israel and—"

"David it is." Pa stopped Delaney's chatter with a finger to his lips as he indicated that Mercy had fallen asleep. "We thought of the same name."

"You did?" Delaney whispered. She smiled at her father and handed the tiny bundle over to him. "Ma would have loved that Dylan has a brother."

Daniel studied his oldest daughter's face. "And she would be proud of the beautiful young lady you've become, just as Mama and I are."

Delaney kissed her pa on the cheek and quietly left the room.

"She's growing up fast, Daniel. They all are." Mercy opened her eyes and looked lovingly at her husband and son. "I want to hold them and keep them just the way they are right now and not let them grow up and someday leave us." A tear slid down her cheek.

"Whoa there, little mother, don't get ahead of yourself. The Lord has blessed us with these children to raise to know him and honor him with their lives. We'll do the best we can by them with his help, and then we'll have the joy of watching them become the people God intends for them to be."

"You're right. I know." She reached for David and cuddled him close to her. "I'm going to enjoy each day, each moment that I have them with me." She put out her hand and cradled Daniel's face. "And I'm going to love growing old with you, watching our children marry and bring us grandchildren to love."

"Grandchildren! Don't age me so fast! But there is a grandpa waiting out there along with some rather excited children who all want to come and meet the newest member of our family. Are you ready for them?"

"I've been ready and waiting for them my whole life."

REFERENCES

Boese, Donald L. and Richard R. (Dick) Cain, and the Itasca County Historical Society. *Grand Rapids Companion, Reflections of the People and Events That Shaped Grand Rapids During Its First 100 Years, 1891–1991*. Grand Rapids, MN: NorthPrint International, Inc., 1991.

Herald Review and the Itasca County Historical Society. *Grand Rapids & Itasca County, Looking Back—The Early Years, A Pictorial History*. Canada: Pediment Publishing, 2004.

Rimmer, Harry. *The Last of the Giants*. 1948; rpt. St. John, IN: Christian Book Gallery, 1998.

For more information about

Tall Timber Trilogy

or

Author Margo Hansen
visit her at www.margohansen.com

Margo would enjoy hearing from her readers.
Send your questions or comments to
margo@margohansen.com

Other books by Margo Hansen:
A Newly Weds Series
(Sky's Bridal Train, Jade's Courting Danger,
Emma's Marriage Secret, Irena's Bond of Matrimony,
Mattie's Unspoken Vow)

Coming Soon:

Only Beloved

Book 2

Tall Timber Trilogy

Margo Hansen